SURRENDER TO THE MISTRESS

SURRENDER TO THE MISTRESS

A collection of four erotic novellas

ALEX JORDAINE

Published by Xcite Books Ltd – 2013
ISBN 9781908262653

Printed and bound in the UK

Cover design by Madamadari

To Mistress G, the love of my life

'Remind me of my place. If I cry, give me reason, show
me no mercy. Force me to my knees and use me
as you will.'
Slave's prayer

Contents

BOOK ONE

GUILTY SECRET

'Every person lives his real, most interesting life under the
cover of secrecy.'
Anton Chekhov

Chapter One

Lauren Wright and her husband, Mark, were naked on top of the rumpled sheets of their bed, both of them as sexed up as could be, in pain with desire. Mark was flat on his back and had a powerful erection, and Lauren knelt over him, smiling provocatively and gazing into his eyes. Her dark hair swung down either side of her lovely face and her full breasts swayed above his chest. Mark was breathing fast and his heart was pumping overtime. He felt indescribably horny, his cock rock-hard and so urgent with need it throbbed fit to burst.

Lauren reached a hand between her quivering thighs until her fingers were wet with love juice and then held them to Mark's lips. He pushed out his tongue and licked her juices away. Lauren then kissed him ardently on the mouth for a moment before pulling her head back and looking down at him again, her big, green eyes shining. 'Do you love me?' she asked.

'More than that,' Mark replied through trembling lips. 'Much more. I worship you.'

Then darkness descended all of a sudden. It was like someone had thrown a switch.

'Lauren,' Mark called out, but there was no reply, only the echo of his own voice in the still night air.

'Lauren, darling,' he called out again, or thought he did. But maybe it was inside his head. The rest of it had been, after all. Mark had been dreaming.

He closed his eyes tight shut and tried desperately to

return to the dream, but it wasn't any good, of course it wasn't. His heart sank like a stone. It had felt so real, that dream. It had been as if they were still together, still the happiest, horniest couple in the world. But no. Mark started to remember, his mind pregnant with memory, his cock still achingly hard from the dream …

The first time they'd met had been a matter of purest chance. Mark had been mooching around the West End of London one Saturday afternoon, just soaking up the cosmopolitan atmosphere of the place. He was feeling blithe, cheerful, glad to be alive.

Mark was a natural urbanite, a real city person. He loved working and living in the centre of London, as he had done over the last dozen years. It was such an exciting mix of the old and new, was so full of energy, had such an incredible buzz.

It was at its best too on that warm bright day in early spring. The cloudless sky was an eggshell blue, a soft breeze was blowing, and the surrounding masonry was doused in the glow of gentle sunlight.

Mark crossed the road, dodging a car that was being driven too fast, and made for The Americas Bar. He'd never been there before but on cursory inspection it looked about right for a quick drink – dark, clean, anonymous and not too crowded.

He ordered a vodka tonic and perched on a high stool at the bar. The ice rattled in the glass when he took his first sip and he felt the cold thrust of the vodka down his throat. Mark took the glass from his lips and glanced to his side, and it happened, that heart-stopping moment.

Mark noticed a woman so stunningly beautiful it made him gasp. She was standing near the end of the bar, nursing a glass of white wine, and was looking at him. Mark thought at first she might be just glancing casually in his direction. But her stare was too insistent for that. He reciprocated, couldn't help himself, couldn't take his eyes off her in fact. The woman was perfect. It was as if she glowed.

Mark let his gaze traverse her body, let it drink her in. Her shoulder-length hair was dark brown and lustrous. She had warm, full lips and strong features with almost Slavic cheekbones. Her neck was slender, her shapely form shown off to splendid effect by what she had on – skin-tight black denim jeans, red high-heeled sandals over bare feet and a maroon short-sleeved top that hugged her contours and exposed a tantalising glimpse of her taut, flat stomach.

This vision of loveliness clearly wasn't wearing a bra and the nipples of her well-shaped breasts were sticking out stiffly. Mark imagined them in his mouth and felt his cock start to swell. Finally he allowed his eyes to meet hers. They were emerald green and large and framed with long lashes.

Mark flashed what he hoped was a winning smile at the beautiful woman. In response she raised her wine glass and smiled back at him, fixing her eyes on his in a way that penetrated behind his pupils and thrust into his body. That smile, that look, induced in Mark straight away something akin to enslavement.

Then she put her glass down and started to walk towards him. He watched her as she glided through the bar. Mark couldn't help noticing how many of the men in the place looked after her, ogling her longingly as she sashayed past. Their eyes lingered on the bounce of her braless breasts, the stiffness of her nipples and the seductive sway of her hips.

'Hi,' the woman said, putting her hands on those shapely hips and flashing Mark that enslaving smile once again. 'Lauren Spencer's the name. I think we should get acquainted, don't you?'

Mark got up from his stool. 'Your place or mine?' he

joked, rather feebly he thought as soon as the words had tumbled out of his mouth. He wished he hadn't come out with that hackneyed, cheesy line. 'My name's Mark – Mark Wright,' he added. 'Can I get you a drink?'

'No thanks, I'm fine,' Lauren said. You sure are, he thought. She went on, 'Nice shirt, by the way, matches the blue of your eyes.'

'Nice everything,' said the master of repartee, eyeing her up and down. Mark wondered what seeing that body naked would be like. It was extremely enticing. 'Lovely day, isn't it?' he added, using another of his brilliant conversational gambits. His mouth seemed to have lost all contact with his brain since he'd started talking to this gorgeous creature.

'Yes, it is a lovely day,' she agreed, smiling.

'What brings you to these parts?' *What brings you to these parts?* Just listen to yourself, Mark thought. How gauche she must think you are. At least he hadn't asked her whether she came here often.

'I live not far away from here,' Lauren said. 'I thought I'd have a fortifying drink before embarking on some serious retail therapy.'

'I see,' Mark said. He wondered what it would feel like to kiss her sensuous lips.

'But plans change,' Lauren went on.

'Eh … right.'

'I said we should get acquainted, didn't I?' she said.

'You did,' Mark agreed.

'And you said, "Your place or mine?"'

'A great wit, aren't I,' he replied. 'Sorry about that. You see, I …'

Lauren cut him short. 'My place.'

'Sorry?' His eyes widened.

'You won't be,' she said. 'Let's you and me go off and get acquainted, Mark.'

And that's exactly what they did. They got acquainted. At her place. Boy, did they ever get acquainted. The sex was joyous. They fucked with an intensity Mark hadn't thought was possible until then.

He remembered it so clearly now, all on his own in the darkness of his bedroom. His groin tightened and he brought his hand to his erection as his body flooded with the memory of that first time …

'Come with me,' Lauren said, starting to make an exit from the bar. Mark put down his half-empty glass in double-quick time and followed in her wake, walking on air. He watched in a daze as she hailed a black cab for them. It took the pair the short journey to Lauren's house, which was in Chelsea, just behind the King's Road. It was in an affluent residential street and was one of a white-stuccoed, black-railinged Victorian terrace. This girl is clearly not short of money, Mark thought vaguely, but it was hardly the first thing on his mind.

Lauren led him from the taxi to her front door. 'Follow me,' she demanded once they'd entered the elegant, expensively furnished property, and he followed her dutifully up the stairs and into her bedroom.

'Let's kiss,' Lauren said next and they did. They kissed with great passion, their tongues flicking together. They lost themselves in that wonderful experience, their first kiss. Lauren broke the kiss eventually, breathless.

'Strip naked,' she said. Mark instantly obeyed, scrambling out of his clothing, and stood before her, his long, thick cock stiffly erect. Lauren's eyes swept over him like a lighthouse beam, lingering on his erection, and she smiled a seductive smile. Then it was time for her to join him in nudity. She kicked off her red high-heeled sandals, peeled off her skin-tight black jeans and the tiny G-string of the same colour she'd been wearing under them. Lastly she pulled her tight maroon top over her head and stood before him in all her voluptuous splendour, utterly, gloriously naked.

Lauren led Mark over to the big double bed. 'Stand right where you are,' she demanded, throwing herself onto the bed. She lay back, head resting on two upright pillows, and began to pleasure herself, spreading her legs wantonly wide apart and rolling her fingers over her clit. All the while she looked straight at Mark, her luminous green eyes staring right at him, hypnotising him.

Mark's cock was steely-hard by now. He felt urgently that he just had to make love to this magnificent woman, this naked, lascivious goddess. But Lauren seemed in no apparent hurry as she continued to pleasure herself, plunging first one and then two fingers into her wet pussy. Then she spread her labia with those two fingers and went back to teasing her clit, this time with the middle finger of her other hand, all the while gazing lustfully into Mark's gleaming eyes.

Lauren stopped masturbating in her own good time. 'Go down on me,' she demanded, reaching out her arms to Mark in a beckoning gesture and he crawled sinuously up the bed to do as he'd been told. He brought his face between her thighs, pressed his lips to her sex and began licking her labia and clitoris as she ran her fingers through his dark hair. His tongue worked ever more vigorously on her sex – and yet still Lauren remained in control.

'Turn onto your back,' she told Mark next and he immediately obeyed. 'I want to suck that big, hard cock of yours while you continue to pleasure me with your tongue.' Lauren swung her hips over Mark's face so that he could carry on eating her pussy while she opened her lips and engulfed his pulsing shaft with her mouth. She sucked his cock so vigorously that Mark became certain he was going to ejaculate at any second, despite the fact he was doing his very utmost, straining every sinew, to hold himself in check.

Lauren stopped, though – almost at the point of no

return for Mark – and gave him a few moments to calm down sufficiently before … 'I want to feel your cock inside me now, Mark,' Lauren gasped as she shifted position and straddled his thighs. 'I want it so much.'

She grabbed Mark's shoulders and raked her fingers over his body. Then, with her thighs pressing wetly against his, she positioned herself so she could manoeuvre the head of his cock against her pussy lips. She slid herself over the length of his shaft, then up and down, up and down, riding him in a mounting frenzy of desire.

Lauren's pussy muscles flexed around Mark's stiff cock, rocking him, her vagina tight and wet, for it was dripping liquid. He reached up to her but she grabbed his arms and pinned them above his head. Mark grunted with her movements as she continued to push her hips up and down, fitting her sex round his hardness. Lauren shoved herself down on Mark with increasing force and he groaned and whimpered and stiffened even more inside her as she rose and fell on him.

Lauren began to moan and flush and rock back and forth, Mark's stiffness rock hard inside her and ready to explode. Then she let go of herself altogether and shuddered frenziedly as exquisite oscillations began to pulse through her.

And as Lauren climaxed Mark allowed himself his own ecstatic release. He began to spasm uncontrollably beneath her before letting out a strangled cry and shooting his liquid, spurt after vigorous spurt, deep inside her sex.

And that was only the beginning of an afternoon and evening of unbridled passion for Mark and Lauren, during which, like the two crazed sex addicts they'd now become, they made love again, and again … and again.

Finally exhausted, they fell into deep, blissful sleep, cradled in each other's arms. They slept like angels. Mark awoke the following day to a shard of early-morning sun slicing through the bedroom curtains. Lauren nudged him fully awake and announced, 'I want you to move in with me.'

'You really do like to get straight to the point, don't you?' Mark replied, giving her a lazy grin.

'Well?' she persisted.

'Consider it done.'

'It's no good,' Lauren then said, her big green eyes glistening. 'I simply *must* have you again.' She guided his mouth to her sex as she fastened her own lips tight to his cock. Mark's tongue moved vigorously over the lips of her sex as his cock became even harder in her mouth, throbbing in her throat.

Lauren took her lips away from his shaft and shifted position. 'I want you inside me again now,' she said and pushed him unceremoniously onto his back. Mark groaned with pleasure as Lauren got on top of him and straddled his thighs. Sliding her moist pussy down onto the thickness of his cock, she ground her hips down and started to ride him. And ride him and ride him.

Lauren looked through half-drawn lids into Mark's eyes as she shoved herself down on him with ever-increasing force, making him groan and stiffen even more inside her with each thrust.

Oh, the memory of it! Mark groaned again and stiffened even more in his own hand as he relived the experience …

He began to thrust his hips upwards rhythmically, pulsing with his imminent climax, and Lauren rocked back and forth on his cock as she began to rub her sticky fingers frantically over her clit.

His cock.

Her fingers.

Her clit.

His fingers.

His cock.

His fingers, stroking away, jerking more forcefully at his cock until it was ready to explode, until he was ready to come.

Then he did come, hard. Mark groaned and tightened his fist, spurting warm seed that splashed over his fingers as he repeated her name over and over into the darkness of his bedroom. 'Lauren, Lauren, Lauren …'

Chapter Two

Mark tried to get back to sleep after that but he had no success. Not long ago he'd been back with Lauren, if only in his dreams and half-dreams. Now he was wide awake, his mind in turmoil. A jumble of thoughts crowded his brain, with but one subject: Lauren, his goddess. And the past closed around him once more …

Mark had been deeply in love, utterly besotted with Lauren from the first moment he set eyes on her. 'I want you to move in with me.' That's what she'd said to him during that sex-drenched weekend they'd first met and for him to have said no would have been unthinkable. As Mark got to know her over the following weeks and months, it became even more unthinkable that he could ever leave her.

Lauren had it all as far as he was concerned. She was warm, intelligent, vivacious, and incredibly beautiful. She continued to be dynamite in bed too – inventive and adroit and unconstrained. She also continued to be something else: commanding, aggressive even, during sex in a way that spoke to some dark need deep inside Mark that he chose to blank from his mind.

Lauren was everything Mark had ever dreamed of in a woman, and so much more besides, and he couldn't imagine life without her. She obviously had similar feelings about him because four months after their first meeting she asked him to marry her. Actually, he'd been about to propose to her, but typically she got in first. Lauren always seemed to be one jump ahead of Mark.

* * *

Mark found married life with Lauren wonderful. She and he were exceptionally close, closer than Mark had ever imagined he could be with another person. They liked the same things – books, films, plays, food, wine, you name it. They had the same sense of humour, shared the same interests. And they were so hot for each other it just wasn't true, making love constantly, often for hours at a time. At first.

Eventually life got in the way and the honeymoon period finally came to an end. The couple were both going from strength to strength in their respective careers, his in marketing and hers in publishing, and as time flew by – one year, two years, more – they became busier and busier at work. They became busier still in the senior positions they both inevitably found themselves occupying courtesy of their successful careers. That meant, among other things, having to work even longer hours, seeing less of each other.

Even so, that usually still left the weekends and Mark cherished his time with Lauren. Sundays were the best. The couple got into a delightful routine: they'd sleep late and when they awoke Mark would go down to the kitchen and make them a continental breakfast. He'd bring it back up on a tray along with the Sunday papers and he and Lauren would lounge around on the bed, eating and drinking and reading the papers.

Then they'd shower and get dressed in a leisurely fashion. If the weather was lousy, in the afternoon they'd watch one of the classic films they had on DVD. If the weather was OK but a bit chilly they'd go for a good long walk, blow away the cobwebs. Because it was Sunday the streets in and around Chelsea were quieter and the pavements emptier. But there was still the simmering energy that never left central London and they both found it invigorating.

If it was sunny but not too hot Mark and Lauren would take a stroll in one of the London parks, Hyde Park maybe, or Regents Park. They'd picnic on the grass and chat and casually people-watch, looking at the couples, the tourists, the joggers, whoever. Then they'd wander back arm in arm through the park in a homeward direction, feeling chilled out but energised, just right.

In the evening Mark and Lauren would go to a nearby Italian restaurant they liked. They'd have vodka tonic aperitifs, a meal – delicious but not too heavy – and some good white wine to accompany the food. They'd finish with coffees and then walk the short distance back to the house for "liqueurs". It was their private joke.

What would happen was this. As soon as they got home they'd go up to their bedroom and strip naked. Invariably Mark would already be very aroused at the prospect of what was to come, his breathing heavy, his heart beating fast. He'd lay on his back on the bed, his hard cock ready and jutting from his body, and Lauren would straight away sit on his face. Mark would stare up, blissfully helpless, as her perfect backside descended before him. Then her thighs would clamp down on his head and his face would be pinned down into her crotch. Soon his nose and mouth would become slick with Lauren's wetness as she used him for her pleasure.

Then she would lean forward and take Mark's shaft in her mouth, all the while continuing to rub her wet sex in his face. As he smothered in her crotch he'd become totally immersed in the aroma and sensation of her pussy grinding in his face. Lauren would suck and suck at Mark's hard cock as she rocked forward and back, rubbing her crotch over his mouth. She would then begin stroking her clit and her wet pussy, her fingers smacking against his chin. And she'd keep on stroking herself, her pussy

14

squelching wetly against her fingers, until she climaxed in spasms. This was Mark's cue to ejaculate into her mouth, which he duly did, his whole body shaking with orgasmic pleasure. Come sprayed out of his cock in liquid bursts deep into Lauren's hot, wet mouth.

But Lauren didn't stop squirming and rocking on his face and didn't stop sucking his cock, didn't stop until she'd sucked him dry. She would withdraw her mouth from Mark's cock, swing round and spit some of the semen into his mouth, keeping the remainder for herself. The couple would then kiss languorously, their mouths creamily wet, as he swallowed his come mixed with hers and she swallowed the same, and it was like they were drinking a fine liqueur, that's what they agreed. It was warm and heavy and delicious.

And they would look directly into each other's eyes when they shared this kinky experience, their Sunday night ritual …

He could see Lauren's great big eyes now, sparkling emerald green, hypnotic in their intensity.

It was as black as pitch in Mark's bedroom, the one he'd shared with Lauren from the day they'd met, and which he now had all to himself. But he could still see her the way he'd seen her then. Hell, he could still see it all – the way Lauren had looked when she first came into his life, the way she'd sashayed towards him in The Americas Bar, picked him up, the radiance of her beauty. He could still remember how she felt – her lustrous dark hair, her angular cheeks, her full lips, her shapely breasts and thighs, her slender neck and hands and feet.

Lauren had been Mark's whole world, his entire universe, for such a long time and now she was gone. What they had shared, that magical thing, was gone. It was history. There were times very occasionally when Mark persuaded himself he was starting, just starting, to get over Lauren. Then there were times like now when he realised all too clearly that he was more obsessed with her than ever. He was consumed by thoughts of Lauren, could think of nothing, of nobody else.

Mark knew he ought to pull himself together and move on. But how, for God's sake? Perhaps he should move on literally, live somewhere else altogether, miles away. Certainly this house, which was his now, simply wouldn't do any more. It had a lot going for it in many ways, Mark couldn't deny that. It was worth a small fortune, apart from anything else. But it was completely suffused with memories of Lauren. How could he possibly hope to get over her if he kept on living here?

All that aside, Mark said to himself resignedly, one thing was certain. There was no way he was going to get back to sleep. He simply couldn't be more wide awake. He switched the bedside light on, got out of bed and padded downstairs, naked.

Mark made himself a mug of coffee in the kitchen and took it into the living room, going over to the PC in the corner of the room. He sat down heavily in front of the screen and booted up the computer. Mark decided to log onto the Internet to look at some porn. Why not? he thought. It would pass the time. And time was something he had plenty of these days now he was not only wifeless but jobless too. He was time rich. He was a fucking time billionaire. Sipping at his coffee, Mark looked for sites featuring BDSM. He surfed around for one most likely to give him the specific fix he needed, and that *had* to be a Femdom site.

He decided on one of the sites he was already registered with and downloaded a short film that looked promising. From the stills it evidently involved a dark-haired beauty in a black leather catsuit, whipping the shit out of a good-looking young guy who was wearing nothing but a slave's collar and the marks of her lash. Mark took a couple of gulps of coffee as the opening credits appeared. He rested the mug on the computer table, turning the sound down so he could concentrate on the images before him and use his imagination more.

As Mark watched the film, he put himself in the place of the man and fantasised that the beautiful woman was Lauren. And that aroused him, no doubt about it. He could feel his breath coming faster. His cock grew hard again and he gripped his hand round it, pushing his fist up and down on himself.

What he was watching was sordid, Mark told himself. *Whip, whip, whip.* What he was imagining was even more sordid. *Whip, whip, whip.* He felt sinful and wicked for having such sordid thoughts ... *Whip, whip, whip ...* And that made him masturbate all the harder, guilt and lust swelling his cock. *Whip, whip, whip.*

He had to rid himself of his guilt. *Whip, whip, whip.* Mistress Lauren, the cruel dominatrix in the film, would force it out of him, beat it out of him. *Whip, whip, whip.*

Mark could feel lust and shame rushing through him now, tight and urgent, as he jerked more forcefully at his hard cock. Then the evidence of his shame burst out of his shaft in a warm rain of sinful semen that splattered down in abundance to anoint his naked thighs.

Chapter Three

Mark thought some more about moving right away from London – not permanently, because he loved the city so much – but at least for a while. He thought about it seriously and he thought about it a lot. He thought about it when he was drunk, which regrettably he often was these days; and he thought about it sober. He decided that, yes, a complete change of scenery for a time represented his best hope of getting his life back together. If things went according to plan, he reasoned, it would provide the cure for what ailed him so acutely.

And Mark knew just the destination to aim for too, the South coast. But not just anywhere on that coast. It had to be Brighton, which, in Mark's view, had the edge over any other resort not just in the South of England but anywhere else in the country. It contained an incredible diversity of people and ideas and was well known as an open society, for its non-conformity and acceptance of all lifestyles. Brighton was irreverent, fun, left-of-centre, alive and vibrant. If anywhere could take him out of himself, help him to recover his old *joie de vivre,* it would be that very special seaside city.

Brighton was replete with history too, a subject that had always interested Mark. George IV had built a spectacular domed palace there: The Royal Pavilion, home to some flamboyant architecture and even more flamboyant interior design. He'd sited it deliberately close to the house of his lover and that was probably where Brighton's reputation as a place for "dirty weekends" first came from. Brighton was louche and sexy; it was sophisticated and easy going. It was where Mark wanted to be.

He took a one-year lease on a furnished apartment there. It was on the second floor of a tall white monolith on Marine Parade, the wide boulevard full of handsome Regency façades – grand five-storey properties, many converted to offices – that runs along a mile of the city's seafront. The apartment itself had a big living room with a fine view overlooking the sea.

Mark put the handful of clothes and other belongings he wished to bring with him into the boot of his car, closed up the house in Chelsea and set off one muggy, rainy afternoon to start his new life. He began the journey a good deal later than he'd planned because the weather was absolutely filthy: rain, rain and more rain.

He had packed the car earlier in the day but had put off the drive until it stopped raining quite so hard. Except the rain hadn't eased off; it was really bucketing down. The sky was heavy with dark grey clouds and the rain was unyielding. It had lacquered the streets black and all but cleared them of pedestrians, if not of traffic.

Mark didn't want to delay any longer. He dashed to his car under the shelter of an umbrella and got in, buckling on his seat belt. He jabbed at the car's ignition, put it in gear, turned on the lights and the windscreen wipers and drove off. The wipers swung across the screen, sweeping the rain from the glass, and the tyres hissed on the wet tarmac.

The drive began slowly; there were an awful lot of cars on the move on those wet roads. It got steadily slower as the traffic leaving the capital turned out to be particularly heavy, virtually gridlocked. As he waited at a stop light, Mark glanced into his rear-view mirror and found himself staring at the reflection of his own blue eyes. They were raw from too much booze and too many sleepless nights.

A web of tell-tale lines furrowed his forehead. Mark brought his gaze back to the rain-lashed windscreen as his car crawled through the wet, congested streets of West London.

The rain was constant, intense, relentless. It pelted down on the windscreen, and Mark drove mainly by focussing on the red taillights of the car inching along ahead of him. The road continued to be blocked with traffic and he continued to move at a snails pace. Mark sat in the line of crawling traffic, rain drumming the roof, his fingers drumming the wheel. He felt tense. He felt impatient. He felt like a drink. His mouth was dry, parched. But water wouldn't have slaked Mark's thirst. He wanted a real drink. Or three.

It was evening now, getting darker by the minute. Mark's car was creeping along the traffic clogged, rain-sodden Western Avenue towards the Hanger Lane underground station. He remembered there was a Crowne Plaza hotel virtually on top of that. What the hell, he thought; he didn't have to get to Brighton today. There was nobody waiting for him there, God knows. He'd stop at the hotel, have a few drinks and a bite to eat, and stay the night. If he could get a room, that is.

He could get a room; the place seemed to be half-empty as far as he could see. Mark booked in, then went straight to the hotel bar. He ordered a vodka tonic on the rocks and a toasted ham and cheese sandwich from the bartender, a man with a strong mid-European accent and an unobtrusive manner. Mark sipped the vodka tonic, the ice cubes rattling in his glass. He gave a sigh of satisfaction as he felt the vodka's cold heat caress his throat and begin to seep through the rest of him.

His toasted sandwich came. Mark ate it, not because he was hungry – he'd lost all interest in food of late – but because he needed something to soak up the drink. He drank a second vodka, ordered another and took his drink to his hotel room.

Mark sipped his vodka tonic and stood at the window of his anonymous room, looking out. It was now completely dark outside apart from the gleam of headlamps and streetlights and the rain tipped it down harder than ever. All was water, driving, drenching, drowning. He watched it running down the window in streams. It took his thoughts back to another exceptionally wet night …

*　　*　　*

Outside the house the rain was coming down in a great hammering downpour. Mark and Lauren were seated side by side on the black leather couch that graced the beautifully furnished living room. Both of them were stark naked, both of them sexually aroused. 'Listen to all that racket outside,' Mark said. 'You realise we're effectively rained-in.'

'Why does that not concern me in the slightest?' Lauren replied, her emerald green eyes glittering with desire. She began kissing Mark on the mouth, doing so aggressively hard. She painted his lips with her tongue and then shoved it inside his open mouth quick and tight.

After a while Lauren stopped kissing Mark and instead moved her lips sinuously over his chest. She licked and sucked Mark's nipples, teasing them with her tongue, as one of her soft hands slipped down his torso towards his erection. She folded her hand around his hot shaft and began smoothing her palm over it, slowly pulling it up and down. Then Lauren parted Mark's thighs slightly and eased herself to the floor. She knelt between his legs and, opening her lips, pressed her mouth to the head of his erect cock.

Lauren licked and sucked the swollen head of his shaft and also stroked its length with one hand. At the same time she began plunging two fingers of her other hand in and out of her wet pussy.

Shifting position after a while, Lauren got off her knees and moved up Mark's body to caress his chest again before kissing him hard on the lips once more, probing his mouth voraciously with her tongue.

'Lay flat on your back on the couch now, Mark,' Lauren directed and, as soon as he'd shifted position, she squatted astride his face, positioning herself above his mouth and slowly sitting lower. Silently, Lauren reached down to pull her labia open, to show him what she wanted from him, and he raised his head so that he could give her what she wanted.

Mark moved his tongue hungrily over the slippery lips of Lauren's pussy, lapping at her, his face glistening with her juices. He continued to lick and lap at Lauren as she ground her thighs down. Then the pleasure exploded through her and, shoving her sex down even harder on his mouth, her orgasm came. Lauren's climax made her cry out and shudder convulsively over Mark's face until she shuddered at last to a halt.

When Lauren had finished hyperventilating she climbed off Mark's face, which was heavily daubed by the spray of her release, her musky scent splattered against his lips. She changed position again, this time lying on top of Mark, facing him. Lauren kissed him once more, letting him taste her mouth as she licked her own pussy juices from his lips.

She then kissed and caressed her way down Mark's body to his hard cock. She knelt between his calves and leant forward to blow him again. Lauren parted her lips and closed her mouth tightly over Mark's erection, letting it slide in slowly. She began to work her mouth up and down, cascading her tongue across the length of his shaft as he trembled with pleasure.

Lauren withdrew Mark's cock from her mouth and slithered part way up the couch to squat above his thighs.

'Fuck me now,' she demanded urgently. Which is what Mark did, pushing his erection inside her, filling her tight, wet pussy with its thickness. Lauren sighed with delight as he forged deep into her sex, fucking her hard.

Mark pushed up into Lauren even harder and she moaned and cried out with his movements, her pussy quivering around his shaft. He began to fuck her faster and faster, his whole body shaking, his stiff cock thrusting deep into her sex. Fighting for breath, Lauren shuddered to a violent orgasm, crying out deliriously as her climax exploded.

Mark was on the very brink of his own climax now and could feel himself building to the peak of excitement. Then the pleasure tightened and exploded through him too. He came long and hard, ejaculating his warm seed deep inside Lauren's sex. He grunted again and again as orgasmic spasms ripped through him like a sound wave. And at last the spasms ceased and it was over …

Yes, it was over. All of it was over, Mark reflected. Over. So why couldn't he accept the situation? Why couldn't he stop thinking about Lauren all the time? Stop living in the past, he told himself. Live in the present.

So, what of the present? Mark thought. It was a very wet evening, wasn't it, an exceptionally wet evening. What would *she* be doing now this wet, wet evening? Was she wet, was her pussy wet? Was it soaking wet? Was Lauren's pussy soaking wet because she was having hot, heavy sex, fucking her brains out? Was she doing that with Sam Lowell right now, right this minute?

Mark gulped down the last of his vodka and put the glass down. He thought about his ex-wife having sex with the new love of her life, Sam Lowell, as he stared at the rain outside lashing down on the dark window pane.

Chapter Four

Mark awoke at the crack of dawn the next day after a night of only intermittent sleep. He had a quick shower and a cup of coffee in his room, then booked out of the hotel, emerging into a grey, drizzling morning. He glanced at his watch. It was just past 5 o'clock.

He got back on the road, half-expecting there still to be traffic queues and driving rain, he'd got so used to them the day before. And it had been pouring with rain through most of the night; Mark could attest to that because he hadn't slept worth a damn. But there were no queues of traffic, it goes without saying, not at that early hour of the morning, and the rain had eased right off. It was now just spitting. He turned the windshield wipers on to low intermittent.

Mark went back to thinking about the demise of his marriage to Lauren. No surprises there – he just couldn't leave the subject alone. He kept scratching away at it like a kid with a scab on his knee, reopening the wound all the time. But he just couldn't help himself. God Almighty, how he missed Lauren, wished somehow that he could turn back time.

Where had it all gone wrong? Why had their marriage fallen apart the way it had? When had it started to fall apart? Mark had no idea exactly when it was that Lauren started her affair with Sam Lowell. As the author of a series of bestselling political thrillers, each one more popular than the last, Sam was one of the leading clients of the publishing house for which Lauren worked. But a client was *all* he was, Mark had thought. When Lauren had left him for Sam it had come as a huge surprise, a real bolt out of the blue. Mark hadn't realised there was anything between Lauren and the darkly handsome, erudite writer apart from a friendly working relationship, blind fool that he'd been.

The rain continued to spit down, specks of drizzle pattering onto the windscreen. How could she do this to me? That's what Mark had asked himself despairingly when Lauren had left him for Sam Lowell. As he drove through the wet grey early morning he remembered how in the first few months after she'd left him he had been in the habit of repeating those words to himself over and over again like a cracked record. How could she do this to me? How could she do this to me?

Lauren had done it to him, though. She'd done something else too. She'd made him a rich man.

Their marriage was now a thing of the past, there was no doubt about that. Mark had the legal papers to prove it, the *decree nisi*. But there was no doubt either that he had done incredibly well out of it financially because when they divorced Lauren had settled a substantial sum of money on him.

A lot of wealthy people seem to believe the edict "if you've got it, flaunt it". The worst kind like to not just flaunt their wealth; they like to rub your nose in it. The best kind are the very opposite of this, wearing their wealth lightly and with consummate ease, and Lauren fell firmly into that category. The swish, expensively furnished house in Chelsea had told Mark from the outset that she was by no means poor. But it hadn't been until after she'd proposed marriage to him and he'd accepted that she informed him just how rich she was.

Lauren was the heiress of a large fortune and had, of course, no financial need to work whatsoever. But she chose to, and had carved out a highly impressive career for herself in the publishing trade. Mark had envied Lauren the evident passion she felt for her work. He'd wished he felt the same way about marketing, but after more than ten years in that most superficial of worlds its appeal to him had palled, to say the least.

Maybe it had been out of a sense of guilt on her part, Mark didn't know, but Lauren had treated him extremely generously when it came to the divorce settlement. She had signed the Chelsea house over to him, which was mortgage free, and also given him virtually all of its contents. Lauren's explanation to Mark of why she'd done this was that she wanted to make a completely fresh start with Sam. But that hadn't been the end of her generosity to him by any means. Mark had emerged at the end of the marriage not only with the house and its contents but with a cool five million pounds in capital gifted to him by Lauren as well; she'd insisted on it.

If Lauren hadn't been so outstandingly generous in this way at the end of their marriage, would he, Mark wondered, have gone on to throw away his career in the incredibly cavalier way he'd ended up doing? Maybe, maybe not. Who knew? One thing Mark did know with absolute certainty was this: he'd give back the house and all the money in the blink of an eye if only he could somehow get Lauren back.

The drizzle had become so light it was barely misting the air now and Mark turned off the windscreen wipers as he motored along. He got to thinking again. He wasn't eating sensibly nor was he getting enough exercise or enough sleep. He needed to put those things right. But more seriously, he needed to get some control over his drinking. It had got completely out of hand.

After his marriage broke up Mark had increasingly used hard liquor as a crutch. If things got really bad, he had told himself – and they had – he could always fall back on drink. Lauren was no longer there for him, but vodka was and it dulled the pain. He steadily increased his drinking until it, and his obsession with Lauren, had all but taken over his life.

At the time of his divorce Mark had been working as a senior executive for Simpson and Gray, a big London marketing agency. He'd risen from the ranks in that organisation to just below director level because he'd proved himself smart, ambitious, and very good at what he did. But he hadn't been able to sustain his ambition, had more than lost his edge. Worse than that, he had started screwing up, getting a reputation for unreliability.

People at the agency couldn't help noticing that Mark had lost much of his old drive and enthusiasm and seemed increasingly distracted. Then they started to notice, more worryingly, that he'd begun to develop a drink problem. Mark's immediate boss, a nice guy called Steve Farrell who was on the board of directors, had a few quiet words with him about it. Mark made all the right noises in response but essentially took no notice, just carried on drinking.

The crunch came when he missed an especially important business meeting because he'd been at home drunk, obsessing over Lauren. The next day Mark got called in to see the company's Chief Executive. David Parsons was a ruthless son of a bitch at the best of times, a man who certainly didn't take prisoners. Sure, like a lot of sociopaths, he could switch on the charm when it suited him. This was most definitely not one of those occasions.

'I have simply this to say to you,' he said, looking Mark in the eye with piercing severity. 'I want shot of you from Simpson and Gray. You're a drunk, which makes you a serious liability to the company.' Parsons concluded their brief one-sided interview with controlled venom. 'You can wait to be sacked or you can go of your own accord, like *right now*.'

He had taken the second option, going straight home without a backward glance. And when he'd got home he'd got drunk, his mind overwhelmed once more with thoughts of Lauren. He'd been drunk, off and on, ever since, this man with five million pounds in the bank; this man who owned outright a beautiful house in one of the chicest and most expensive parts of London; this man who had so much and yet had nothing. Mark's life felt utterly empty and he drank to try and fill the void. He'd become someone without any sense of purpose, floundering in a sea of alcohol. Money can't buy you love, as the saying goes. By the same token, when you've found love – real true love – and then lost it, money doesn't come remotely close to being a satisfactory substitute.

Mark was well past the ragged edges of London now. He passed through suburban Surrey and on into the lushness of rural Sussex towards the undulating open countryside of the South Downs. There were wide hills with long smooth summits and shadowy hollows. Then he saw it stretched out before him: the vast urban sprawl of Brighton and, beyond, a shimmering strip of sea, the English Channel.

Mark drove into a seaside city that was in the process of waking up, and he made for the front. He gave a glance down to the dashboard when he got there and saw that the display on the digital clock said 7.05. He drove along the front, past the white sea-facing frontages of hotels and offices and apartment blocks, toward the block that contained his new home.

Forget the past, look to the future. That's what Mark said to himself as he put his key in the front door lock of his new apartment. But the future is as difficult to predict as the past is to leave behind. The future had some very big surprises indeed in store for Mark. And the past had by no means finished with him yet.

Chapter Five

After Mark had let himself into the apartment he unpacked, which was hardly a mammoth undertaking given the small number of belongings he'd chosen to bring with him. Then he familiarised himself with his immediate surroundings, his new home. And that's what this spacious, well furnished apartment was, for the next year anyway, Mark told himself. It was his home. It wasn't Lauren's home or Lauren's former home. There was nothing here to remind him of her at all.

Mark decided to have a nap to try and catch up on some of his lost sleep, ended up sleeping much longer than he thought he would and awoke feeling genuinely refreshed. He had a coffee, shaved and went out for a bracing walk along the seafront. He looked out at the broad grey expanse of the sea, its waves slowly ebbing and flowing. Above him gulls soared and swooped and cried out. Mark breathed in the sea air, could taste the tang of salt on his lips.

Then he crossed back over Marine Parade and walked toward a part of Brighton he'd always loved. He wandered round the wonderfully confusing narrow passages and cobbled streets that make up the Old Lanes. Finding a vegetarian restaurant there that looked quite promising, he decided to give it a try. Feeling positively virtuous, he asked for mineral water rather than alcohol to go with his meal. He then went to a supermarket and bought some essential supplies, which included a couple of bottles of

Red Smirnoff vodka – he wasn't feeling *that* virtuous – and returned to his apartment.

Mark ran himself a hot bath, the rush of the water breaking the silence of the apartment in a pleasant, soothing way. He had a good soak, dried off and put on a terrycloth robe. He ambled into the kitchen and twisted open one of the newly purchased bottles of vodka. He got some ice from the fridge, put it into a glass and poured some vodka over it, adding a couple of splashes of tonic. He let the glass stand on the kitchen table for a little while. He wanted to savour the moment.

This was the second day in a row since he couldn't remember when that Mark had refrained from having his first drink of the day until the sun was over the yardarm. Licking his lips in anticipation, he picked up his glass and walked into the living room. He took his first swallow and the drink slid down his throat, pure cold heat. Oh my, Mark said to himself with a sigh of satisfaction. That was worth the wait.

He was clearly wide open to accusations of being in denial, he knew that, but Mark honestly didn't think he was an alcoholic as such. He didn't think he'd have to give up drinking altogether to cure his undoubted drink problem. To cure his Lauren problem was a different matter. Now that *would* require total abstinence. Mark was only too aware that he had to achieve closure as far as Lauren was concerned if he was going to get his life on track again. That's what the move to Brighton had been all about, hadn't it. And maybe, just maybe, he could find the inner strength to draw a line under their relationship once and for all and move on. Completion, Mark told himself, closure. That was what he needed.

Mark shook the ice cubes around in his glass and drank some more. One of the difficulties was that in her own way Lauren seemed to be finding it as hard to let him go as he was in trying to shake off his obsession with her. Even though they were no longer married, she still kept in touch with him, although it was only intermittently and always by phone. Even though they weren't together any more they could still be friends, Lauren had insisted on more than one occasion since their break-up. But Mark was quite sure he could never be her friend and nothing more. It just wouldn't work. To him Lauren wasn't friendship material. She was someone to worship, a goddess.

He sat down on one of the comfortable armchairs that had come with the apartment and sipped his drink. He needed to be strong to get over Lauren. The drink made him feel strong. Mark tried to simply feel the strength and look ahead to his future existence, free of his obsession with Lauren. He could do it. He would be strong, was strong.

There must be no more phone calls, that's what he'd tell her. He didn't want her to think he was ungrateful for her considerable generosity to him in the divorce settlement because that wasn't the case. He was extremely grateful. He certainly didn't want her to go away with the wrong idea about that. But he did want her to go away. Didn't he? How else was he ever going to get over her and get his life back, for Christ's sake?

And that was when Mark's mobile phone rang. He couldn't ignore it. He could see it and hear it. It was sitting on the coffee table in front of him, making its presence felt with an insistent trill. He leant forward and picked it up. There was a pause and then he heard Lauren's familiar voice.

'Mark?' she said.

'Lauren.' He kept his voice flat, neutral. He was being strong. He didn't want her to phone any more, he'd tell her. It wasn't a good idea. They were finished as a married couple and trying to be friends was a compromise that wouldn't work for them, they both had to accept that. They both had to be strong.

'I'm all on my own tonight,' Lauren said.

God, she sounded sexy, Mark thought, his resolve already beginning to slip. 'Really?' he said.

'Yeah,' she said. 'So, how are you, Mark? How are you settling in?'

'Great,' he said. 'I moved in this morning and really like the place.' He drank some more vodka, felt its icy heat massage his throat.

'What were you doing when I phoned?' Lauren asked. She must have heard the ice cubes in his glass clink, Mark thought. Was she checking up on him? He knew his excessive drinking had been worrying her a lot; she'd said so. She'd phoned him a couple of times when he'd been so smashed she hadn't been able to get a word of sense out of him. It had alarmed her greatly, she'd told him.

'Honestly, what was I doing?' Mark said. Thinking about asking you – no, *telling* you – to stop phoning, Lauren. Telling you, politely of course, diplomatically, that there can be no friendship between us.

Maybe this was the time to tell her that.

And maybe it wasn't. He didn't think he could find the right words.

'Yes, honestly,' Lauren said. 'What were you doing when I phoned?'

Mark told the truth, sort of. He said, 'I was sitting in an armchair and thinking about you and having a drink – my first one of the day, I hasten to add.'

'Glad to hear it, really glad,' Lauren said and he could tell from her tone of voice when she spoke those words that she meant it. She continued, her tone subtly changing. 'Want to know what I was doing when I phoned you?'

'Uh-huh.'

'Sitting in an armchair and thinking about you and having a wank – my first one of the day, I hasten to add,' she said. 'And which, I'm still doing, by the way. I've rubbed myself all wet and sticky and I just can't stop.

Want to know what I'm wearing?'

'Yeah.' Mark gulped. His cock had sprung up violently beneath his robe. What was she trying to do to him?

'I'm wearing absolutely nothing,' Lauren said, her voice thick now, husky. 'And you?'

'A bathrobe,' he replied. Mark's heart was thumping, his hard cock was pounding, his palms had become wet.

'Put down your drink and take off your robe.'

'Pardon?'

'You heard.'

'OK,' Mark said, his breath quickening by the second. 'Your wish is ...'

'My command,' Lauren interrupted. 'That's right. And don't you ever forget it.'

'What do you want me to do now?' Mark breathed rather than spoke into the phone. 'I've done as you said. I'm as naked as you are.' He could feel his blood rushing through his veins, making his cock ever more rigid, making it throb even more.

'Make yourself hard.'

'There's no need,' Mark gasped. 'Believe me on that one.'

Lauren let out a throaty laugh. 'Make yourself harder then.'

He obeyed instantly and grasped hold of his aching shaft. He could feel electric sensations rippling up through his fingers from his cock as he started to push his fist up and down on himself.

'Do you feel good?' she said.

'Mmm.'

'I feel good too,' Lauren said with a moan. 'Shall I tell you how good I feel?'

'Yes please,' Mark replied, his voice raspy with desire.

'My nipples are hard, my thighs are all quivery, my clit is stiff, and my pussy is so wet that my hand is all glistening, really sticky. Just imagine, Mark, how juicy I

33

look bucking away in my armchair, finger-fucking myself.'

He could imagine it all right, could see her using her fingers on herself, plunging them in and out of the wetness between her thighs, could see it all. He could hear it too, the sound of her fingers in her sex, wet and urgent. It filled him with immense passion. Mark was panting, he was so incredibly turned on. He screwed his eyes shut. His fist continued to pump and pump as the images of Lauren having sex with herself rolled behind his eyes.

'I don't want to wait any more,' Lauren said with a moan of pleasure. 'I'm going to come now and I want you to come too.'

Mark jerked more forcefully at his cock as he listened to Lauren's orgasmic cries. His nerves were singing and his body was shaking as his hand moved furiously over his cock. Faster and faster he masturbated; it felt *so* good. He stroked himself even more quickly. Then the pulse came and he cried out, spasms ripping through him like a mighty wave. Sperm spurted out of his throbbing cock and into his fist, creamy and liquid.

Mark sat there, his heart still pounding from his orgasm. He was panting heavily and so was Lauren. Finally she stopped panting and spoke. 'I don't want to lose you,' she said, her voice almost a whisper. Then the line went dead.

After she'd hung up Mark put down the phone and sat looking at it. What Lauren and he had just done together had been amazing. It was over now but the experience still reverberated through his body; he felt wonderful. But what now? Was there hope, after all, that they would get back together? *I don't want to lose you.* Or was occasional phone sex with her ex-husband when her new lover wasn't about Lauren's bizarre idea of how they might achieve the elusive status of just being friends?

Mark stood and picked up his nearly empty glass. He

took a long breath and went back into the kitchen to wash the come off his fingers and make himself another drink. He washed and dried his hands and added some ice to his glass and splashed in some more vodka and tonic. Closure, Mark said to himself as he lifted the glass to his lips. Completion, he added as he gulped down his drink. Closure. Completion. Bullshit. Who had he been trying to fool? He was even more in thrall to Lauren than ever before. She'd just made perfectly sure of that. *I don't want to lose you.*

Chapter Six

Mark sat on the balcony of his apartment with his chair tilted back. It had been a glorious spring day, hot and bright. There was still not a cloud in the sky and the usually murky English Channel was continuing to give a fair approximation to Mediterranean blue. The salt air was warm and soft, the heat of the day fading. The sky remained blue but the light was beginning to dim as the sun started its stately progress to the dark horizon.

Mark smiled and sipped his vodka tonic. He was quietly rather pleased with himself. He'd been living in Brighton for nearly three weeks now and he was slowly but surely getting healthy. He was eating sensibly, getting loads of fresh air and exercise, reading a lot in order to keep his mind occupied, and sleeping much better than he'd been doing for a very long while. He was limiting his boozing to the evenings too, although he knew he was still drinking too much. The next stage, Mark thought, would be to switch from the hard stuff to wine. It wouldn't scramble his mind to the same degree.

He turned to look into the apartment and caught sight of his reflection in the glazed sliders. He looked at the handsome fellow staring back at him and raised his glass to him. 'Here's to you, Mark,' he said. 'Keep up the good work.' He took a long pull of his vodka tonic. He could feel a warm sensation creeping down his throat and chest, hitting his stomach. Nice. It wouldn't be quite so easy to switch to wine, he thought. It wouldn't have anything like the same kick. Maybe he'd reduce his intake of vodka instead. It was as broad as it was long. Either way, he'd make sure he got his alcohol consumption down to the sensible level it had been before Lauren walked out on him.

Ah, Lauren. *I don't want to lose you.* Mark leant back in the chair, holding the vodka in both hands, and gazed out across the blue expanse of the sea once more and got to thinking about the same old subject yet again.

There are an endless number of reasons why a marriage can hit the rocks. What had happened to theirs? Sam Lowell had happened, that's what. Which was crap and he knew it, Mark chided himself. If he was to have any hope of getting Lauren back – and that last phone call he'd received from her *had* given him hope – he would have to be honest with himself about why she'd left him in the first place.

Because it had been he, not she, hadn't it, who'd first started getting dissatisfied with the marriage – with its sexual side, to be exact. Why? Because after a while the sex had begun to feel too predictable to him, too familiar, and – more to the point – far too *tame.* Mark loved having sex with a dominant woman and Lauren was that all right; there was no doubt on that score whatsoever. The trouble was their lovemaking had only ever involved vanilla sex. And that hadn't been enough for Mark, he'd discovered to his alarm. As time went on he found he wanted more, *craved* more – much more.

Mark wanted Lauren to tie him up and beat his arse black and blue. He imagined her tying him spread-eagled to the bed on his front and then standing above him wielding a whip. He imagined her laying furiously into his backside with that whip while he moaned and wailed in pain and struggled uselessly against his bonds.

But Mark didn't just want to be tied up and beaten by Lauren. He wanted her to do other things to him too. He wanted her to buckle on a strap-on dildo and fuck him in the arse with it, make him her slut. Mark imagined Lauren pushing and pushing the dildo deep into him, and him pushing back on it until they both came in a sweaty delirium of lust.

He wanted more still, though. Mark wanted Lauren to humiliate him, really humiliate him. He imagined her shoving him down onto his knees and watching her haughty expression when he whimpered before her in abject, grovelling shame. Because that's where he wanted to be: grovelling on his knees beneath Lauren – where he belonged.

Mark wanted … But what was the use? How could he possibly ask Lauren to abuse him in such perverted ways? If he did ask her, wouldn't she think at best that he'd taken leave of his senses and at worst that she was married to one sick fuck? On the other hand, maybe Lauren would be as turned on by the idea of their developing a sadomasochistic relationship as he was. Or she might not.

Would she instead be positively repelled by the idea of sadomasochistic sex, disgusted with him for suggesting it? Could his asking for it do irreparable damage to their relationship, destroy it even – or do no damage to it at all, quite the reverse? Oh, why did he have to be so indecisive? Just ask Lauren, Mark told himself. Stop vacillating. It can't hurt to ask, surely. Or maybe it would hurt. A lot. And not in a nice way.

And so indecision continued to hold him. Mark carried on wavering and procrastinating to his own infuriation until he finally made up his mind. Kind of. Nothing ventured, nothing gained, he said to himself resolutely, and decided to muster up the courage to broach the subject with her. When the time was right.

Then a chance comment by Lauren one weekend made Mark seriously think again. She pointed to the page of the Sunday newspaper she was reading.

'Listen to this,' Lauren said, her full lips pursed slightly. '"The ex-girlfriend of Kurt Anson, the Hollywood superstar with the ultra-macho screen image, has 'told all' about their sordid sex life to a US scandal magazine. She said that Kurt had liked having anal sex with her – not giving but receiving, with her riding him rough with her strap-on dildo. He was also forever asking her to tie him up and thrash the living daylights out of him, she claims."'

'Well, there's a turn-up,' Mark said, genuinely surprised. The action-man movie star didn't seem obvious submissive material, not at all.

'What a pathetic creep,' Lauren said, her tone derisive. 'I can't stand the guy.' She gave a little shudder of disgust. Then, without looking up from the paper, she turned to the next page, the subject evidently forgotten.

Mark breathed a sigh of relief. Thank goodness he'd not mentioned his masochistic cravings to Lauren. She'd made it obvious what she thought about guys who were into being tied up and beaten and buggered with strap-on dildos – guys like Kurt Anson. They were pathetic creeps, she couldn't stand them.

Mark invariably deferred to Lauren. He always tried his best to accommodate what she did and didn't want and she obviously did not want to get into BDSM. Lauren didn't have to spell it out; Mark had got the message loud and clear without even so much as bringing the subject up with her. So, that was that, he told himself. He would have to forget all about it. Except that proved an awful lot easier said than done.

Chapter Seven

Mark started to become obsessed with the idea of being dominated sadistically, couldn't get it out of his head. What on earth could he do? If Lauren wouldn't do those deliciously painful and humiliating things to him perhaps he could go to a professional dominatrix and have her do them to him instead. He would only go to a pro ome the one time, just to see what it was like, Mark told himself. Where was the harm in that? In fact, it would be positively beneficial, would get the idea out of his system.

But Mark knew it wasn't possible, not even once. He wouldn't be able to tell Lauren what he was going to do; that would defeat the object. He would have to do it clandestinely and that felt like betrayal, would have *been* betrayal. And he wouldn't do that to Lauren.

No, he wouldn't, couldn't do that to her. And another thing: just for argument's sake, what if he *did* do it and Lauren ever found out? Christ, the ramifications of that for their relationship didn't bear thinking about.

Mark tried to forget about the idea – put it right out of his mind – he really did. He tried to convince himself that a professional dominatrix was just a glorified prostitute and he would never consider visiting one of those, now would he? But Mark could not convince himself. The more he denied himself the poisoned fruit, the more he felt tempted by it.

Then Mark thought he'd found the answer. OK, Lauren clearly wasn't interested in sadomasochism. He could work round that. When they were having sex Mark started to pretend that Lauren was not Lauren at all but a really sadistic pro   ome. When they made love at night in the darkness of the bedroom, Lauren as uninhibitedly assertive in her passion as ever, Mark imagined that his fantasy dominatrix was disciplining him, pulling at the metal clamps she'd attached to his nipples, making him squirm with pain.

He imagined her going further, imagined her whipping him harshly on the back and rear, her violence making him burn with pleasure. And he imagined the dominatrix going further still, fucking him in the arse brutally with a gigantic strap-on dildo, plunging into his narrow anus then withdrawing, then plunging in again, his insides screaming in protest.

His body was so marked now, so stretched, so damaged. It felt as if it was broken in pieces. The excitement was too much, too fucking much … It made Mark come, his orgasm overwhelming him – and inflaming the unwitting Lauren who climaxed too, her body convulsed by a long, shuddering spasm.

And the beauty of it was that Lauren really was none the wiser. Why would she be? She had no reason to believe that her devoted husband was dreaming up such depraved fantasies while they were having sex. And the strategy worked. The fantasies kept Mark from thinking about using the services of an actual pro   ome. For a while.

Then the craving came back even stronger. So Mark allowed himself to fantasise a little more. He started surfing the Net, looking for pornographic sites involving female domination. Mark told Lauren he was working on his computer in his attic study when in reality he was looking at Femdom websites, the more extreme the better.

Mark's favourite among the various MPEGs he downloaded during this shamefully furtive time was called

41

Dungeon Torment. It involved the torture of a man whose wrists were manacled to chains that were hanging from the ceiling of a dark dungeon.

The man was leather-hooded and gagged but otherwise naked and he had a giant hard-on, which was oozing precome. His nipples were clamped and lead weights were hanging from the clamps.

A gorgeous dark-haired dominatrix in a tight-fitting leather bodysuit was beating the man's backside savagely with a heavy whip, the strands of which were inlaid with small pieces of *bone,* for fuck's sake. Each time the whip landed, another red streak appeared on the man's flesh, joining the angry pattern of lacerations already there.

Mark felt a strange trembling at the base of his spine and an ache in his groin each time he watched that MPEG. He felt overcome with excitement as he imagined it was *him* in the dungeon, manacled to the chains hanging from the ceiling, *him* leather-hooded and gagged, his chest clamped with weighted nipple clamps, *him* receiving such excruciatingly vicious treatment from the gorgeous, whip-wielding dominatrix.

There was no harm in what he was doing, Mark rationalised to himself. He was just fantasising, everyone did that. It wasn't like he was cheating on his wife in that or indeed in any other way, nor would he. But another powerful voice inside his head fuelled his sense of guilt, told Mark he shouldn't be lying to Lauren about what he was doing on his computer, told him he was disgusting for getting excited by such extreme porn, asked him how he could possibly enjoy looking at those kind of degrading images when he was living with such a goddess. Mark resolved to stop. And he did.

But the temptation to visit a professional dominatrix did not go away. It got stronger. The thought of it excited Mark and terrified him in equal measure and that was a heady mixture. He felt he needed to experience for himself

42

what it would be like just one time. And it *would* be just the once. He wouldn't make a habit of it, honestly he wouldn't. But he didn't want to cheat on Lauren and that's what he'd be doing when it came right down to it. Mark couldn't do that, he just couldn't.

Eventually there was something else Mark couldn't do. He couldn't get a hard-on when Lauren wanted sex – no matter how much he let his sadomasochistic imagination run riot, or *tried* to let it run riot. The memory of it after all this time still made Mark go cold with shame. And not at what had happened either, but at the fact that he hadn't had the guts to tell Lauren *why* it had happened, come clean about the state he'd got himself into. Maybe they could have worked something out if he'd only found the courage to do that.

Because it had been bound to happen at some time. Mark's ploy couldn't go on working forever. Finally even fantasising that Lauren was not Lauren at all but a sadistic professional dominatrix doing unspeakable things to him hadn't been able to get him hard when they were trying to have sex. Mark made light of it at the time and, in fairness to her, so did Lauren. He'd had too much to drink, they agreed. He was very tired, working too hard. These things happened, blah, blah, blah.

Lauren had then gone off to have a shower, leaving her apparently exhausted husband to go to sleep. But as soon as he was on his own Mark had grabbed his cock and started masturbating. His penis, previously so stubbornly flaccid, had become hugely erect in no time as he thought about being dominated by his fantasy pro ome, while he stroked and pulled at himself. His eyes had been screwed shut and there had been a rushing noise in his ears but he'd seen what she did and heard what she said so clearly as he'd masturbated more and more quickly.

He'd seen her whipping him and whipping him and whipping him, heard her calling him her slut, calling him

43

her bitch. She had inflamed him with the dark passion that was his secret guilt as she'd told him what to do. *Come for me now, slut*, she had ordered, her voice as sharp as a stiletto. *Come for me, bitch.* And Mark had obeyed, shuddering with terrible desire as he shot out his sinful, hot semen into the air.

Chapter Eight

Mark lied to Lauren, told her he'd lost his libido because he was having to work so damned hard on a major project at the agency that it was sapping all his energy. There was an upside though, Mark explained. If he came up trumps this time for the company there was talk of him being given a place on the board of directors.

Lauren's response was all Mark could possibly have wished for. She wrapped her arms around him and said she understood entirely. It was OK, he mustn't worry. She didn't mind at all. This was his big chance, she said. He should grab it with both hands. She was sure his loss of libido was only temporary, that it would soon be a thing of the past and they'd go back to having a normal sex life again. What Mark would have liked more than anything else, of course, was an *abnormal* sex life. But needless to say he kept that thought to himself.

Actually, what Mark had told Lauren contained a strong element of truth. He *was* having to work extremely hard on the project to which he'd recently been assigned. It was a major advertising campaign for a big insurance company, and a directorship with Simpson and Gray was definitely in the offing if he kept his eye on the ball. And he was determined to do his best.

Soon Mark was working even harder than he'd been doing at the start of the project. He was getting into the office by eight o'clock every morning, often earlier. Most nights he wasn't getting home until nine or ten o'clock.

Mark was working weekends too. Forget about those special Sundays he and Lauren had once enjoyed. They were a thing of the past now, an ever more distant memory. He couldn't have worked any harder during this incredibly hectic period if he'd tried.

Lauren couldn't have been more understanding either. She never once complained about Mark's excessively long hours, the fact that she hardly ever saw him, that when she did he was completely distracted, that not just the sex but all the intimacy seemed to have gone out of their marriage these days. She was patience itself. Or appeared to be.

Arguably Mark didn't have much choice than to be a complete workaholic during this time. It could be the big breakthrough of his career if he played his cards right. But the truth was that Mark liked it, although for all the wrong reasons. Work was rapidly becoming his only world. He'd become wedded to it. It replaced sex – the kind of sex he wanted. And that was a good thing, Mark told himself, because he didn't want to be the sort of person who wanted that kind of perverted sex. His total absorption in his work, which was not of itself innately absorbing to him by any means, was a kind of comfort blanket for his mind. It blocked out all thoughts of deviant sex.

It couldn't stop that very troubling erotic dream Mark had, though. It was recurrent – virtually every night – and always the same. In the dream it was night time and there was a full moon. Mark was naked and being pursued by a beautiful brunette, also naked, who was carrying a whip. At first she pursued him across a sinister stretch of empty rutted land and then down a mud path in an equally creepy forest. Mark could hear the woman's footfalls getting closer and closer to him and the sound of her panting breaths, getting louder and louder. He was running and running down the path but with every heartbeat he knew she was closing in on him.

Then he stumbled and fell, landing on his hands and

knees. She'd caught him now and Mark realised to his shameful excitement that he *wanted* to be caught. He waited there on all fours, feeling vulnerable and exposed but unbelievably turned on. He found himself pushing his rear towards the woman, yearning for her to do whatever it was she was going to do to him. But she did nothing. Moments passed with excruciating slowness and the anticipation Mark felt became so intense it hurt.

But not half as much as the first lash of the woman's whip. Or the second or third or fourth …

On and on she berated his back and rear with savage blows. Each one was a flash of pure pain that made Mark tense and squirm more and more as the full effect of the whipping spread through his body. The woman kept on beating him in this ferocious way until the pain that was lacing through him was overwhelming. He felt as if his agonized body was on fire and he began bellowing in pain. Only then did she stop beating him.

Mark remained on all fours, facing ahead. He didn't dare look back at the woman or even move. But he could hear her masturbating, plunging her fingers noisily into the wet parts of her sex. Mark then felt her spread her wetness over his anal hole, lavishing it with her lubrication.

She stroked his backside several times before suddenly pushing the pommel of the whip with which she'd recently beaten him so savagely deep into his anus, making him groan with pain – and pleasure.

The woman gripped Mark by the hair and began sodomising him with the smooth pommel, wet from her pussy, entering and re-entering his anus. She made the implement move faster, made him burn with pain and with pleasure, with *pleasure-pain*. He felt totally degraded. He felt totally himself.

Mark would wake from these dreams with his heart pounding wildly in his chest and his cock ragingly hard. But his excitement would morph all too quickly into anxiety and worry and he'd lose his erection. Mark didn't want to be the man he was in those dreams, the kind of man – the kind of *pathetic creep* – Lauren would despise.

He'd tell himself he was being absurd, that he had no reason to be anxious. After all, they were just dreams. He wasn't that man in reality, and thank God for that. But Mark knew in his heart of hearts he was lying to himself. He knew exactly why the dreams made him feel such anxiety, but he didn't want to admit it. Because he knew that if he admitted it, he'd have to confront it.

The trouble was that after a while Mark started having flashbacks during the day. His recollections of those incredibly vivid dreams began to increasingly haunt his waking hours. They started to come between him and his work, his world. He began to lose his focus on that important project, started fouling up, making stupid errors.

Mark could feel the directorship he'd coveted slipping out of his grasp, so near and yet so far. But did he really care?

The vision of himself being beaten and sodomised by that dream dominatrix was far more seductive than being one of the top dogs in the artificial world of marketing. All the energy he'd been throwing into that felt bogus somehow, like displacement activity.

Finally Mark decided to properly confront his demons – the deviant fantasies and dreams that he kept so guiltily secret from his wife, from the world. He'd find a London-based professional dominatrix on the Internet and book a disciplinary session with her, just the one.

He'd get all this shit out of his system once and for all. All the main pro ome seemed to have their own websites, he remembered from the time when he used to regularly surf Femdom sites whilst pretending to Lauren that he was working on the computer in his attic study.

Mark went home early from work for once and, as soon as he entered the empty house, went straight up to his study. He switched on his computer and sat there staring at the screen, butterflies fluttering in his stomach. He logged on to the Internet, found Google and started his search.

Chapter Nine

Mark drove up toward the high-walled house in Kensington that was his destination and pulled his car to a standstill next to the curb. He was very nervous, his mouth so dry he could hardly swallow. He was about to do that thing he'd been resisting with every fibre of his being for such a long time. He was about to use the services of a professional dominatrix. He'd had a preliminary meeting with her and that had gone well. Very soon now it would be time for the real thing.

Mark would have been the first to admit that he hadn't had much of a clue when it came to choosing a pro   ome. He'd decided on Mistress Simone mainly because, from the photos of her on her website, she was beautiful, and also because she was relatively expensive. His logic had been that the service he was looking to purchase was essentially the same as any other: you got what you paid for. That was the way of the world, like it or not.

When Mark had met Mistress Simone in person, though, she had come as a surprise to him because she was very pleasant. It wasn't that he'd been expecting to be greeted by some sort of ogress. But he had been expecting someone stern, commanding, obviously sadistic. Mistress Simone hadn't been like that at all – on that occasion, anyway. She'd been warm and friendly and understanding.

She'd also proved to be even more beautiful than the photographs on her website. These had revealed a woman with strong features, big midnight-blue eyes, full lips, lush, dark hair hanging to her shoulders, and a curvy, perfectly proportioned figure. What the photos hadn't revealed was that Mistress Simone was a woman who radiated a great deal of charisma too. It shone from her like an aura.

She had also proved to be thoroughly professional and had wanted to find out what made her new client tick sexually before she'd embark on disciplining him in any way. At that preliminary session they'd just sat together in her living room and talked, or to be more precise Mark had done most of the talking with some judicious prompting from her.

Mistress Simone had asked him what his most frequent sexual fantasies were and he'd told her, revealing the recurrent masochistic dream he'd been having of late too. She'd asked him about his previous experience of being disciplined and he'd admitted it was non-existent. She'd wanted to know whether he wished to be "tied and teased" or something stronger and whether he minded if she left any marks. Something stronger, Mark had replied, and no, he didn't mind if she left any marks. He'd taken a calculated risk based on the fact that he was seeing so little of Lauren these days he could easily disguise any fading bruises and the like from her as long as he was reasonably careful about it.

Mistress Simone had given Mark instructions about the ablutions he should carry out before presenting himself to her to be disciplined. She'd also made it clear that there was no question of Mark being permitted to fuck her, that wasn't the kind of service she was offering, and he'd assured her he understood absolutely. Finally, she'd told him he must always address her as "mistress" when speaking to her.

Then they'd parted company and Mark had waited with eager anticipation for their appointment a week later. In fact, he'd been unable to get Mistress Simone out of his mind, had fallen right under her spell, and those seven days had dragged like an eternity. He certainly had not been able to concentrate at work, a fact that hadn't gone unnoticed by the powers-that-be at the agency. Mark had known he was hammering a few more nails in the coffin of his chances of getting onto the board of directors. But he couldn't have cared less.

Lauren hadn't notice the change in Mark's behaviour, though, couldn't have. This was for the simple reason that whenever he'd been at home during that waiting time, he'd had the place to himself. Lauren had been away at a publishing conference in Hamburg, apparently.

Eventually the waiting was over and there Mark was in his car outside Mistress Simone's house, his heart racing, his mouth dry, the palms of his hands damp. He glanced at his watch. It was time to make a move. He stepped from the car. This was it: crunch time.

Mark walked through the high gates and up to the entrance, rang the bell, and a few anxious moments later the door was answered by Mistress Simone who flashed him a welcoming smile. She looked magnificent in a figure-hugging black leather top and matching skirt, which was extremely short. She also wore a tight-fitting pair of tall black leather boots with pointed toes.

Mistress Simone took the cash that Mark discreetly proffered, then led him into her living room. 'Strip naked without delay,' she ordered, her tone suddenly strict.

'Yes, mistress,' he replied submissively.

'We're going to my dungeon playroom now,' Mistress Simone announced once Mark was completely nude. She then took him down a corridor at the end of which she opened a door.

Mark followed Mistress Simone into the large, dimly-lit room beyond, which was decked out with dungeon equipment. This included a vertical torture chair, a leather-covered bondage table and a whipping bench. Hanging from the ceiling by a set of chains was a metal spreader bar with manacle attachments at either end of it. The room also contained an open cabinet of dark wood up against one of its walls upon which there hung a large collection of canes, whips, paddles, chains, clamps, and other disciplinary implements.

'Do you like my dungeon playroom?' Mistress Simone asked.

'I love it, mistress,' Mark replied enthusiastically, feeling his cock stiffen.

'Now for a little of what you've come here for,' she said. 'Get over the whipping bench right away.'

Mark's mind had begun swimming and his eyes had gone blurry as he got into position and braced himself. Here it came, what he had fantasised about for so long but had never yet once experienced. And Mistress Simone did not disappoint. She used her hand first, each hard smack to his backside a sharp stab of fire. For a long while that dungeon playroom echoed with the sound of hand on naked flesh as she followed one stinging blow with another in quick succession.

Mistress Simone then switched to a black leather paddle. She brought the paddle down onto Mark's backside with remorseless energy, each blow landing like an explosion and smarting vividly. He tensed and squirmed with pain as the searing heat burned his flesh.

The dominatrix then replaced the paddle with a leather flogger, throwing it against Mark's backside with great force. He moaned and cried with the explosive pain it delivered. She sliced the flogger down again with even more vicious force six more times, the savage impact cutting abruptly through Mark's cries.

Simone next told Mark to come away from the whipping bench. She pointed towards her feet, demanding that he grovel there and lick her boots. He knelt down on the floor, bent his head low, and pressed his lips against the pointed toes of first one and then the other of her boots.

He slid his tongue along the pure leather over and over, luxuriating in his humiliating task.

In due course Mistress Simone ordered Mark to stop licking her boots but to remain on his hands and knees. 'I told you that under no circumstances would you be allowed to fuck me, didn't I?' she said, grasping him by the hair and gazing into his eyes with laser-like intensity.

'Yes, mistress,' he replied, his lips trembling.

'But that doesn't mean I can't fuck you.'

Mistress Simone then removed her tiny leather skirt, revealing that she'd not been wearing panties and her sex was completely shaven. The dominatrix took hold of a strap-on dildo harness and buckled it on. She went on to liberally douse with lubricant the black silicone dildo now jutting from her crotch.

Positioning herself behind Mark, she gently worked the thickness of the dildo in and out of the opening of his anus a few times, pushing it in a little further with each thrust and stretching his reluctant sphincter. He suddenly felt the dildo spasm into him. At the same time his hard cock ejected a throb of precome onto the shiny wooden floor beneath him.

Mistress Simone spread Mark's rear cheeks wider, pushed herself forward more and slid the strap-on dildo slowly even further into him. Its length slipped ever closer to the depths of his anus, accentuating his arousal with each further inch of its penetration.

Having started slowly, the dominatrix went on to bugger Mark hard. Her hands gripped his hips as she thrust energetically in and out. As she continued pounding into him, increasing the pace all the time, his sexual excitement grew stronger, his erection stiffer. Then she slowed down the rhythm of her thrusts, only to speed up again. The sensation as Mistress Simone speeded up sent a jolt of pleasure through Mark's frame and he pushed back against her, giving himself over to the dizzying excitement of the experience.

As she forced herself deeper still into Mark's anus spasms of delight began to rush through his body. His anal muscles squeezed and released deliciously around the large intruder she was pounding into him. Her rhythm was ever stronger, each thrust going deeper into his anus, filling him, penetrating him, giving him more and more pleasure.

When Mistress Simone brought her right hand to the front of Mark and began masturbating him while continuing to sodomise him hard with the strap-on it was not long before he tumbled over into an orgasm that racked his body with spasms of delight.

Shuddering deliriously, he climaxed, sending out one thick spurt of hot come after another onto the floor beneath him until at long last he spurted to a stop. Only then did Mistress Simone remove her hand from Mark's shaft and also stop fucking him in the arse with her strap-on dildo.

And so ended Mark's much anticipated disciplinary session with a professional dominatrix. It had greatly exceeded his expectations and left him feeling wonderfully elated. It wasn't Mark's first and last disciplinary session with Mistress Simone, though, as he'd told himself it would be. How could he possibly have left it at that? It had been an incredible experience and he wanted more, couldn't wait for more. He booked another session with her straight away.

Chapter Ten

As soon as Mark had arrived at the Kensington address for that second disciplinary session with Mistress Simone and had paid her for what he was about to receive, she took him to the living room and told him to strip naked as before.

Then she led him once again down the corridor to her dungeon playroom. Considering what had happened to him on his first visit, Mark was both excited and frightened about what might befall him there this time. He could feel beads of perspiration stinging his upper lip and there was a hollow, fearful feeling in his chest.

As soon as they were through the door Mistress Simone got him to stand underneath the metal spreader bar with manacle attachments, which hung from the ceiling by chains. She told him to stretch his arms out, then manacled his wrists to either end of the spreader bar.

The dominatrix went behind Mark, took hold of a rattan cane from her rack of disciplinary implements in the open wall cabinet, and immediately got to work with it. As she swiped it across, it made a loud swishing sound, then there was a crack like a rifle shot as it struck his rear. *Swish-crack!* At first Mark felt nothing at all, but a fraction of a second later the burning sting that flooded across his rear was so agonizing all he could do was gasp.

Swish-crack! went the cane again. The sensation was even more agonizing. Mark felt as though someone had laid a red-hot poker against his flesh and was pressing down on it hard.

Swish-crack! Swish-crack! Swish-crack! went the cane again and again and again. Every one of Mistress Simone's skilfully aimed strikes was very painful indeed, intensely sharp and stinging. Mark thought it could only get worse but, in fact, the reverse happened. As Mistress Simone continued to bring the cane down, he felt the sharp, hot pain he was suffering start to become a suffuse red heat that seeped through his body, connecting with the hardness of his cock. Mistress Simone carried on beating Mark with the cane for a long time and the resounding swish and crack of each blow mingled with his moans and muffled grunts of pleasure-pain.

Mistress Simone put the cane to one side, replacing it with a whip. Mark gasped when she sliced the whip against his backside. She immediately delivered another blow to his rear and he cried out loudly in response, revelling wantonly beneath the whip's fiery sting. The dominatrix slammed the whip down even harder the next time, the thongs of the cruel implement cracking savagely against his rear-cheeks. Mark released a roar of pleasure-pain.

Tremors shivered down his spine as, with another vicious blow, Simone brought the whip down on his rear again. Mark stiffened in his bonds, releasing a tortured gasp as he tried to cope with the punishing impact of the whip. Her next blow forced a sob of ecstatic agony from Mark, its shivers trembling through his frame like an earthquake.

Eventually Mistress Simone released his wrists from the spreader bar. She then picked up the rattan cane once more. 'Bring yourself off while I cane you again,' she ordered, and Mark moved to obey, taking hold of his stiff cock with his right hand. He encircled it with his fingers and began to masturbate, his hand coming and going in brisk, short strokes. Then Mistress Simone started beating him on his backside with the rattan cane, laying into him so harshly with the implement this time that each strike made him shudder and cry out loudly. It wasn't long before out-of-control spasms began to shake his body as he stroked his shaft to a gushing climax. Squirts of come leapt out of his cock and spilled onto the floor beneath him as the dominatrix finally stopped caning him.

So ended Mark's second disciplinary session with the redoubtable Mistress Simone. And what had built to another intense high turned into a depressing low as he was plunged back again into a world of tedious conformity – until his next appointment with her.

Chapter Eleven

When Mark entered Mistress Simone's dungeon playroom for his third disciplinary session with the dominatrix he felt, if anything, even more nervous than he had at the beginning of his two previous sessions. What in God's name was she going to do to him this time? he wondered in trepidation.

Mark swallowed hard as he surveyed yet again the frightening array of instruments of correction that lined the open wall cabinet as well as all the imposing, not to say terrifying, dungeon equipment. His legs were unsteady and his heart raced. He felt a powerful electric sensation, a combination of fear and desire, start to vibrate within him.

'I want complete silence from you in here today, Mark, unless the pain gets unbearable for you and you have to beg for mercy,' demanded Mistress Simone, her dark eyes gleaming. She was in a tight black leather catsuit on this occasion. It accentuated her shapely form exceptionally well, moulding itself like a second skin to her perfect curves. 'Do you agree to this?'

Mark nodded that he did. Once again he was wearing nothing at all, his cock now rock-hard.

Mistress Simone attached two metal clamps to his nipples and four similar clamps to his ball sack, causing him to tremble with pain. Taking hold of a whip in her right hand, she told Mark to kneel forward onto all fours. When he had done so she raised the whip.

Mark readied himself for the flogging he knew he was

about to receive, tensing his body and gritting his teeth. Then it began, and the sharp pain burned into his flesh as Mistress Simone's whip came crashing down. He barely had time to catch his breath before her second strike landed. Again the pain swept through him as the flogger landed explosively on his rear. Mark could feel the heat burning on the cheeks of his backside, the skin raised and imprinted with the pattern of the whip's thongs. Simone continued flailing his backside like this until pain burned like a scorching flame into his flesh.

Next she led Mark crawling over to the vertical torture chair. She strapped him on his back into the chair, which left his legs widely parted and his erect cock exposed. Mistress Simone removed the metal clamps from his chest, leaving angry indentations where they had been. She alternated between squeezing his nipples hard and rolling a multi-spiked stimulator over this area of his body. As instructed, Mark made no sound while he endured this cruel punishment.

Mistress Simone then removed the four metal clamps from Mark's ball sack, and started to slap his shaft with the flat of her hand, concentrating her spanks on its head. She went on to whip his swollen cockhead with a small flogger, only stopping when his body was quivering constantly in its bonds in reaction to the intense pain he was suffering.

Simone released Mark from the vertical torture chair and led him, still trembling uncontrollably, over to the leather-covered bondage table. She told him to lie face down on it with his arms and legs apart, then secured him to its four corners by means of its manacle attachments. The dominatrix began to beat Mark's rear with a heavy leather tawse. The quick-fire snapping sounds as its thongs connected for the first time with his backside echoed through the dungeon playroom.

Mistress Simone brought the sturdy implement down

hard on Mark's flesh for a long time after that, the sharp sound of heavy leather thongs snapping against his backside continuing to fill the room.

The dominatrix then took hold of the leather flogger again and immediately put it back to use. The first crack of the whip flew through the air, shocking Mark with its ferocity. He bit back a cry of pain, the cheeks of his backside stinging where the flogger's thongs had landed.

Simone brought the whip down again and a blistering jolt of pain racked Mark's frame once more. Then it came down again. Mark braced himself for the impact of the flogger in the split second before it arrived but his effort was futile. The blow stung agonizingly, leaving a vivid red imprint in its wake. Still Mark remained obediently silent, though, the only sound to come out of him that of his laboured breathing.

As Mistress Simone kept on whipping Mark his rear began to smart with a fire that made him jump and tense within his bonds as the full effect of the beating spread through his body. Mark bit into his lip to keep himself quiet. It was the only way he had to stop himself screaming out his agony.

Mistress Simone at last stopped beating Mark with the flogger – but only to replace it with a riding crop. She used the crop to beat Mark's backside viciously hard, stroke after agonizing stroke. The dominatrix built up the frequency and harshness of the beating still further, one red hot strike after another, until the fire on Mark's severely punished flesh bit very deep indeed into his body. He was utterly frantic by this stage, completely desperate.

'Mercy, mistress, please, please,' Mark cried out, his anguished words ricocheting around the walls of the room, and Mistress Simone immediately stopped beating him. At the same time, the intense pain he'd been suffering became subsumed into throbbing desire which began to sweep through his body, connecting with the pulsing hardness of his cock. Mark climaxed then, shaking without control within his bonds as creamy come sprayed from his punished cock in spurts onto the leather covering of the bondage table beneath him.

And that brought Mark's third disciplinary session with Mistress Simone to an end.

'Anything you'd like to ask me?' the dominatrix said once she had freed him from the come-smeared bondage table.

Mark looked at her with shining eyes. 'Yes, mistress,' replied the man who'd vowed to himself that he'd visit a professional dominatrix once and once only. 'When's the earliest you can see me again?'

After that next appointment came the next one, and the one after that and the one after that … During the time that intervened between these disciplinary sessions Mark could think of little else and his work performance continued to suffer accordingly.

As for Lauren, if she noticed the change in him she never said anything. But in truth she and Mark were hardly seeing anything of each other by that stage. They were just ships that passed in the night. Ever more frequently, those ships were not even passing during the night, Lauren was away on business so much. That's what she said she was doing anyway.

Chapter Twelve

Mark ended up visiting Mistress Simone two, sometimes three times a week. He was grateful both for the fact that he was pretty well off and also that Lauren and he had separate bank accounts, because he was withdrawing more and more from his account in order to feed his secret habit. This was money that couldn't have been better spent as far as he was concerned.

On some occasions when he knew for certain Lauren wasn't going to be around and therefore wouldn't suspect anything, Mark would attend lengthy – and expensive – evening sessions with Mistress Simone. On other occasions there would be equally lengthy, equally expensive afternoon sessions with her. And if attending them meant cancelling meetings, or taking bogus sick leave, or otherwise lying to his colleagues about his whereabouts, Mark didn't care. And as for that formerly coveted directorship with the company, fuck it. Mark was a man in the iron grip of an obsession.

Two months, two *feverish* months, that was how long it took for the obsession to ride its course. That was the duration of Mark's flight from sanity. He was well and truly hooked on Mistress Simone during that crazy time, or to be more exact, he was well and truly hooked on the service he was buying from her.

Mistress Simone was clearly someone who loved her job with a passion and was undoubtedly extremely expert at it. But it was a job nonetheless.. Even when he'd been at the height of his obsession with her, Mark had harboured no illusions about that. It was a paid service she was providing to him, and an expensive one to boot. He wasn't Mistress Simone's lover or even her friend. He was simply one of her clients and paid her handsomely for her services. There could be no getting away from that fact.

Even so, he said to himself as those two extraordinary months finally drew to a close, wouldn't it be wonderful to live in a loving relationship with a superb dominatrix like that? He would be happy – ecstatically happy – to give himself to such a woman completely; happy to surrender to her every demand, no matter how cruel and degrading. He wanted to give his all to a really magnificent dominatrix. He wanted to forget about everything except being worthy of his sadistic lover, his goddess. He wanted...

Oh, who the hell was he trying to kid? He wanted *Lauren* to be his dominatrix. He'd wanted it for ages and ages, perhaps subconsciously from the very moment he first met and fell in love with her.

There was only one thing for it. He was going to have to be brave and ask her. After all, he'd finally plucked up the courage to go to a professional dominatrix and look how well *that* had turned out.

He was starting to really miss Lauren's company too. They'd been like virtual strangers these last few months, seeing less and less of each other. That had to be put right. His guilt about lying to Lauren was really getting to Mark as well. It was time to put his cards on the table, be completely honest with her about everything. He must at last reveal his secret self, his *real* self to her. There was nothing else for it.

Strangely enough, Mark wasn't nervous about telling Lauren he was a sexual masochist, telling her he'd been regularly visiting a professional dominatrix for the past two months, telling her about what she'd done to him during those visits.

He wasn't nervous either about asking Lauren – begging her – to be his dominatrix. No, Mark wasn't nervous about coming completely clean with Lauren in this way, not now he'd decided to do it. Instead he felt oddly calm.

But it was the calm before the storm. For what Lauren would have to say to Mark when he saw her next would shatter his world. And after what was to happen Mark realised just what a deluded fool he'd been. He could never bring himself to pay for the services of Mistress Simone again after what Lauren had to say to him, or visit any other professional dominatrix for that matter. It would have been far too painful for him, and not at all in a nice way.

Chapter Thirteen

Mark was fine about at long last spilling the beans to Lauren. That is, until about half an hour before she was due home. Then he started to get nervous. Doubts began to set in, then more than doubts – pure panic. He broke into a sweat and his heart started pounding hard. What if Lauren's response to his revelations and that all-important entreaty he intended to make of her was one of appalled disgust? He'd have burned his bridges by then, he'd be completely fucked.

But he mustn't think about it that way, Mark told himself. In fact he mustn't think about it at all, he must just do it. And it must be now or never. Mark had built up the courage, hyped himself up, to tell Lauren all about his sexual masochism and plead with her to be his dominatrix and he didn't know if he could find that courage again.

Mark got up from the couch in the living room and went to the kitchen. He got a bottle of vodka from the cabinet and poured some over ice, adding a splash of tonic. If ever there was a man in need of a bit of Dutch courage it was him. He sighed as he took some of his vodka in and felt it seep through him. Then he walked back to the living room and over to the window.

Sipping a little more of his drink, Mark glanced down the street to see if Lauren's car was coming. There was no sign of it yet. The evening was prematurely dark for summer, he noticed, the sky heavy with black clouds. It was also drizzling and for some moments he stood and watched the trickles of rain running down the window.

Mark bit his lip and waited impatiently. He sipped some more at his drink, then sat back down on the sofa. Then he got up again. He was like a cat on a hot tin roof. He tried to find some stillness within him. Mark stood and stared intently into his glass as if the answers to all life's questions could be found in its colourless contents. He sipped some more from his drink, almost drained the glass.

Then time slipped ahead as if in a dream and Lauren was standing in front of him. Mark was still cradling his nearly empty glass and was about to offer to get Lauren a drink while refreshing his own. But she dropped her bombshell before he'd even had time to open his mouth. 'I'm leaving you for Sam Lowell,' Lauren said, her jaw set in a determined line.

Then Mark couldn't speak anyway, was momentarily struck dumb, in a state of complete shock. He just stood there, stunned, his head reeling. Finally, after that endless agonizing interval, he said, 'I'm sorry, what did you just say?'

Lauren's face became even more rigid. 'I said I'm leaving you for Sam,' she replied stiffly.

'I don't get it,' he said, his stomach churning.

'What's not to get?' she replied.

'How long has this been going on?' Mark asked. His voice was so tight it seemed half-strangled. He still couldn't take it in.

'Long enough,' Lauren said, whatever the fuck that was supposed to mean. Let's face it, Mark thought, it could have started any time in the last few months or so and he wouldn't have been any the wiser. He'd been so wrapped up in the displacement activity of excessive work and latterly his obsession with the service being provided to him by Mistress Simone that his eyes had been shut to everything else.

Mark's eyes were wide open now. He knew exactly

what was important to him and what wasn't. His work meant nothing to him. It was superficial and meaningless in its essence. Mistress Simone meant nothing to him. Theirs had been a strictly business arrangement, that was all. Lauren meant *everything* to him, everything in the world. But she was leaving him because she was in love with another man.

Mark could feel himself completely losing his grip, could feel the bottom falling out of him. His face had gone white, bloodless. There was perspiration on his upper lip. His arms and hands felt week and the hand holding his glass began trembling. 'How could you do this to me?' he said, his voice thick with emotion.

Lauren did not reply but in the awful silence that followed his question she gave Mark such a sad smile it nearly broke his heart. She then turned on her heels and walked out of the room, out of the house.

Mark stood for a long time in the empty living room before walking to the window and looking out. It was as dark as midnight now and the earlier drizzle had turned to straight, steady rain that reflected the comfortless light of the streetlamps as it poured down.

Finally Mark walked heavily to the kitchen. He sat down on a wooden chair and put his glass on the kitchen table. He rested his arms on the table, his head bowed, and began to cry. Mark cried his eyes out, couldn't stop himself. Tears were streaming down his face. They were running down his neck, reaching the collar of his shirt. His body was shaking all over as he cried and cried.

This had been meant to be a brand new beginning for Mark. Instead, he found himself at the lowest ebb he'd ever been in his entire life. He had at long last discovered who he really was, what he really wanted out of life, and it had all been for nothing. All his fantasies and hopes and dreams had come crashing down around him. What was he going to do now? His whole world seemed to have fallen apart. He felt utterly desperate, as if he had nothing left to live for, not without Lauren.

How could she do this to me? How could she do this to me? Mark wailed to himself over and over again miserably. How could she do this to me? But she could and she had.

Chapter Fourteen

Weeks and months of Mark's new life in Brighton went by and what had been a patchy spring turned to an even patchier summer. It was anyone's guess from one day to the next what the weather would do. A day might start with real promise: deliciously warm with a clear blue sky and a gentle sea breeze. Tables and chairs would appear outside the cafés, bars and restaurants, soon to be occupied by people of all walks of life chatting, watching the world go by, listening to the cries of seagulls.

It was like being at a sophisticated resort on the Mediterranean, as if Brighton really was England's Riviera, as it had long billed itself. But time and again the sun that had seemed such a permanent fixture at the start of the day would disappear in the afternoon behind leaden grey clouds that came out of nowhere, and a howling weather front would move in off the Channel. This would sooner or later be accompanied by a heavy downpour of rain that would lash the windows of all those cafés, bars and restaurants, and drum down on the now empty tables outside them to make a further mockery of Brighton's Riviera claim – until the next bout of glorious sunshine and balmy breezes.

Come rain or come shine that summer, though, there was one constant for Mark. There were no more phone calls from Lauren. Whether Mark would ever have been able to force himself to ask her to stop phoning – certainly after that last call – is extremely unlikely. His heart simply wasn't in it. But it became academic. Lauren appeared to have stopped of her own accord. So why had she said those words, "I don't want to lose you"? Mark kept asking himself. Had she been playing games with him, messing with his mind? He was loathed to admit it but he guessed she had to have been.

Alone in his apartment, waiting for the phone call that never came, Mark's misery over the failure of his marriage started to turn into something else. He began to veer between the awful ache of loneliness and a bitter resentment towards Lauren that could somehow exist simultaneously with an inability to fall out of love with her. With the passage of time he started to take a more jaundiced view of their break-up.

He conveniently massaged over in his mind his own major part in the failure of their marriage. Mark now convinced himself that Lauren had been determined to leave him for Sam Lowell and had been manoeuvring herself away from him for some little while with that end firmly in mind. It was Lauren who had destroyed their marriage, not him. She was the one who'd gone off and had a full-blown affair, for God's sake.

What he'd done hadn't been in the same league at all. There was no excuse for her unfaithfulness. She was to blame for almost everything really, he told himself. Well, he'd show her. If Lauren could live apart from him quite happily with someone else, he'd go out and find himself someone else too and be just as happy.

Chapter Fifteen

Brighton is famous for its night life, and its beachfront is a hot spot for many of its best known clubs, such as The Honey Club and The Beach. And it was to a club on the front called Bang! that Mark set off late one Saturday night. By the time he arrived there the place was heaving, packed with party people moving their bodies sinuously to the music that washed over them in waves.

Mark spotted the girl almost immediately. She was alone on the dance floor and had black hair cut in a retro-pageboy and a very attractive face with dark oval-shaped eyes, full lips, and a strong jaw. She also had a fine body with shapely breasts and hips on an otherwise slim frame. The girl was all in black: a tight, short-sleeved top, even tighter leather shorts and knee-length boots with high heels.

Mark really liked the look of her and decided to cut to the chase before anyone else beat him to it. He wandered straight over to the girl. 'Hi, I'm Mark,' he said.

'And I'm Paula,' she said, her face lighting up with a seductive smile.

'Dance?'

'Sure,' Paula replied.

As they moved among the throng of dancers, Paula pressed against Mark, moving her hips sensuously, and he responded by pulling her in against him further. Mark could feel the sexual tension building in him, could feel his cock starting to get hard.

As they danced, Mark began to bring his hand down the thin fabric of Paula's black top, pulling her even further in against his body. He was beginning to feel very turned on, almost dizzy with lust.

'You are *so* sexy,' he said.

'So are you,' Paula replied. 'Want to come back to my place?'

Mark looked into her dark shining eyes. 'Lead the way,' he said. Something very similar to this had happened to him once before, he couldn't help recalling. But this was not the time to be thinking about Lauren.

They took a taxi up past the enormous cast-iron structure of Brighton railway station to a modest street of semi-detached houses nearby. Paula had a ground floor apartment in one of these. It was late and the street was still. They went in. The place was small: living room, kitchen, bedroom, and bathroom.

As soon as they were in the bedroom Paula switched on the bedside lamp and pulled the curtains tight shut. She and Mark then hastily stripped and, standing naked together beside the bed, began masturbating one another. 'I'll bet I can bring you off before you bring me off,' Paula challenged with a mischievous giggle, pulling hard at his erection.

'Oh yeah?' Mark replied, finger-fucking her harder.

'Yeah.' Paula's hand went faster and it would have been anybody's guess which of them would climax first.

Mark determined that it wouldn't be him. He wasn't going to let Paula make him spill his seed until he'd made her climax; no way was he going to do that.

We'll see about that, the look in Paula's shining eyes appeared to say, and she began to work up a furious rhythm on his cock.

Mark's whole body was shaking and his heart was racing. Still he kept his resolve, willing himself not to climax whilst working away at Paula's sex, plunging his fingers in and out now like ramming rods until he knew she was ready to go over the edge. Paula came at that point in noisy spasms, her wet pussy contracting tightly around his fingers.

Then Mark got his reward. Paula got onto her knees and took his hard cock in her mouth just as he shot out his seed. She swallowed it down greedily, Mark's cock pulsing in her throat.

The couple fell onto the bed and kissed one another wetly for a while, pearls of jism passing between their lips. Eventually Paula pulled her mouth away from Mark's. 'I want you to bring me off again, Mark,' she said, leaning over and opening the drawer to her night table. Paula took a purple vibrator out of the drawer and handed it to Mark. He switched it on, as she lay on her back with her legs spread apart.

Mark crawled down and positioned himself between Paula's thighs so he could lick her clit while working the vibrator in and out of her slippery sex. He pressed his tongue forward, stiff and wet, and it and the vibrator began to work their miracles of delight on her pussy.

Paula played with her nipples for a time and then replaced Mark's tongue on her clit with her own fingers, tremors of excitement running through her body. She rubbed her clit hard while Mark worked the vibrator feverishly in and out of her soaking wet pussy while kissing and licking her inner thighs.

Paula's breath was coming quickly, her pussy drenched and creamy as she continued to roll her fingers over her clit insistently while Mark plunged the vibrator in and out of her sex. Finally she was overwhelmed by a delirious climax, quivering in ecstasy and letting out a long moan of erotic delight.

Shortly afterwards, Mark switched off the vibrator and handed it back to Paula who returned it to its drawer. 'I'm sleepy now,' she said.

'Me too,' yawned Mark.

'Goodnight,' whispered Paula, turning away from him, and they both went off to sleep.

But not for long.

Mark awoke as if from a fainting fit to find Paula's lips fastened tight to his cock once more, her own sex hovering invitingly over his face. He brought his mouth to her pussy and began licking, his tongue moving wetly over her labia and clit as she continued to suck his shaft.

Paula then changed positions and sat astride his thighs, facing him. 'Fuck me now,' she gasped, and he placed his hands on her slender waist and pushed up into her. Paula groaned with pleasure as Mark's erection slid in and out of her and she started grinding her hips down on him with force, really bucking. She opened her legs wider to grip him harder, drawing him layer upon layer even more deeply inside her sex.

Mark's hard cock twitched, throbbing inside Paula as she squeezed her pussy around it and continued moving up and down until Mark was pulsing with an imminent climax. And as he ejaculated, spilling and shuddering, the sensation of his hot semen gushing into Paula's sex pushed her over the edge, causing her to climax in great shivering spasms.

Mark and Paula disengaged their bodies then and slept – really slept this time, all the way through to late in the morning ... And then they fucked again. And so it went on in the afternoon too.

Mark prised himself away from Paula eventually and returned home that evening, wanting by then to be back on his own. But he arranged to see her the next day.

Chapter Sixteen

The apartment was very still when Mark arrived home. He got a bottle of vodka and one of tonic out of the sideboard in the living room and made himself a drink – light on the vodka, heavy on the tonic. That was how he was mixing his drinks these days. Mark carried his glass to the refrigerator in the kitchen and added ice cubes.

He went back to the living room and stood at the window sipping his vodka tonic, looking out at the sea and at the lights on the Palace Pier. Lauren and I are equal now, Mark said to himself. She's got her precious Sam to fuck and I've got Paula to fuck. Then he cursed himself. Why oh why did everything always have to come back to Lauren?

For the next few weeks Mark forced himself to obliterate Lauren from his mind as best he could, tried to make himself forget about everything except meeting Paula and getting to know her better and having hot, steamy sex with her. But it became obvious before long that their relationship wasn't going to work. As Mark got to know Paula more fully it soon became clear that apart from their mutual sexual attraction they had precious little in common.

For a start Paula was seriously into new technology, designing software for a living; whereas Mark wasn't interested in computers in the slightest. As far as he was concerned the one in his apartment was just sort of *there*, like the television set and the microwave oven.

Mark liked quiet. Paula by contrast wanted to go out clubbing all the time. Mark was an introvert, Paula an extrovert. Mark liked reading. Paula didn't. Paula seemed a little too fond of recreational drugs for Mark's liking. Mark never took recreational drugs. His drug of choice was alcohol and he had that well under control now, thankfully.

Mark liked – no, *craved* pain with his pleasure. Paula wasn't into BDSM in any way. She found it a complete turn-off, something she made clear in no uncertain terms when Mark oh-so-tentatively broached the subject with her.

The fact was, though, that even if Paula had been into BDSM she and Mark would never have lasted for any length of time as a couple. The two of them just didn't gel together when it came right down to it. As things worked out the sex between them, which had been so hot right at the start, went off the boil quite quickly and their relationship petered out soon afterwards. Deep in his heart Mark knew what his affair with Paula had been all about. He'd found yet another displacement activity for what he really yearned for, *who* he really yearned for; that had been all.

First it had been Femdom fantasy and porn, then workaholism, then Mistress Simone, then the demon drink, then contrived resentment towards Lauren. Then there had been his brief foray onto the south coast club scene to find himself a girlfriend, which had led to a short-lived affair with Paula, who was certainly extremely sexy but with whom he was fundamentally incompatible. Indeed, there was only one person in the whole world he was truly compatible with as far as Mark was concerned, only one person who was his true soul mate.

Mark hoped desperately that Lauren would phone again soon. He prayed and prayed that she would, because time wasn't proving to be the great healer he'd hoped it would be, not at all. The more time went on, the more Lauren consumed Mark's thoughts, the more overpowered he felt by his desire for her. 'I don't want to lose you.' That's what she'd said. So, phone, Lauren, please, please for God's sake, phone.

Chapter Seventeen

Late one weekday afternoon Mark decided to take his car out for a spin. He wasn't intending to go anywhere in particular, had nowhere to go *to*, really. His life was completely aimless without Lauren. He existed in a constant state of suspended animation as he waited for her call. Mark drove past the smart hotels and apartment blocks and offices that line the Brighton seafront, past the city's large grey-brick Conference centre, past the weather-beaten Regency town houses of Kemp Town.

Then he drove onto open road, high above the cliffs, past the neo-Gothic pile that is Roedean School for Girls. Mark got as far as the Art Deco building of St Dunstan's Home for the Blind before driving into a lay-by to check his phone. He also wanted to quench his thirst by having a drink from the bottle of mineral water he'd brought with him.

First things first; the phone. Damn, the thing was dead. It needed recharging. What if Lauren was trying to get through to him? Cursing his luck, Mark tugged out the bottled water from the door pocket, twisted off the cap and took a swig. He replaced the cap and jammed the bottle back.

Mark turned the car round and started to drive back to Brighton. He drove past the home for the blind again. There are none so blind as those who will not see, he said to himself scornfully. When the fuck was he going to get it into his thick head that Lauren wasn't going to phone, not ever? Christ, it had been months since that last call. He should give it up, should give *her* up. But he knew he couldn't do that, he simply couldn't.

Half an hour later Mark drove his car into his underground parking bay. He climbed out of the car. The air in the basement parking area was laced with the smell of engine oil. Mark trudged towards the lift and took it up to the second floor. He let himself into the silence of his apartment. He plugged his phone into the charger and dialled his voicemail box. There were – huge surprise – no messages for him.

Mark got himself a diet Coke from the fridge and poured it into a glass. He didn't feel like anything alcoholic. He was, rather to his amazement, gradually losing his taste for it. Alcohol had been a false friend to him, Mark realised very clearly now. He walked through to the living room and took a couple of large swallows of Coke before putting the glass on a side table.

Then he hunched down in the chair in front of the computer and booted it up. The little clock at the corner of the flat screen said 18.55. Mark decided to log onto the Internet, use it as an encyclopaedia. He thought he'd find out a bit more about the seaside city that was currently his home. Hadn't Brighton been a smugglers' town centuries ago? How had that come about? What sort of legacy had it left?

Almost the minute Mark logged on, there was the double ping of an incoming email on the screen. He checked it and immediately all thoughts of local history vanished from his mind. It was from Lauren. Mark sat bolt upright, thrilled beyond measure at the contact.

His pulse racing wildly in his chest, he read what Lauren had written. It said, *Hi Mark, I phoned a couple of times about twenty minutes ago but got no answer. What I've got to tell you I couldn't possibly say to your answering machine so I decided to email you instead. I'm sorry it's been such a long time since I contacted you but I felt after the last time that I wasn't being fair on you – on either of us – by continuing to phone you, so I forced myself to stop altogether.*

Although there have been many times since then that I've been tempted to phone you again, I stuck to my resolve. But things have changed now and I'll get straight to the point. I've walked out on Sam. There is no question of a reconciliation with him, it's over. I'm currently staying in a suite at Claridges hotel while I look for another place to live. Anyway, enough about me. How are you? Are you healthy, are you sober, are you happy? Look forward to hearing from you. Lauren.

Mark sat at the computer screen and re-read the message he'd just received. He pored over it, excitement pulsating in the pit of his stomach. *She's broken up with Sam, she's broken up with Sam.* Then he pressed the reply icon and began to tap at the keyboard. He wrote, *I cannot tell you how delighted I am to hear from you, Lauren. I'm completely over the moon that you've got in touch again. How am I? you ask: healthy, sober, happy? Well, two out of three's not bad, I suppose.*

I'm healthy – all that sea air and plenty of exercise. I'm sober – only one drink a day nowadays, sometimes not even that, would you believe. I won't tell you I'm happy, though. I miss you so much it's like a physical ache to my heart. I won't pretend I'm sorry you've split from Sam either. How did it happen, if you don't mind me asking?

Hey, Lauren, I've just had a brainwave, Mark typed. *Rather than live out of a suitcase while you're looking for another place, why don't you move back into the house in Chelsea. It's just sitting there empty and is much as you left it when we parted. I hardly changed a thing, not even the combination on the burglar alarm. I certainly didn't change the locks, so if you've still got your set of keys, well, what could be simpler? Why not move back in, at least for a while. On the other hand, a suite at Claridges isn't exactly roughing it! Anyhow, it's just a suggestion. Let me know what you think. Mark.*

Mark looked again at what he'd typed, pronounced it reasonably satisfactory and pressed the send icon. He waited for Lauren's reply, listening to the hum of static from the computer. What he hoped was that she was still sitting in front of her computer screen, had received his email and would give him an immediate reply. If she wasn't, he hoped it wouldn't take her long to respond.

Another double ping sounded. Lauren had answered his email more or less straight away. Mark read what she'd written. *What a good idea about the house. It is very kind of you, Mark. No, I didn't ever get rid of the keys. I've still got them in my handbag actually. So I think I might very well take you up on your suggestion.*

I split with Sam because he was cheating on me. I was furious about it, could have killed the bastard, frankly – or at least done him some serious damage. It was only when I'd calmed down that I decided I must be the biggest hypocrite going. Because essentially he had merely done to me what I did to you.

All I can say in my defence, Mark, is that you'd been extremely distracted and our sex life non-existent for quite a while and that by the time I decided to leave you for Sam you'd become completely unreachable. I just couldn't get through to you at all. It was like all the lights were on but there was nobody home. What was going on with you back then, for heaven's sake? I've often wondered. Was it the booze?

I'm so glad you're sober again, I was very worried about you there for a while. Like I've said before, I don't want to lose you. I'll sign off now for the time being and wait here at my laptop for your reply. Lauren.

Mark's fingers hovered over the keyboard for a second or two. Then, without thinking, he launched into his response, typing the words in a great outpouring of candour. *No, it wasn't the booze that made me like that, Lauren,* he wrote. *I started abusing alcohol after you left me, not before. What happened was that I had a guilty secret I was keeping from you, that's the truth of the matter. I'm going to tell you about it now, not before time. And I'm going to do that even though I think it will shock you, maybe even disgust you I'm afraid.*

I'm a sexual masochist, that's what I've got to tell you. I tried desperately to repress that part of myself in so many ways, you wouldn't believe. But the desire, the compulsion, kept returning stronger and stronger every time.

I gave up the struggle to resist it eventually, couldn't help myself despite all my efforts. I ended up going regularly to a professional dominatrix for about two months. Mistress Simone, she's called. I found her on the Internet. She lives in Kensington and her house has got what she calls a dungeon playroom. She is very expert at what she does and for a time I couldn't get enough of her services, kept going back to her for more. I became obsessed with Mistress Simone for a while – with the service she was providing to me anyway.

But eventually the penny dropped for me. I realised that the only person I wanted to dominate and discipline me, Lauren, was you. I think it's always been that way actually. It still is. I love you with all my heart and soul and if you'd only come back to me I'd agree to any terms you wanted to make. I really mean that. You're by far and away the best thing that ever happened to me in my life. I worship and adore you, I always have and I always will. I want you back so much it's driven me more than a little crazy, I can't deny it.

So there you are, now you know the awful truth. Your ex-husband is a raging pervert and a raving lunatic who would do anything – agree to anything – to get you back.

Where do we go from here? Mark.

Mark had thoroughly spilled his guts in writing all that. The thing was, he'd typed it but could he actually send it? With his heart thumping away in his chest, he moved the cursor to the send icon. Then moved it away again. He couldn't send the email, he just couldn't. It was far too raw. He'd highlight the text and delete it, that's what he'd do. He'd replace it with something more ... More what? Faint-hearted? Dishonest?

Mark closed his eyes tightly, trembling. He took several deep breaths and tried to summon up all his courage. He opened his eyes and found he could barely read what he'd written now, his vision had become blurred. His mouth had gone dry too and his heart was pounding away like a jack-hammer. *Courage, Mark, courage.*

He moved the cursor back to the send icon. He sent the email ... And waited with bated breath for Lauren's reply. Apart from the static haze of the computer screen the room was silent. You could have heard a pin drop. The anticipation Mark felt was incredibly intense. He was shaking all over, couldn't stop himself.

He didn't have long to wait for Lauren's reply, though, and it didn't take him long to read it either. It went, *You've given me a lot to think about. I'll be in touch. Lauren.*

'God Almighty, that was brusque,' Mark said to himself in dismay. He feared he'd really blown it now, irrevocably screwed up any chance he might have had of getting Lauren back. Real panic set in with him then and dread gripped his insides. He sat at the computer desk for ages, still trembling, reading and re-reading what Lauren and he had written to one another.

Finally Mark turned off the computer and just sat there staring at the blank screen, his trembling reduced now to an occasional spasm. *I'll be in touch.* Those had been Lauren's last words. Was that her way of saying "don't call us, we'll call you?" Was it the ultimate brush off? Only time would tell.

I'll be in touch. Repeating those words over and over in his head like a chant, Mark went back to doing what he'd been doing for such a painfully long time already: playing the waiting game. But he didn't reach for the vodka bottle.

Chapter Eighteen

Lauren didn't email Mark again. She didn't phone either. He didn't hear a thing from her for two agonizing months, two agonizing, *sober* months. Then he received a package from her, which was delivered by a courier. It contained a small tape machine within which, Lauren informed him in the briefest of accompanying notes, was an audio cassette recording she'd made. Mark set the tape machine down on the table before him, pushed play and sat listening intently to what she had to say to him.

'Well, Mark,' she started, and despite his nervousness about what he was about to hear he found it indescribably good to hear her voice. 'Like I said in my last email, you've given me a lot to think about. Now it's my turn to get you really thinking. First, it will surprise you to know that I didn't find your revelations about your sexual masochism shocking. On the contrary, I found they resonated with something in my own nature that I've only recently begun to recognise. I always realised I was a very dominant kind of woman, sexually in particular. I now understand I'm an awful lot more than that. I'd just been sublimating it. I see that with great clarity now. But I'm getting ahead of myself ...

'Let's go back to that thought-provoking email of yours,' Lauren went on. 'Actually, it turned out to be a lot more than thought-provoking. It prompted me to embark on a personal voyage of discovery. I used the house in Chelsea as my base – thanks again for that, by the way –

and my first and, as it turned out, most important port of call was in Kensington. I went there to try and get acquainted with Mistress Simone. She wasn't difficult to track down. You found her on the Internet, as you told me in your email, and I did the same.

'I took to Mistress Simone from the word go, I must say, and I think the feeling was mutual. Certainly once she realised I was entirely sincere she couldn't have been more helpful. She became my mentor in all matters sadomasochistic, in fact. I feel I understand you an awful lot better as a result of the time I spent with her. I understand myself a great deal better too.

'You said in your last email that if I'd come back to you, it could be on any terms I cared to make. Well, listen up. I'm going to spell out those terms in this tape and you need to be aware from the start that they *won't* be subject to negotiation. It's all or nothing at all.

'If I come back to you, Mark,' the taped message continued, 'it will not be as your wife but as your dominatrix. And what will you be? You will be my slave, yes, *my slave*, and I as your mistress will do exactly as I see fit with you. I will require complete obedience from you at all times. You will always have to do exactly as I tell you without question, no matter how humiliating and degrading that might be for you. Heady stuff, huh? But a little non-specific, you may think. Well, keep listening, Mark, and it will all become clear.

'I ought to say at this point that if you agree to all of this you'll be in safe hands. You see, I've just completed a six-week sabbatical from work, and during that time I paid Mistress Simone to train me thoroughly in the art of erotic domination. It's been kind of a crash course, very intense.

'It's been very successful too. Under her skilful tutelage I've learned one hell of a lot. I've learned all about safe domination from A to Z: how to use a variety of whips, paddles, canes, and clamps, about the different types of bondage such as rope, handcuffs, body bags, suspension machines ... I could go on. She also let me loose on a number of her clients – with their consent, I hasten to add. It was great!

'Mistress Simone's trained me very thoroughly. In fact she's been fantastic – put considerably more hours into my training than I could have hoped for or indeed than I paid her for. She told me it was a labour of love and, you know, I believe her. She is clearly passionately committed to what she does. I'm not surprised you became obsessed with her for a while there, Mark. She really is rather a remarkable woman.

'Anyhow, I am now officially a dominatrix, with all the necessary skills. And I need a place where I can fully exercise those skills. While I was receiving my training I dealt with that specific need by doing something, strictly speaking I suppose, I shouldn't have done, Mark, given the house in Chelsea officially belongs to you. I was being a bit premature, one could say. But I thought it highly unlikely you'd object, under the circumstances.

'What I did – again with the benefit of Mistress Simone's invaluable advice and assistance – was to turn the empty basement area into a dungeon. I had it fitted out with all the equipment I'll need to discipline you with, and lined its walls with my newly acquired and extensive collection of disciplinary instruments. If you agree to be my slave, Mark, you can expect to spend a lot of your time in that dungeon being disciplined by me.

'The basic ground rules for our new relationship will be extremely strict, make no mistake about that. When we are on our own together you will be expected to always call me "mistress" when you address me. You will also be required to obey me at all times without question. You won't be allowed to masturbate without my permission or to have an orgasm unless I say so, and it will have to be clearly understood that I can punish you exactly as I see fit. In short, I will have *total control* over you.

'Finally, you'll have to sign a slave contract that covers all I've just described and you'll be expected to abide religiously by its conditions at all times. If you don't do so I will leave you again and this time I won't *ever* come back. I hope that's crystal clear.

'That's all I have to say, Mark,' Lauren concluded tersely. 'Think extremely seriously about all this. If you want me back those are the terms I'll require, *nothing less*. I'll contact you again in a week's time and you can give me your decision then.'

The taped message ended at that point. Mark sat and shook his head slowly from side to side, dumbfounded by what he'd just heard. He was thunderstruck, stunned, totally amazed. He pressed stop and then rewound the tape so he could listen to it again. Mark listened to it again and again over the next week. He listened to it so many times that eventually he knew it off by heart.

Chapter Nineteen

Mark could feel the tension progressively building inside him as the time drew closer for Lauren to make contact with him. He did his best to push the feelings back. After all, he knew exactly what his answer to her would be. But he wasn't at all successful in calming himself down. The more he tried, the tenser he became during that interminable week.

He tried to masturbate on a couple of occasions as a means of relieving the almost unbearable tension, but he stopped both times. It felt like disobedience somehow. Even though Lauren's incredibly strict regime was not yet in operation, Mark knew that when it was in place he wouldn't be allowed to masturbate without her permission. He felt he ought to start as he meant to go on, that Mistress Lauren would expect that of him.

Mark awoke very early in the morning of that fateful day, the one that would change his life forever. The first tepid rays of sun had only just filtered through the bedroom blinds when he climbed, bleary-eyed, from his bed. He showered and dressed and had a light breakfast. Then he went out for a long walk. The streets were vast and still at that early hour. There was hardly another soul about. He made for the Old Lanes. It was a magical place at that time of day, the seagulls and the strange light of early morning piercing through its empty alleyways.

Mark wandered around the city centre for hours, just

killing time, something at which, God knew, he'd become thoroughly expert. After a promising start, the weather was turning grey but it remained pleasantly mild. By mid-morning the city was as busy as usual, its heart pulsing with life, with humanity. The pavements and streets had become busier and noisier. Floods of cars now clotted the roads. Mark left all the hustle and bustle of the city centre and the roar of the traffic and returned to the peace and quiet of his apartment. To wait.

Once home, he made straight for the kitchen where he put coffee into the filter basket of the coffeemaker. He added water and turned it on. He put a slice of bread in the toaster and made himself some toast, which he smeared with blackcurrant jam. Mark sat down at the kitchen table and drank his coffee and munched his toast and jam. As he did so, he flicked through a magazine. He couldn't concentrate on its contents at all.

This has *got* to be the day I hear from Lauren, Mark thought. She'd said she'd be back in touch in a week's time and that had been exactly seven days ago. Mark picked up a triangle of toast from its plate and bit off a corner. He chewed and swallowed and put the toast back down on the plate. He took a long sip of coffee. When would Lauren make contact? he wondered. There wasn't much left of the morning, so would it be this afternoon or this evening? And *how* would she make contact this time? Lauren never did what Mark expected. He should have got used to that by now, he told himself. But he couldn't help wondering nonetheless.

When he'd finished his toast Mark topped up his coffee from the round glass pot. He picked up the mug and walked into the living room. He stood silently, looking out of the window of the still, quiet room. He sipped at his coffee, which had become stronger sitting in the pot. As usual for this time of day, most of the parking spaces across the road were filled now, Mark noticed. One or two of the cars were very smart, most weren't. The shingle beach beyond was almost empty and the sea was as grey as the sky. It heaved in a slow, turbid rhythm. Mark stared out through the window at its blurry expanse, waiting and waiting.

He took another sip of his coffee. His mug was empty now and he went into the kitchen and emptied it in the sink. As Mark was wandering back into the living room, his mobile phone rang. He pulled it immediately from the pocket of his jeans, nearly dropping it, his fingers were so nervous. When he answered the phone there was a pause and then he heard Lauren's voice. This was it. He could feel his breath coming faster.

'Mark, three questions,' she said curtly. 'One, have you listened to the tape? Two, have you thought deeply about what I had to say to you on that tape? Three, are you willing to accept unconditionally my terms for coming back to you?'

'Yes to all three questions, mistress,' Mark replied. His voice was quavering with emotion.

'No reservations?' Lauren probed. 'No questions you want to ask before it's too late?'

'None, mistress,' he said, still struggling to get his trembling voice under control.

'Well, *I* have another question for *you*,' Lauren said. 'Why were you so certain I'd be shocked, disgusted even, if I found out you were a sexual masochist?'

Mark was silent for a moment, frowning, as he reflected on the answer he would give. 'It was mainly about my own self-image for a long time, I think, mistress,' he said. He'd got his voice under control now. 'I was alarmed and troubled by the way I was and I assumed you would be too, to the extent of it seriously damaging, perhaps even destroying our relationship. It took me a very long time to come to terms with who I really am and not be ashamed about it. I tried very hard to repress it, deny it, and simply couldn't bring myself to tell you about it. I did nearly muster up the courage to talk to you about it once but before I said anything you made that remark about Kurt Anson – you know, that macho-man film star – when you read that he'd been "outed" as a sexual masochist by his ex-girlfriend.'

'Remind me about this remark of mine about that Anson idiot,' Lauren said. 'I don't remember it.'

'You said that he was a pathetic creep, mistress, and that you couldn't stand him and ...'

'I do think those things about him. I always have,' Lauren interjected. 'But not because he's been exposed as a masochist. I hate the aggressive image of masculinity he portrays in his films. It's pitiful and so is he. What you did there, it seems to me, was to add two and two together and make five.'

'I see, mistress,' Mark said, thinking he must have got it all wrong.

'Having said that, I must be perfectly honest,' Lauren went on quickly. 'I think you were right to have been worried about talking to me about it. I'd be the first to admit I haven't been exactly brilliant in the self-knowledge department until recently. Better late than never for both of us though, Mark, huh?'

He smiled gently into the phone. 'Yes, mistress.'

'Anyway, this is where things get interesting,' Lauren said. 'I want you to do something for me now.'

'Anything, mistress,' Mark said and he could feel his heart start to beat even faster.

'Walk out onto the balcony,' Lauren said and, pushing back the sliding doors, that's what he did. 'Look over the road at the red open-topped sports car parked on the front.' Mark had vaguely noticed the car earlier because it looked like a new model. But he hadn't noticed whether it had been occupied. He wouldn't have been able to see anyway as its top had been up then and it had darkened windows. It was certainly occupied now. Oh my, was it occupied!

Lauren, her phone to her ear, gave him a broad smile and a wave. It was wonderful. Mark felt a huge tug at the centre of him at the glorious sight of her. God, the sheer joy of being able to look at her again after such a long time. She was, he thought, more beautiful, more radiant than ever.

Mark felt himself stiffening beneath his jeans at the sight of Lauren. And no wonder. She looked incredibly sexy in the black leather coat she was wearing.

'Do you like my coat?' she asked, almost as if she was reading his mind.

'Yes, mistress,' Mark said. His eyes were shiny now, his face flushed. His breathing had started to become laboured.

'Want to know what I'm wearing under it?' Lauren asked, looking across the road at him seductively, smiling that enslaving smile of hers.

'Y-yes, mistress,' he stammered.

'Sweet. Fuck. All,' she replied.

'Mistress …' Mark gulped. He felt a sharp pang of desire in his groin.

Lauren went on, 'See the black leather holdall next to me on the passenger seat?'

'Yes, mistress.'

'Would you like me to tell you what it contains?' She gave him an expectant gaze.

'Yes, mistress.' Mark could feel his cock swelling further.

'A dildo-gag, half a dozen metal pegs, nipple clamps and an assortment of paddles and whips,' Lauren said, continuing to gaze across the road at him. 'These include a heavy leather flogger, a vicious little cat o'nine tails and two paddles, one of which is studded. Want to know what I'm going to do with the contents of my holdall once I come up to your apartment?'

'Yes, mistress,' Mark replied, breathing heavily.

'First of all I'm going to thrash you severely, using each of the whips and paddles in turn,' Lauren said. 'I'll beat you and beat you and beat you until you plead with me for mercy. I will then stop beating you. Do you know what I'll do then?'

'No, mistress,' Mark gasped.

'I will attach the nipple clamps to your chest painfully and the metal pegs to your scrotum even *more* painfully. I will then gag you with the dildo-gag and will require you to pleasure me with it for a *looong* time. Once you have given me as many orgasms as I require, I may remove the clamps from your nipples and the metal pegs from your scrotum, or I may not. I'll have to see. Whenever I do remove them, though, you can be sure of one thing – it's going to hurt like the devil. Finally, I *may* milk you, bring you to a climax. On the other hand, I may not. I might just leave you drooling instead. I haven't decided yet. I'll see how I feel at the time. Is all that understood?'

'Yes, mistress,' Mark panted. He'd never felt so excited. His tongue snaked out to lick at his lips. Sweat had broken out on his palms. His cock was achingly hard beneath his jeans, its throb hot and insistent.

'Go back inside now, Mark,' Lauren instructed. 'Take all your clothes off. Tell me when you're completely naked.'

A few moments later he gasped into his phone, 'I'm naked, mistress.'

'Is your cock hard?'

'Rock-hard, mistress,' Mark replied, speaking nothing but the truth. His long, thick cock was now throbbing and urgent with need, its bulbous head glistening with precome.

'I make it 11.56,' Lauren said. 'What time have you got?'

Mark looked over at the clock on the wall. 'Eleven

95

fifty-six also, mistress.'

'While you were stripping naked I left my car,' Lauren informed him. 'I'm standing at the main entrance door to the apartment block now. Buzz me up and open your front door, leave it ajar. Then go back to your living room and get onto all fours. I will walk into the apartment at twelve noon exactly, and at that time you will officially be my slave. The first thing I want to see as I enter your living room is your splayed arse ready to be severely beaten. Is all that clear?'

'Yes, mistress.' Mark could smell the strong scent of his own sexual excitement now; it filled the room. He was acutely conscious of his pulsing stiffness too, of the way it leaked precome in an almost constant stream.

Mark did everything that had been instructed of him, finally getting down on his hands and knees. He felt his hard cock against his stomach. It was continuing to throb and to drizzle precome. Mark glanced at the clock: Eleven fifty-eight. In two minutes he would no longer be free, would never be free again, in fact ... Free to be lonely and miserable and bereft. In two minutes – nearer one minute now – he would be enslaved to Mistress Lauren.

From that time on he would be totally at her mercy, would have to do *everything* she required of him at all times or he'd lose her for good, something he would never, ever allow to happen. He would exist solely for Lauren's pleasure, to be used and punished and humiliated according to her whim. And Mark knew that he'd absolutely love it, adore it; he had no doubts about that whatsoever. Why? Because his desire for Lauren to be his sadistic mistress, his dominatrix, was absolute now. It was *all* he wanted, all he would ever want.

Mark knew he'd adore being the slave of a woman who was nothing less than a goddess, would adore meeting the demands of the cruel dominatrix who owned him body and soul. He felt a sensation of blissful happiness erupt through him. It was overwhelming, uncontainable. He was incandescent with joy.

It was seconds away from 12 o'clock now. The clock on the wall was tick-tick-ticking. Mark continued to kneel on all fours, waiting, waiting, waiting. His hard cock throbbed even harder, rivulets of precome moisture dripping constantly from its slit. He heard the front door he'd left ajar creak open and then close shut.

It was noon exactly. Mark's stay in purgatory had finally come to an end and he was about to enter a paradise of pain. His excruciating wait in limbo was over at long last. His time had come. Mistress Lauren had arrived. Mark's life was about to begin.

BOOK TWO

CRUEL DENIAL

'How do you know I'm mad?' said Alice.
'You must be,' said the Cat, 'or you
wouldn't have come here.'
Lewis Carroll

Chapter One

Alice first met Sarah at a party, but that's not important. It doesn't matter where Alice met Sarah or how she met her, just that she met her. That's the important thing. Because if she hadn't met her, she wouldn't have met Mistress Gale and if she hadn't met Mistress Gale none of the rest of it would have happened. And Alice as like as not would have ended up as sane as the next person.

Alice was young and she was lovely, a honeyed blonde with full, sensuous lips, a pert nose and soft grey eyes that were large, expressive, and without guile. She also had a wonderful body, sumptuous and well proportioned. As for Alice's character, it was playful, affectionate, sweet, and exceptionally submissive. She was as honest as the day is long too, someone who couldn't tell a lie to save her life. That was all part of her naïve charm.

Alice was an instant hit with Sarah, who like herself was bisexual. Sarah fell in lust with her in no time at all. Likewise Alice was very taken with the forthright and alluring brunette she had just met. She found her a major turn-on without a doubt. The two women started a passionate affair, with Alice invariably taking the passive role in their feverish bouts of lovemaking.

As they got to know one another better Alice became increasingly fascinated by Sarah's thrillingly explicit accounts of her masochistic experiences at the hands of a cruel dominatrix called Mistress Gale. She was amazed that such an obviously alpha female like Sarah would allow herself to be treated so sadistically by another person. The more Alice thought about it the more she felt that it sounded much more like *her* sort of thing.

Alice wanted so much to have more extreme sexual experiences of the kind that Sarah had been describing to her in such graphic detail. She imagined how erotically frightening it must be to be disciplined by someone as sadistic as this Mistress Gale person. Alice desperately wanted to experience such sensations for herself.

She told Sarah this one day and asked her whether there was any chance that Mistress Gale might be prepared to dominate her as well. Sarah agreed to ask the dominatrix the next time she saw her and was as good as her word.

Mistress Gale didn't need much persuading, truth be told. She listened to what Sarah had to say, took a look at the photo of Alice she showed her and unhesitatingly gave her assent. And so the die was cast.

Chapter Two

The sky was just starting to blue into black when Sarah and Alice arrived at the gates of Mistress Gale's large house. The property, which was built of grey stone, was set well back from the road and wasn't overlooked from any direction. It was completely secluded. Despite the fact that Alice was wearing a red leather coat that kept her perfectly warm she could not stop herself from shivering as she anticipated what this visit might bring. Her throat was tense with excitement and her heart was beating hard.

Entry to Mistress Gale's imposing residence was initially through a set of high wrought iron gates. Sarah and Alice walked through the gates and made their way to the front entrance of the house. Sarah rang the bell and a few moments later the door was answered by Mistress Gale herself.

Alice was mesmerised by her first sight of the dominatrix. She gasped at how hypnotically beautiful she was with her lustrous brown hair, high-cheekboned face and large blue-green eyes. Mistress Gale also had silken skin as pale as alabaster. And if all that were not enough, she absolutely radiated charisma. It was those luminous blue-green eyes that did it. They drew Alice into an orbit all their own once they fixed on hers. One look from Mistress Gale was really all it took. Alice was completely in her thrall from that moment on.

Mistress Gale excited Alice immensely and so did the way her well-shaped figure looked in the black leather

103

dress she wore. It was very tight and very short, barely skirting her thighs. She also had on a pair of pointed shoes of shiny black leather with sharp stiletto heels.

Alice admired the swell of Mistress Gale's beautiful breasts, her stone-hard nipples pushing against their leather covering, her long, shapely legs. Alice was incredibly turned on, wet with desire. Her breath quickened and her nipples stiffened and her clit pulsed with a hot, insistent throb as she gazed in lustful awe at Mistress Gale's magnificent body.

The dominatrix ushered Sarah and Alice into her elegant living room – all dark leather and antique mahogany – and told them to remove first their high-heeled shoes and after that every stitch of their clothing. 'Come with me,' she then ordered and, obediently following the dominatrix, they padded out of the living room. The three women went down a longish corridor and descended a spiral staircase to another, shorter corridor at the end of which was a heavy oak door.

Chapter Three

Mistress Gale opened the door, flicked at a light switch, and led Sarah and Alice into the big, cavernous room that was her dungeon. Alice was both frightened and excited by the ominous gloom of the place, which was made more threatening by the long wooden rack bolted to one of its dark walls. This contained a terrifying collection of straps, whips, canes, clamps and other instruments of correction.

And then there was all the sinister looking metal and black leather-covered dungeon equipment that the big, dimly-lit room contained. This included a horse, an upright torture chair, a bondage table, and a whipping bench. One of the walls was dominated by a St Andrew's cross and another by a metal cage. Chains hung from the dungeon's high ceiling, a number of them attached to metal spreader bars.

Mistress Gale, her stiletto heels clicking purposefully on the shiny dark wood floor, took Sarah and Alice over to the whipping bench. She told the two naked women to kneel over it, side by side.

The dominatrix then picked out an extra-long rattan cane from the rack of disciplinary implements and immediately got to work with it on Sarah and Alice. She sliced it through the air in a graceful arc that cracked hard against their backsides. The two young women experienced twin flashes of pure pain that caused both of them to inhale sharply.

The   ome's second strike whistled through the air,

cracking hard against their rears and bringing those twin flashes of pain once more. A third stroke of Mistress Gale's cane followed the second one before either of them had time to recover. Gale continued to cane them relentlessly, stroke after painful stroke, until intense pain burned into their flesh. Then – mercifully – she stopped.

Mistress Gale next led Sarah and Alice away from the whipping bench and over to the wall-mounted St Andrew's cross. She got Sarah to assist her in securing Alice face forward to the cross, strapping her tightly to this piece of equipment at the wrists, upper arms, waist, thighs, and ankles.

The dominatrix then took hold of a heavy leather flogger and, with Sarah looking on with rapt attention, began to whip Alice's backside. She went on to beat her at length and with ever-increasing ferocity, one hot strike after another. Each of her searing strokes produced a sharp, fiery sting and Alice's rear, which was already marked with red stripes from her caning, reddened considerably more.

Alice's beautiful grey eyes were spiked with tears of anguish but, weirdly, something very strange was happening to her. The agonizing pain she was suffering was beginning to dissolve, starting to transform itself into something else entirely: overpowering desire. Alice could feel her blood begin to run even faster. She had become so sexually excited she was soaked, threads of love juice dripping from her labia. She could feel trickles of wetness running down the inside of her legs as she revelled wantonly beneath the fiery sting of Mistress Gale's flogger. Alice was now consumed by lust. It made her writhe and buck against her bonds in erotic delight as the lashes from the flogger continued to land across her rear.

Then, much to Alice's surprise – and to Sarah's too – Mistress Gale suddenly switched tack, handing the flogger over to Sarah. 'I want you to whip her arse now,' she said.

Chapter Four

Sarah's initial blows were quite tentative, which was unsurprising given that this was the first time she had ever beaten anybody. However, she soon picked up the rhythm and warmed to the task. To her shock and surprised delight she found it incredibly exciting to be whipping her lover. As her excitement escalated, her blows became increasingly ferocious, each stroke landing explosively on Alice's rear.

Harsh stroke continued to follow harsh stroke in quick succession and agonized moan followed agonized moan from Alice. Soon a pattern of deepest red was imprinted on her backside, the colour of this and her previous punishment stark against her pale skin.

Once again intense sexual arousal began to take Alice over, the pain she was experiencing at Sarah's hands blurring with pleasure, agony and ecstasy combined. She felt as though her body was on fire, the sharp, hot pain on the cheeks of her backside reaching a peak.

Finally it all became too much for Alice and, writhing in her bonds with agony and sensation, she begged for mercy. At the same time she climaxed violently in a long, savage orgasm, its spasms and contractions seeming to go on for ever.

While Alice's orgasm was still raging Mistress Gale grabbed hold of Sarah, who was so stunned by what she'd just done that she had dropped the flogger to the dungeon floor. Gale kissed her hard on the lips, shoving her tongue inside her open mouth quick and tight.

Mistress Gale stopped kissing Sarah and pushed her hand into her sex instead. Sarah's breath came faster as she moved against her hand. Gale pressed down hard on Sarah's clitoris and started rapidly working two, then three fingers in and out of her ever more slippery sex. She masturbated Sarah furiously until, her heart pounding and her vision flashing, she trembled to a convulsive orgasm.

Gale removed her fingers, glistening wetly with love juice, from Sarah's dripping pussy. 'You are clearly a "switch". There's no doubt about that in my mind,' she informed the still gasping young woman. 'But I'd go further than that. I'd say that your future is not as a submissive at all but as a dominatrix. Believe me, I know about such matters.' She added, 'Now help me release Alice.' The two of them then unbuckled the various straps that held her to the St Andrew's cross.

Mistress Gale eyed Alice with an imperious look. 'Kneel before me,' she ordered, pointing to the space between her feet, and Alice obediently scrambled into position. 'What have you to say to your mistress?'

'Thank you very much, mistress,' Alice replied, her voice a husky whisper. Her big grey eyes were bright and feverish with desire as she looked up adoringly at her tormentor, her goddess. 'Thank you so very much for the discipline.'

Mistress Gale told Alice to get onto her hands and knees, then led her to the metal cage inside which she locked her. She next took Sarah over to the leather-covered bondage table. When she got there, she kicked off her stiletto-heeled shoes and removed her short leather dress, underneath which she'd been gloriously naked.

Mistress Gale's nude body was utter perfection, Alice thought as she gazed at her through the bars of the cage. As well as having a slim waist and wonderfully shapely thighs she had fantastic breasts; large, beautifully belled, with broad areolas and long, erect nipples. Gale's voluptuous body looked incredibly enticing to Alice.

'It's time I had some pleasure now, Sarah,' the dominatrix said as she lay down on her back on the bondage table in all her naked glory, spreading her legs and lifting her knees. 'Lick my pussy.'

Sarah obeyed immediately, leaning forward and bringing her face between Gale's thighs. She fastened her lips to her sex and started licking her clitoris, teasing the hooded pearl of pleasure over and over with her sinuous pink tongue.

Mistress Gale luxuriated in the sensation, her whole body rippling with pleasure. She ran her hands up over her stiff nipples as Sarah's mouth continued to work tirelessly on her clit.

Alice knelt in the cage and watched all of this from behind its bars, masturbating in a fever of lust. She rolled the fingers of her right hand over her stiff clitoris fast and hard, then pushed them in and out of her sex. She dug them in deep, plunging into all her juicy wetness over and over. Her fingers soon became very wet indeed, soaked with the sap of desire.

As the fingers of Alice's right hand plunged noisily in and out of her pulsating sex, soaking her palm and wrist, the fingers of her left hand started to pinch first one of her engorged nipples and then the other as hard as she could bear. She felt insatiable, every sexual part of her swollen with desire.

At that moment Alice's erotic imagination was in total overdrive. She thought how wonderful, how joyous, how utterly perfect it would be if somehow she could remain within Mistress Gale's dungeon domain for ever.

Beware of what you wish for, a voice inside Alice's head warned. But she deliberately ignored the warning voice, blocked it out as she used her fingers on herself ever more frantically, eddies of sexual delight trembling through her body. What she wished for was a kind of madness, an erotic dementia, but she didn't care. *Beware of what you wish for.*

Alice had never felt so alive. Pleasure-pain spiked up through the fingers pinching her stiff nipples while her other hand continued to plunge and plunge into the wetness between her quivering thighs.

Blood was rushing through Alice's veins from her self-ministrations. Her heart pounded inside her ribcage and the waves of its beat roared through her ears like the ocean, completely drowning out that warning voice still trying to make itself heard inside her head.

Chapter Five

Sarah and Alice in their different ways had really set Mistress Gale thinking, and she soon had plans for them both that she lost no time in putting into effect. Mistress Gale reiterated to "switch" Sarah that her future was not as a submissive but as a   ome. She went on to tell her that with the right kind of training she had the potential to be a very fine dominatrix indeed, one of the very best.

Sarah accepted what she'd been told, which was after all not only true but also extremely complimentary.

Mistress Gale next made her an offer she couldn't refuse: to be flown off with all expenses paid to that international bastion of female supremacy, The Femdom Kingdom, there to train – and afterwards remain – as a top dominatrix.

All this took no little organizing on Mistress Gale's part and cost the dominatrix a lot of money. How very generous it was of her to do such a thing for Sarah, how very kind. Well, actually, no. Mistress Gale didn't *do* kind. She did charismatic, she did seductive, she did enigmatic, she did mercurial, she did powerful, she did devious, and above all else, she did cruel. But she didn't do kind. The wily dominatrix had an ulterior motive in spiriting Sarah away permanently like this and it was all to do with Alice.

Mistress Gale, you see, had decided that she wanted Alice all to herself: to be her sex slave. Gale already had two such slaves living with her, but they were both male. She now wanted a female one as well. She wanted Alice.

And whatever Mistress Gale wanted Mistress Gale got. That was the golden rule by which the dominatrix lived.

Whether Alice would want to be her sex slave was frankly beyond dispute. It was a given after that cathartic, apocalyptic first time she'd spent in her dungeon. Whether she'd be able to last the distance – now *that* very much remained to be seen.

Alice received the summons by phone. 'Pack a few essentials in a small suitcase,' Mistress Gale told her. 'But do not pack any clothing – I require my sex slaves to be naked at all times. Make sure you are wearing the red leather coat you had on when you visited here last time but on this occasion I want you to be nude underneath it. Once you've arrived I shall – eh – "introduce" you to one of the two other sex slaves who live here under my control. His name is James.'

Chapter Six

When Alice arrived at her new home she was buck-naked under her red leather coat, exactly as she'd been told to be. Mistress Gale answered the door naked herself to all intents and purposes, wearing only a black leather and diamante choker and black high-heeled leather boots. Her gorgeous appearance provoked Alice's lust like a lightning bolt. She felt a jolt of desire, a sharp twinge between the legs at the delicious nude-elegant sight of her beautiful mistress, her *owner*.

After Alice had put down her small suitcase and removed her leather coat and high-heeled shoes, Mistress Gale took her into the living room and helped her into a slave's collar and wrist and ankle cuffs, all of red leather. Every nerve in Alice's body was jangling with anticipation by now. She felt really moist between the thighs, ready for any sexual humiliation the cruel and wonderful woman who was now her mistress might decide to inflict upon her.

She also felt curious. Alice wondered about James, what he looked like and where he was; how exactly she was going to be "introduced" to him, and where. It would take place in the dungeon, she assumed. Alice could feel the sexual tension building even more as she contemplated all this. Her heart started pumping hard. She could hear it in her chest, and in the sound of her breathing, heavy and strained. Her clitoris stiffened further and her pussy became wetter still with desire.

Mistress Gale led Alice out of the living room and into

the corridor. But she did not take her downstairs to the dungeon as the young woman had expected. Instead she took her up the main staircase to a large high-ceilinged room, the thick curtains of which were drawn. Wall lights illuminated the room's darkness with a soft amber glow.

There was an open cabinet against one of the walls that was hung with various implements of correction: whips, canes, clamps and the like. Hanging from the ceiling of the room were two sturdy ceiling hooks from which hung two chains that were attached to either end of a metal spreader bar.

But what drew the eye more than anything in the room was the big double bed at its centre. It had four posts of carved mahogany, each with a leather anchor strap attached to it, a number of leather cushions, and bed covers of black satin. It had no bed head as such. This was evidently not a bed for sleeping in but for playing on.

Against one of the room's walls was a closet of dark wood. Alice assumed that it must be packed with Mistress Gale's fetishwear or other kinky items, but she was quickly disabused of such a notion, because the dominatrix went on to open it wide to reveal that kneeling inside the otherwise empty closet was the object of Alice's curiosity, James.

And Alice liked what she saw. A lot. James had thick, shiny black hair, a chiselled chin and glittering mahogany-brown eyes. Alice couldn't tell what his mouth was like, though, as he'd been tightly gagged with a black leather tongue-gag that obscured his lips.

She let her gaze traverse James's kneeling form and could see that he had a fine body: broadish shoulders on a slim frame. Alice could also see from the angle she was looking at him that his wrists had been strapped behind his back and his ankles had been bound together with another buckled leather strap.

James was stark naked. He was turned on too; that was

perfectly clear. She could see his excitement from his hard cock, thick and ready, jutting from his smooth body. Gazing at James made Alice even wetter between the thighs, drenched.

Chapter Seven

Mistress Gale brought Alice's attention away from James and back to her by sitting on the side of the bed and ordering the young woman to get over her lap. 'You will play with your pussy while I am spanking you,' she told her. 'But under no circumstances are you to allow yourself to come.'

Alice's backside was raised high for the dominatrix, its curved cheeks offered for punishment. At the same time her fingers were planted between the lips of her pussy, poised to begin rubbing.

Mistress Gale lifted her hand and brought it down forcefully. The sharp slap was so hard that it left a distinct red mark on Alice's flesh and made her cry out with pain. Simultaneously Alice began to rub the opening of her vagina, her fingers sticky in her sex.

Mistress Gale spanked her a second time, lifting her hand high, then bringing it down swiftly to make contact with her rear, leaving another red mark on her flesh and making her cry out again. She delivered a third heavy stroke, which smarted even more painfully and left a deeper red mark.

During the course of these further strikes Alice continued to masturbate as she'd been ordered to do. Her fingers worked rhythmically as she rolled them over her stiff clitoris and into the pulsating slipperiness of her pussy.

Mistress Gale hand-spanked her vigorously, beating

hard, flat strokes across her punished flesh. And all the while Alice's fingers continued to work at her stiff clit and wet, wet pussy. The pleasure she was bringing herself with her fingers was intensified by the pleasure-pain she was experiencing from the spanking, its ecstatic heat radiating through her being.

By now the overexcited young slave felt devoured by lust and was finding it increasingly difficult not to climax. She was much relieved when Mistress Gale stopped spanking her and allowed her to remove her fingers from her soaked pussy.

The dominatrix next walked Alice over to the metal spreader bar that hung by chains from the ceiling. She told her to raise her arms and used trigger clips to attach her wrist cuffs to either end of the bar. Mistress Gale then extracted a leather flogger from the open cabinet of disciplinary implements, and wasted no time in putting it to use.

Alice gasped as the first red-hot strike from the flogger landed across the middle of her backside. She gave another gasp of pain as Mistress Gale's next stroke planted a second line of fire across her rear. The beating continued unremittingly, causing the cheeks of Alice's backside to smart with a fire that made her tense and squirm and gasp in pain.

Eventually Mistress Gale released Alice from the spreader bar. 'I am going to allow you to bring yourself off with your fingers shortly, slave. And I require you to do it in front of James. You can see from his hard-on that he is extremely sexually excited, can't you?'

'Yes, mistress,' Alice replied.

'I took him to the edge of orgasm half a dozen times before your arrival today,' Mistress Gale went on. 'Now see if you can finish the job and make him come at the same time that you do. You are not to start masturbating until I give you the word,' she added. 'And you must also ensure that you do not climax until I tell you to.'

Chapter Eight

Alice stood before the fettered and gagged James, kneeling in the open closet. She opened her thighs slightly, put a hand down on herself and waited for the go-ahead from Mistress Gale. 'Start masturbating now,' the dominatrix ordered, and Alice began to rub. She plunged her fingers between her pussy lips, feeling sticky wetness, the thrilling pulse of her clit.

Alice finger-fucked herself in a mounting frenzy of desire, breathing heavily, as wet as anything. She was careful to keep herself from climaxing, though, always holding something in reserve.

But this was not easy and, as she continued masturbating, the delirium she was experiencing mounted further. It was unavoidable, especially as she was doing as she'd been told, trying her best to excite James to such an extent that he'd climax when she did. Alice's breath was coming even more quickly, her pussy even more drenched and creamy as her fingers plunged in and out of her sex.

James struggled in vain against his bonds, his cock painfully erect, as he watched this gorgeous blonde vision of licentiousness doing everything in her power to make him as sexually excited as possible – and succeeding in spades.

Alice stopped playing with herself momentarily. She lay on her back on the floor in front of James, opened her legs wide apart and immediately went back to masturbating. The fingers of one of her hands dipped in and out of her oozing slit while she pushed down on her clitoris with the other, the engorged bud rotating and sliding against her slippery touch.

Alice knew how juicy she must look to James, how fucking hot. She could see the effect she was having on him, the way sweat was prickling on his brow, the way he was panting beneath his gag. She could see the glazed look in his dark, gleaming eyes, could smell the scent of his excitement.

She could see his massive stiffness, which was now glittering with wetness as if it had just been withdrawn from a sopping pussy – *her* sopping pussy. His shaft had begun pulsing constantly too.

'Alice, come for me now,' Mistress Gale commanded, adding quickly, 'James, you are *not* permitted to come.'

Alice obeyed Gale's command, using her fingers, fast and furious, to bring herself to a shuddering climax. As orgasmic pleasure exploded through her, James screwed his eyes shut and a guttural moan came past his gag. His cock spasmed again and again, silvery precome spilling from its head. Clearly this was one incredibly excited sex slave. But all credit to him: he didn't come.

'Nice work, Alice,' Mistress Gale remarked approvingly. 'And well done, James.'

Chapter Nine

After allowing a moment or two for Alice to recover her composure – and for James to do likewise – Mistress Gale told her to get to her feet. She then walked her over to the bed. 'Lie on your back with your arms and legs outstretched,' she told her before clipping her wrist and ankle cuffs to the anchor straps attached to the four corner posts of the bed.

Next Mistress Gale went over to the open closet and got on one knee in order to release James from his bondage, also removing his gag. Getting to her feet herself, she told him to get up from his knees and come over and stand by the side of the bed.

'Say hello to James,' she instructed Alice.

'Hello there,' said the spread-eagled slave, looking up at him with shining eyes.

'Hello Alice,' James replied, giving her a crooked smile. It was a lovely smile, Alice thought. He had a lovely smile and a lovely mouth and a lovely voice. He had a lovely body too, fluid and toned, without an ounce of excess. All in all James was a very appealing man. And that was one hell of a hard-on he was still sporting. It was continuing to drizzle precome too.

'Do you like the look of Alice?' Mistress Gale asked James.

'What's not to like, mistress?' he replied, giving Alice another sexy, lopsided smile. He then switched his gaze back to the dominatrix.

'Would you like to help me torture her?' Mistress Gale asked next and saw his smile disappear, if not his erection.

'No, mistress,' he replied, wetting his lips uneasily. 'I would not.'

'Will you help me torture her if I tell you to?'

'Of course I will, mistress,' James said simply. 'I'll do anything you tell me to, you know that.'

'Just checking,' Mistress Gale said, arching an ironic eyebrow. 'Now go to the head of the bed and clamp Alice's nipples.' James's erection, thick and hard as a rock, continued to drizzle a rivulet of precome, which leaked onto Alice's face as he leant over to do this. The tiny teeth of the clover clamps he attached bit hard into her sensitive nipples and her beautiful face, now spattered with his precome, winced with pain.

Mistress Gale used a small flogger with suede thongs to beat Alice's pussy. Each blow made her shiver within her bonds with pain and desire. When the blows landed it was as if her sex was being beaten and caressed at the same time. And all the while James, on Mistress Gale's instruction, pulled at Alice's painful nipple clamps, his hard cock waving obscenely in her face and continuing to splatter it with precome.

The dominatrix then told James to remove Alice's nipple clamps and he immediately did so. This caused her a sharp burst of pain as oxygen rushed like quicksilver back into the previously constricted flesh.

Mistress Gale unclipped Alice's wrist and ankle cuffs from the anchor straps at its four corners. She told her to turn over onto her front and edge forward on the bed, positioning her face as close as possible to James's erection and then to open her legs. After she'd done that Gale climbed lithely onto the bed and knelt between her spread thighs. Looking down at Alice's heavily thrashed rear, she trailed her fingers lightly over the young woman's inner thighs, which were soaking wet.

James remained standing in front of Alice, his hugely erect shaft pulsing in her face. 'Now suck his cock, Alice,' commanded Gale.

As Alice engulfed James's pulsing shaft tightly with her mouth, Mistress Gale plunged her fingers into the wetness between the novice slave's thighs. She began pushing her fingers in and out of her pussy fast and hard, making her tremble with delight.

Faster and faster Alice blew James, sucking ever more violently on his stiff cock. And faster and faster Gale masturbated her from behind, her fingers making an increasingly liquid sound.

Mistress Gale's fingers were working Alice's pussy like pistons now and she plunged three of them deeper inside her. She drove them in hard, plunging into the hot, liquid velvet of her pussy as all the while Alice sucked and sucked at the throbbing tautness of James's erection.

Alice's pulse began racing wildly in her breast. She was getting more and more excited, small explosions of erotic delight sweeping through her. Alice knew she was going to climax any moment and that the experience would be a thrilling eruption. Perversely, though, the orgasm wouldn't come.

Then all of a sudden Mistress Gale's grinding fingers, slick with Alice's juices, pressed hard on her G-spot. This caused the young slave to climax immediately, her body shuddering in sexual ecstasy as the orgasm racked through her body.

And still she kept on blowing James ...

'Come in Alice's mouth now,' Mistress Gale ordered him.

'Yes, mistress,' James gasped. He began to tremble without control before yielding to the ecstasy of release. His handsome face screwed up and he cried out in satisfaction as hot seed burst out of his shaft deep into Alice's encompassing mouth.

She drew down the semen that spurted onto the back of her tongue, taking it into her throat and swallowing. It was like nectar, delicious. *James* was delicious. He was definitely to her taste in more ways than one, she told herself deliriously as she gulped down the last of his jism, his cock still pulsing in her throat.

Alice wondered whether she'd feel the same way about her other fellow sex slave, whoever he might be. She wondered how long it would take Mistress Gale to "introduce" her to him, and how it would happen. She didn't have long to wait. It was that evening in the dungeon when it happened. His name was Alex.

Chapter Ten

Flash forward to the evening. Mistress Gale, who on this occasion was wearing a minuscule chain mail bikini and pointed leather shoes with sharp stiletto heels, was standing in the middle of the dungeon, admiring her handiwork so far.

A naked Alice, her grey eyes wide and glassy, lay on her back on the leather-covered bondage table. Mistress Gale had ensured that her arms were bound to her side by attaching together with trigger clips the red leather wrist and thigh cuffs she was wearing.

The dominatrix had clipped the chains at the end corners of the table to the red leather ankle cuffs Alice also had on. This had achieved the effect of spreading her legs widely apart. Alice's pussy was completely exposed. It was moist and silky, dripping with liquid, and her clit twitched.

Alex, a blond-haired Adonis with gleaming pale blue eyes and chiselled features, was naked apart from red leather wrist and ankle cuffs and was also in bondage. Mistress Gale had beaten him very thoroughly already and now had his lithe, lean body strapped tightly into the upright torture chair. His thick, long cock was rigidly erect, its bulbous head coated with precome.

Mistress Gale strode towards the leather-covered bondage table to which she had Alice secured. Her shapely thighs quivered and rubbed together provocatively as she moved and her stiletto-heeled shoes clicked decisively against the dungeon floor.

It was Alice's turn to be disciplined now and the novice sex slave knew it. She could feel her heart thumping and her pussy began to tighten moistly, her clit to twitch still more. Her breath came fast and furious.

Mistress Gale didn't start Alice's discipline with anything even approaching a warm-up. Instead she began whipping her breasts and pussy hard with a small but vicious leather flogger. It hurt like anything, that flogger. Each harsh strike caused Alice to jump and shudder in her bonds, crying out constantly as the pain flashed through her.

If this was the way Mistress Gale was going to start her discipline tonight, Alice thought in trepidation, what in God's name was she going to do to her after that? Her eyes started to brim with tears, pain and fear colliding in her punished body.

The dominatrix stopped beating her then, though, detaching her from the bondage table and removing her thigh cuffs at the same time. She released Alex from the torture chair too and led the pair of them to a part of the dungeon where four chains hung from the high ceiling to about four feet from the ground.

Chapter Eleven

Mistress Gale placed Alex and Alice standing back to back either side of the chains, and took hold of a box of red pegs. She used all of these, attaching them painfully to their nipples, Alice's pussy lips and Alex's ball sack. She saved the last peg to attach to the small flap of skin just beneath the underside of Alex's precome-smeared cockhead.

Mistress Gale then told the two sex slaves to turn round and stand face to face but without meeting one another's eye. She clipped their wrist cuffs to the end of a chain each, then winched the chains up so that their arms were outstretched above their heads. Finally she clipped Alice's ankle cuffs to either end of a wooden hobble bar and attached Alex's ankles to another hobble bar in the same way.

Next Mistress Gale used a red fibreglass cane to thrash their backsides, alternating six stripes per slave. She sliced the cruel implement through the air in one quick swipe after another. The blows of the cane cracked hard each time against their flesh and made them wince and squeal and buck within their bonds.

Mistress Gale steadily increased the severity of her caning until they were both shuddering violently in agonized ecstasy – and then she stopped abruptly, dropping the fibreglass cane to the floor where it landed with a clatter. The dominatrix marched away from the two slaves to the door of the dungeon and left, zapping off the lights as she went.

In the darkness, Alice lifted her lips to Alex. He kissed her on the mouth, his lips pressing hard against hers. Alice felt the tip of his tongue probe her lips. Alex moved his mouth away a fraction, then brought it back. He kissed her open mouth again, this time pushing his tongue into hers, sliding it over and over.

Alice felt incredibly horny, the heat of desire sweeping through her body. Her sex was throbbing and wet. Her clit was buzzing, burning as if Alex's hard cock was already thrusting away inside her. She was ripe, ready. Alex felt ready too, more than ready.

He and Alice would have loved to fuck then, *loved* to. They *imagined* fucking, imagined doing it again and again with amazing intensity: Alice and Alex and Alex and Alice. Alex on Alice and Alex in Alice. Alice on Alex … But their bondage – the taut chains, the hobble bars, the pegs attached to Alice's labia and the single one attached to the flap of skin beneath the underside of Alex's cockhead – made anything like that a physical impossibility.

Even so, the two sex slaves, their systems awash with endorphins, managed to bond very well indeed. In their fashion. They continued to kiss deeply, Alice letting Alex explore her mouth still more with his tongue, letting him breathe her hot breath. They kissed for a very long time. They kissed and kissed and kissed. They didn't converse, though – not one single word. Words weren't necessary.

The talking came afterwards with both Alex and James as Alice got to know the dishy duo over the ensuing few weeks. But she never actually got to be fucked by either of them – disciplined with them, yes, on numerous occasions and in numerous outlandish permutations – but not fucked by them.

She hoped it would not be too much longer before that situation was rectified. It was up to Mistress Gale, though, completely up to her. That went without saying. Mistress Gale called all the shots in this deviant household, there was no question about that whatsoever. She, Alice, was a mere slave. Hers was not to reason why. Even so, you would think …

Chapter Twelve

Alice and Alex were alone in Mistress Gale's living room, seated together naked on her sumptuous black leather couch. The French window opposite them at the end of the room looked out on a neatly landscaped rear garden, which was bordered by a high stone wall. 'I'd love it if you'd fuck me,' Alice suddenly announced right out of the blue.

'Don't beat about the bush like that. Say what you really mean,' Alex replied teasingly. But he felt a tingling in his loins. He'd love it if he'd fuck her too – once Mistress Gale allowed that to happen, whenever that might be. The thought of it brought on the beginnings of an erection, a slow, luxurious rush of blood to his cock.

'Ha ha, very funny,' Alice said, her big grey eyes twinkling. 'I'd also like very much to be fucked by James,' she went on.

'You don't want much, do you?' Alex said with the same bantering tone. His cock started to swell all the more visibly, though, belying the sardonic approach he was trying to affect. He now had a medium hard-on.

'I'd love to be fucked by both of you, one after the other,' she continued.

Alex chuckled. 'Alice, what are you on?' he asked. His big cock said something else, however. It was now fully erect.

'I'd like my double-fucking by you two handsome studs to be supervised by Mistress Gale in her own inimitable way,' she concluded with a straight face. 'I think she'd want that.'

'That's thoughtful of you,' Alex replied drolly. He was still trying to be Mister Sardonic but already sexual excitement had crept its way across his features. Alice could see that quite clearly, could see quite clearly too his stiffly erect cock.

'Do you think there would be any chance of Mistress Gale agreeing to my idea?' Alice said, parting her lips quizzically. 'I mean, honestly, what do you think?'

'Why don't you ask her yourself?' came a voice from behind the two slaves, making both of them start. At some stage Mistress Gale had quietly entered the room. Her demeanour was as regal and self-assured as ever but her voluptuous body was as gloriously naked as those of the two slaves.

Alice's cheeks flushed. 'Oh God ... I apologise, mistress,' she said, her voice cracking as the words stumbled out of her mouth. She was certain that she'd overstepped the mark with her flippant, borderline-disrespectful comments. Mistress Gale waved the apology away as she sashayed towards the two slaves. Her unbound breasts jiggled and her hips swayed enticingly as she moved. She stood before Alice. 'No need to be sorry,' she reassured the nervous sex slave. 'In fact, I respect the initiative you've taken here. It's somewhat out of character for you, though, wouldn't you agree?'

'Yes, mistress,' Alice replied, smiling at her tentatively. 'I guess it is.' She was normally passivity personified, as she'd have been the first to admit. What on earth had got into her? she wondered in dismay.

'Well, I'm going to reward that initiative,' said Gale. 'I'm going to indulge you on this occasion.'

'Thank you, mistress,' Alice said in surprise and delight – and no little relief that she hadn't incurred the displeasure of the formidable Mistress Gale on this occasion. It could so easily have been otherwise.

'I had intended to put James and Alex through their paces in the dungeon this evening, but not you,' Mistress Gale said. 'I've changed my mind in the light of your interesting proposals. You can now join us – and will be allowed your specific wish.'

'Thank you very much indeed, mistress,' Alice gushed. 'I'm so grateful.'

'You're welcome,' said Gale, adding with a soft chuckle, 'I'm not cruel all the time, you know – just most of the time. Now, I have things to do, so I'll leave you randy pair of sex slaves to do what comes naturally.'

'Are you sure, mistress?' asked Alice uncertainly.

'Quite sure,' the dominatrix replied. Her eyes narrowed with amusement as she noted the way Alex's cock, already very swollen, had begun to pulse insistently. 'All I can say to you is enjoy yourselves. Oh, and Alex –' she added, turning to him as if as a complete afterthought.

'Yes, mistress,' he replied, looking up at her, his pale eyes shining.

'You're not allowed to come. I hope that's quite clear. I'm indulging Alice today, not you. Is that understood?'

'Yes, mistress,' he replied resignedly.

'Good,' the dominatrix said, emitting a dry laugh. And with that she exited the room, leaving the two horny sex slaves alone, sitting there side by side on the leather couch.

'Is that OK with you, Alex?' Alice asked, giving him a look of concern.

'It has to be,' Alex replied with a shrug of his shoulders. 'I was half-expecting Mistress Gale to give me that instruction anyway. She's *always* doing it to her slaves, as you know all too well by now. Orgasm denial is one of the main means she uses to keeps us under her thumb. And she uses it constantly, trying to push our limits further every time. It's very much her *thing*. So, yeah, it's OK with me.'

'Well, as long as you're sure,' said Alice.

Chapter Thirteen

'Now, where were we, Alice?' Alex asked, shaking his head in mock-confusion as he edged closer to her. 'Remind me. What was that you were saying to me originally?'

'I said I'd love it if you'd fuck me,' Alice replied huskily, easing herself into his embrace.

'Well, let's see what we can do about that.' Alex pulled her all the way into him and kissing her on the lips. Her mouth was warm and he probed it quick and tight with his tongue, kissing her hard. And Alice kissed him right back, her tongue and mouth as ardent as his.

Then they broke the kiss and Alice looked down at Alex's erection. 'Mmmm, what a nice big cock you have,' she commented lasciviously before licking a warm trail down his abdomen and taking his shaft into her mouth. She surprised Alex by immediately engulfing it all the way down to his balls. Alice deep-throated him for a blissful while, her head working all the way up and all the way down as he moaned with her movements.

Then she switched gears, withdrawing Alex's erection completely from her mouth. She went on to press against its swollen head with her tongue while massaging its length with her fingers.

'You are so hot, Alice,' Alex said, his breath coming quickly, his eyes gleaming with desire.

'So are you,' she replied, licking a pool of precome from the head of his cock. 'Delicious,' she remarked, ostentatiously licking her lips. 'But, Alex, don't forget Mistress Gale's instruction to you not to come.'

'Remembering it is not the problem,' Alex replied, his voice raspy with arousal. 'It's all too easy to remember. It's going to be nowhere near so easy to achieve. Mind you,' he added quickly, trying to sound philosophical about his situation, 'Mistress Gale is so hot on her slaves exercising orgasm control that I've certainly had plenty of practice in the time I've been with her. So – what the hell – you go ahead.'

Alice gave Alex a long look, her eyes glinting with desire. 'You quite sure?' she said.

'I am,' he replied firmly.

'All right,' Alice shrugged and went back to blowing him, concentrating again on licking and sucking the head of his shaft. She flicked her tongue tantalizingly over its come-slit, precome trickling from the corner of her mouth.

Then she cupped Alex's firm balls with one hand and started to rhythmically masturbate him with the other, her fingers moving increasingly swiftly over the hardness of his cock. The shape of his veins pulsed beneath her fingertips as she briskly worked her hand up and down his erection.

Alex was getting more and more sexually excited and so was Alice, who now felt overwhelmed with desire. She moved her body away from Alex but only so she could get onto all fours on the couch. 'Fuck me,' she said, looking over her shoulder at him seductively. 'I simply can't wait any longer,' she added, wiggling her backside for him, cream oozing from her pussy lips.

Alex got into position behind Alice and, running his hands over the smoothness of her rear, pushed his hard cock into her willing pussy. He began to fuck her, forging deep into her sex, the strokes of his cock slow and powerful. Alex pushed into the hot warmth of Alice's pussy and she pushed back. They thrust together hungrily until …

'I like to take it from behind every which way,' Alice announced breathlessly, disengaging her body from Alex's and rising to her feet. 'Sit back down on the couch.' He did and Alice, facing away from him, positioned herself so that she could manoeuvre the head of his hard cock against her pussy lips, against her clitoris. She rubbed herself against Alex's cockhead gently at first and then more vigorously.

Alice slid herself right down onto his shaft, feeling its thickness impale her sex once again. Alex gave out a soft groan and whimper in response and she could feel his cock stiffen even more inside her. Alice began to slide up and down on him vigorously, grinding her hips down hard.

Alice felt on fire with sexual excitement and so did Alex. The two sex slaves continued to fuck in a mounting frenzy, each full of their own need. Then Alice suddenly stopped dead.

'I'm sorry, but I can't do this any more, Alex,' she said, emotion colouring her voice. Alice disengaged herself from him and rose shakily to her feet. She turned and looked down at Alex, her big eyes glistening.

'But why?' he asked in stunned amazement. He could feel his heart pounding hard, and as for his erection …

'Look, if we carry on as we have been doing, I'm going to have the most massive orgasm. I just know I will.'

'Eh … Alice, isn't that the general idea?' Alex asked, more bewildered than ever, and more in pain with lust too.

'Yes, but at what cost?' Alice said. 'I'm worried that if I climax, it will either tip you over the edge into having an orgasm yourself, which will mean that you'll have disobeyed Mistress Gale's instruction – and God knows what revenge she'd take.'

'Or?'

'Or you'll manage to control yourself like I know you're determined to do, but it'll leave you half-demented with unfulfilled lust.'

'Alice, believe me, that's what I am right now anyway,' Alex protested, gasping.

'Well then,' she reasoned, 'think how much worse you'll feel if we go on.'

'But – but, Alice,' he stammered.

'No more "buts", Alex. 'That's my final word. You know you'd do the same for me.'

'I would too, you're right, I have to admit it,' he acknowledged with a heavy sigh. 'Aren't we both wonderful?'

'Yes we are.' Alice laughed. 'Now, let's just calm down and look forward to this evening in the dungeon.'

So "calm down" is what they both did to the best of their abilities. It wasn't easy.

Chapter Fourteen

Jump cut to that evening. Mistress Gale and her three sex slaves were now in the dungeon. What little the dominatrix was wearing was all of soft black leather: an "open" bra that left her magnificent breasts completely exposed, the nipples bullet-hard; a miniscule G-string and a tight-fitting pair of tall boots. She was holding a riding crop in one hand; and by her side, on her knees and naked, was Alice.

'Do you like what I've done to your two fellow slaves, Alice?' Mistress Gale asked, gesturing with the crop in the direction of James and Alex.

'Very much so, mistress,' Alice replied excitedly. There was an ache between her legs and her sex felt slippery-wet.

This is what Alice could see:

James was strapped by the wrists, waist and ankles to the wall-mounted St Andrew's cross. He was facing out on the dungeon, his nipples clamped with clover clamps and his cock rigidly erect.

Alex was standing in the centre of the dungeon, his arms outstretched to his side, his red leather wrist cuffs clipped to a pair of chains that hung from the high ceiling. Movement in Alex's legs was much restricted by the short length of chain clipped at either end to his ankle cuffs, which were also of red leather. Mistress Gale had attached half a dozen black pegs to his ball sack, above which his hard cock reared.

'Let's go and say hello to your partner in crime,' said

Mistress Gale to Alice, swishing her riding crop as she led her crawling across the floor to Alex in his chained bondage.

The dominatrix gave him a look, amused, mocking. 'Feeling horny by any chance, Alex?' she asked, pushing his chin up with the end of the crop.

'Yes, mistress,' he replied. 'Extremely.'

'You must be, after exercising such admirable self-control this afternoon,' Mistress Gale said, now running the crop up and down his thighs. 'Those poor aching balls of yours,' she added, flicking several of the pegs attached to his scrotum with the leather tip of the crop and making Alex cringe in discomfort.

'And your poor cock,' she continued tauntingly. 'It's so hard and red, it looks positively angry. I do hope it's not angry with me, because if it were I'd have to punish it. In fact, just to be sure …'

Mistress Gale immediately started to beat the head of Alex's shaft with the leather tip of the crop, her rapid-fire blows coming down in swift succession. His body jerked sharply as he struggled uselessly against his bonds in reaction to the intense pain she was inflicting on him. Then the dominatrix stopped as quickly as she'd started.

Mistress Gale removed the pegs from Alex's ball sack with care. 'Alice,' she said, turning to the kneeling slave. 'Crawl forward, and suck Alex's punished cock.'

Alice crawled into position, opened her lips and pressed her mouth to the head of Alex's shaft, tracing her tongue under it at first. Then she closed her mouth around his cockhead, sucking it.

While she did this Mistress Gale stood behind Alex, using the riding crop to beat his muscular rear, which rapidly reddened under her onslaught. However, the dominatrix seemed to tire of this after a short while. 'I feel that I'm being too lenient with you, Alex,' she told him ominously. 'I must put that right *tout de suite*.'

Mistress Gale switched to whipping Alex with a heavy leather flogger, each of her blows a sharp explosion of pain that made him shudder and squirm. Meanwhile Alice's bright lips remained fastened tight to his hard cock, sucking and sucking it. He gasped as the blissful sensations Alice was arousing with her lips merged with the burning of the marks that now covered his punished rear.

Alex writhed and squirmed in his chains with a combination of pain and desire. For a time, though, pain went into the ascendancy. It mounted agonizingly as a result of the vicious whipping Mistress Gale was continuing to give him with the heavy leather flogger. The pain was burning Alex's flesh more and more until he was on the point of crying out his safeword. However, when it came to it that was not necessary. Again Mistress Gale suddenly stopped beating him.

'Alex thinks I'm showing him mercy but he's wrong,' she told Alice, who looked up at her while continuing to suck Alex's shaft. 'It's just that I can sense James on the cross there is in need of my attention. While I'm dealing with him, Alice, carry on blowing Alex.'

And as she did just that Mistress Gale got on with torturing James on the St Andrew's cross to which he remained securely bound. She squeezed his clamped nipples and his handsome face twisted into a grimace of pain in reaction.

'I think I can improve on that, James,' Mistress Gale told the anguished slave before attaching metal weights to his nipple clamps. It made his dark eyes tear over with agony. 'And look at that big cock of yours, standing so majestically proud,' she added. 'Such arrogance! It's simply asking to be slapped down.'

Mistress Gale went on to beat James's hard cock with the leather tip of the riding crop. Each blow to his aching shaft made him flinch and shudder. Finally he started to shake his head rapidly in desperation. Mistress Gale immediately ceased beating him, knowing this to be his safe gesture.

'Crawl over here, Alice,' she called to her. 'I've another slave's punished cock in need of your soothing lips. You, on the other hand, are well overdue for some discipline.'

Alice withdrew Alex's pulsing erection from her mouth and crawled on hands and knees towards the St Andrew's cross. The lovely young blonde was poetry in motion, her beautiful naked body moving sinuously across the dungeon.

Chapter Fifteen

When Alice had crawled to the cross she covered James's stiff cock with her lips. She fastened tight to it with her mouth as she lapped up his precome, before sucking, sucking, sucking …

While Alice was giving James this four-star blowjob, Mistress Gale whipped her back ferociously with the heavy leather flogger, causing pain to sear through her. Alice could feel the heat burning on her flesh, the skin raised and imprinted with the pattern of the whip's thongs. She could not cry out in pain. All she could do was suck even harder on James's thickened cock. Until …

'Stand up now, Alice,' Mistress Gale demanded and Alice withdrew James's erection from her mouth and got to her feet. 'Now wank him. Do it as hard as you can.'

Alice began to masturbate James with all the energy required of her, her fist working up and down in swift, urgent rhythms over his stiffness. At the same time Mistress Gale used the heavy leather flogger to thrash her quivering backside until it was covered with welts as angry as those already covering her back.

On and on Gale continued beating Alice. And as she wrestled desperately with the sharp spasms of burning pain suffusing her body, she continued masturbating James ever harder.

Alice's fist worked up and down faster and faster, pulling him into a lascivious state of sweat and sex and grip. James's shaft was so engorged now that it seemed likely to erupt at any moment with the strength of his sexual arousal.

Then Mistress Gale stopped beating Alice and told her to stop masturbating James – and not a moment too soon as far as he was concerned.

After putting the heavy leather flogger back in the rack of disciplinary implements and picking out a studded leather paddle in its place, Mistress Gale returned her attentions to Alex in his chained bondage.

She brought the studded paddle swinging across in a smooth, curved path to smack hard on Alex's backside. It connected with his flesh with a sharp report that echoed around the dungeon. A second harsh stroke followed the first, Mistress Gale paddling him even harder on his rear.

The dominatrix continued to beat Alex until his body was enveloped in intense pain. Then she began masturbating him as well, squeezing his rock-hard cock and pulling it up and down fast.

Harder and harder Mistress Gale paddled Alex's backside with one hand. Faster and faster she jerked away with the other, stroking and pulling him into a state of furious arousal until it looked as if he was about to climax, that he was right on the very brink.

Which was when Gale abruptly ceased beating and wanking him. 'Oh no you don't, Alex,' she snapped. 'I haven't given you permission to come. You know the rules.'

Mistress Gale freed Alex from his chained bondage, immediately afterwards winching up and out of the way the chains that had been clipped to his wrist cuffs. Then she beckoned Alice to crawl over to join them, telling her to remain on her hands and knees.

'I want you to fuck Alice now,' Mistress Gale told Alex. 'After all, that's what she said she wanted. Are you happy with that, Alice?'

The young woman let out a deep, shuddering breath. 'You bet, mistress,' she replied, looking up at the dominatrix with eyes shiny with intense excitement.

'Good,' said Mistress Gale. 'By the way, Alex,' she added matter-of-factly, switching her gaze to him, 'you still won't be allowed to come.'

Chapter Sixteen

Mistress Gale watched as Alex positioned himself behind Alice's splayed rear. 'I know you must think what a cruel dominatrix I am, Alex,' she said, in a suspiciously conciliatory tone. 'But not too cruel for you, I hope.'

'No, mistress,' he replied distractedly as he plunged his cock into the inviting wetness of Alice's pussy.

'A cruel dominatrix,' Mistress Gale explained in a tone of sweet reasonableness, 'would do as I have done: make sure you were in a state of frenzied sexual excitement and then instruct you to fuck this beautiful girl but *not* to climax. Agreed?'

Alex's breathing deepened. 'Agreed, mistress,' he said as he pushed and pushed inside Alice, his shaft soaking wet in her sex.

'But a *really* cruel dominatrix would go further than that, wouldn't she?'

'Yes, mistress,' Alex replied uncertainly, continuing to push and push, thrusting deep inside Alice's pussy.

'Knowing how being in pain just intensifies the lust of a sexual masochist like you, she would give you a really severe beating while you fucked this horny little bitch. Isn't that the case?'

'Yes, mistress,' he replied in an unsteady voice, still pushing and pushing as Alice rocked her hips back to meet his thrusts.

'Thanks for the confirmation,' Mistress Gale said with a cruel laugh, 'because that's exactly what I'm going to do. And you, dear Alex, are going to fuck Alice *really* hard from this point on.'

And he did. The frantic slave began to plunge his cock vigorously into Alice's sex, holding onto her hips as he thrust his own forwards and backwards fast.

At the same time Mistress Gale used a cat o'nine tails to rain blow after stinging blow upon Alex's rear, each of her lashes ferociously painful and harsh. He moaned and gasped at the sharp pain as she increased the strength of the beating and he fucked Alice even more energetically.

Open-mouthed and panting, Alex felt waves of pleasure-pain flooding his body as he got ever closer to the climax he was willing himself with increasing desperation not to allow to happen.

Then came his biggest test yet. Alice shuddered uncontrollably to a huge orgasm, her wet pussy contracting in spasms around his hard cock. Alex closed his eyes and summoned every ounce of determination he possessed, shudders rippling through his frame. He managed to restrain his climax. Just. My God, it had been close, though.

'Well done, Alex. What an obedient slave you are, even in the most difficult of circumstances,' Mistress Gale commended him, putting the cat o'nine tails to one side. 'You can withdraw your cock from Alice's pussy now. But let's not forget that she's said she wants a double fucking on this occasion: that she wants to be fucked by James as well as you. And today is all about indulging Alice, isn't it?'

'Yes, mistress,' he agreed, panting and gasping. 'Yes it is.'

Chapter Seventeen

'Alex, I want you to do something else for me now,' Mistress Gale said. 'I want you to come and help me release James from the St Andrew's cross.'

'Yes, mistress,' he said, his breathing still laboured.

'Alice –' the dominatrix turned to the young slave '- crawl over there to the middle of the dungeon.'

'Yes, mistress,' she said, and did.

Alex assisted Mistress Gale in removing James's weighted nipple clamps and in unbuckling the straps that bound his wrists, waist and ankles to the cross. Mistress Gale then led James and Alex by their hard cocks over to Alice. 'Blow the two of them for a while,' she told the kneeling sex slave.

Both men were hugely erect, their cocks urgent with need. Alice took Alex's erection into her mouth first and, closing her lips around it, began to blow him languorously. Then she did the same to James. She expertly, sensuously blew James and Alex separately and together.

'Lie flat on your back on the dungeon floor, James,' Mistress Gale commanded next. 'Alice, you sit on his hard cock and let him start fucking you, then go back to sucking off Alex. And I do mean sucking off, not like your recent lazy efforts,' she said sternly. 'This time put some real effort into it, girl, like the effort I want James to put into fucking you. I want you to do your very best to suck Alex to orgasm, Alice. Understood?'

'Understood, mistress,' Alice replied, her big grey eyes

glazed with lust. She fell onto James and he pushed his swollen cock inside her pussy, immediately beginning to fuck her hard.

As Mistress Gale had instructed, Alice went back to blowing Alex but with considerably more vigour this time. She worked her mouth over his stiff shaft, moving fast. At the same time James continued thrusting up and down vigorously, his erection steely-hard inside her.

Mistress Gale waited a decent – correction, *indecent* interval until she judged the time was right, then issued her next edict.

'Alex, James, Alice,' she said, 'I absolutely *forbid* any of you to climax until I say so. Clear?'

'Yes, mistress,' all three replied frantically, Alex's response in particular sounding almost manic.

Mistress Gale looked Alex in the eye and could plainly see how desperate he was by now. In response she simply picked up her riding crop and held its leather tip to his lips. 'Kiss it, slave,' she told him and he of course obeyed, bringing his lips to the implement.

As James continued to thrust up hard into Alice's sex, she carried on voraciously sucking Alex's shaft as it throbbed and spurted out precome into her mouth. At the same time Mistress Gale beat Alex's backside with the riding crop in an avalanche of relentless ferocity, one red-hot strike after another. And all the while the frenzy of her three sex slaves mounted and mounted until it reached boiling point.

'James, climax now. Alice, stop blowing Alex and climax now,' came Mistress Gale's sudden staccato command and the two slaves obeyed immediately. Both of them climaxed together in noisy convulsions of release, James shooting his creamy load, spurt after vigorous spurt, deep inside Alice's sex.

'Alex …,' Gale then said, pausing for what seemed like an eternity. Alex's heart was beating like a hammer. His face was flushed, his mouth wide open, his breathing rough and ragged. His ragingly hard cock was pulsing fit to explode. 'I want you to climax now,' the dominatrix said at last. 'Come all over Alice's face.'

Oh, the incredible, the monumental relief! Mistress Gale had been indulging Alice so much that day. But, now at long last it was Alex's turn and, it has to be said, he really did splash out on her.

Chapter Eighteen

Flash forward a couple of days. Alice was one happy sex slave. She loved Alex and James, thought the dishy duo were adorable. And as for Mistress Gale, Alice worshipped the ground she walked on, regarded her as not merely a goddess but as the *supreme* goddess.

Yes, Alice was happy all right, ecstatically happy. But she was feeling more than a little disorientated. You see, she was in Mistress Gale's dungeon – this time with James – but all was total darkness. The dominatrix had left them kneeling in the pitch black inside the cage, which she'd locked.

'James,' Alice said.

'Yes.'

'I'm trying to work out exactly where you are.'

'Have a grope about,' James suggested.

'I am. Oh … What's that?'

'As if you didn't know!'

'It feels nice – really big and hard,' Alice said, smiling mischievously into the darkness. 'Do you mind me rubbing it like this?'

'Not if you don't mind me doing this to you.'

'Not at all. It's just what I need.'

'You have a lovely wet pussy.'

'Thank you, James. It'll get wetter still if you keep rubbing it like that. Mmmm, that's nice.'

'Alice.'

'Yes. Oooh, right there, that's perfect.'

'What do you think Mistress Gale is doing at the moment?'

'Goodness knows,' said Alice. 'I'll tell you something, though.'

'What?'

'She isn't as cruel as we sometimes think she is.'

'How can you possibly say such a thing, Alice?' James said, his voice dripping with incredulity. 'I could give you any number of examples to refute what you've just said. But merely look at our current situation if you will. She has got us on our knees locked up in this cage in the pitch dark, wearing nothing but our collars to remind us of our enslavement to her. And there's no knowing *when* she'll let us out.'

'Yes,' agreed Alice. 'But she has left our arms and legs free and she hasn't gagged us.'

'That's true,' James acknowledged. 'I can play with your pussy and that's what I'm doing.'

'And I can play with your hard cock and that's what I'm doing.'

'I can also caress your breasts like this.'

'Yes, and we can kiss like th –'

At that point the lights went on and the two startled slaves turned their heads to see Mistress Gale standing inside the dungeon by its door – where she had been all along.

The dominatrix looked stunningly beautiful. Her skin was more porcelain-perfect than ever. Her dark hair had an extra-glossy sheen to it and her wonderful figure was enhanced by the highly seductive outfit of black leather she had on. It consisted of an extremely short, tight-fitting dress, underneath which she was naked, and thigh-length boots.

Mistress Gale began to stride towards the cage, her high heels click-clicking against the dungeon floor. 'Turn right round to face me, slaves,' she ordered, her voice calm – and all the more unnerving for that.

'Yes, mistress,' James and Alice replied in unison, shuffling round nervously on their knees.

'Surprised to see me, Alice?' Gale asked.

'Yes, mistress,' Alice said, her grey eyes as wide as saucers.

'You too, James?'

'Yes, mistress,' he replied, also wide-eyed. 'How did you manage that?'

'Easy,' Mistress Gale replied. 'When I locked the pair of you in the cage you had your backs to me, I simply switched off the lights and shut the dungeon door.'

'And we jumped to entirely the wrong conclusion, mistress,' said James.

'That's right.' The dominatrix passed her tongue from cheek to cheek. 'And I was able to listen to your interesting conversation. But it raised a couple of worrying concerns in my mind. First, I didn't give you permission to play with each other, yet you did. What do you have to say for yourselves?'

You didn't tell us we *couldn't* play with each other, mistress, the kneeling slaves both felt like saying. But they kept their thoughts to themselves. This was no time to be a smartarse. Indeed there was *never* such a time with Mistress Gale.

'Sorry, mistress,' they chorused shamefacedly, looking up at her through the bars of the cage.

'Oh, believe me, you're going to be sorry, slaves – very sorry,' Mistress Gale said sharply, fixing them both with a penetrating gaze. 'Particularly when you consider the second and by far the most serious of my concerns. Do you know what it is?'

Alice made an effort to swallow. 'Is it what I said about you not being as cruel as we sometimes think you are, mistress?' she asked.

'Right first time,' Gale replied, her voice heavily edged

with sarcasm.

'That was me being stupid, mistress.' Alice's tone was wheedling. 'I know I shouldn't have said something like that. It's just that I'm so very happy with you and …'

Mistress Gale interrupted. 'That's true, Alice,' she said, the threat of retribution in her piercing gaze. 'You shouldn't have said something like that – something that I regard as a fucking insult. You still have so much to learn about being a good slave, that's very clear. However you need to be aware that I'm going to make you both suffer for what you've done.'

Alice tried not to tremble beneath the ferocity of Mistress Gale's gaze. 'I'm really, really sorry, mistress,' she grovelled, her voice cracking.

'Like I said, you're going to be – both of you,' the dominatrix replied, her words as sharp as razor wire.

Chapter Nineteen

'Punish me severely, mistress. I know I deserve it. But, please, not James,' Alice pleaded. 'I wouldn't want him to suffer just because of my foolishness.'

Mistress Gale looked down at her for a long moment, her expression more fearsome than ever. 'What you want and what you don't want is entirely immaterial to me,' she finally said, unlocking and opening the door to the cage. 'The fact of the matter is that on this occasion I've decided to treat both of you equally. Equally badly, that is. Now, crawl out of the cage, slaves. You first, James, then stand up.'

James did as he'd been told. Alice followed and also started to stand. Mistress Gale pushed her roughly to the dungeon floor.

'Wrong again, Alice,' the dominatrix said, glaring down at her. 'Get back onto your knees and crawl to the front of James.'

'Yes, mistress,' replied the chastened slave through trembling lips.

'Now, do you know what I want you to do, Alice?' Mistress Gale asked.

'No, mistress.'

'I want you to suck his cock for all you're worth,' Gale said, adding curtly, 'James, look at me.'

'Yes, mistress.'

'You know very well what you're not allowed to do when she does that, don't you,' the dominatrix said. 'I don't even need to say the words, do I.'

'No, mistress,' he replied softly. *Of course* he knew.

Alice closed her lips around James's cock and started to blow him vigorously. She worked her mouth up and down fast, cascading her tongue across the hard length of his shaft.

Mistress Gale picked up a thick leather strap and began to whip James's backside, bringing the sturdy implement down so hard on his flesh that each stroke made him cry out in agony. Harsh stroke followed harsh stroke in quick succession and agonized cry followed agonized cry.

But his cries had evidently begun to irritate Mistress Gale. 'Shut the fuck up,' she rasped, bringing the strap down extra hard to emphasize her words.

The dominatrix carried on strapping James ferociously until he was in such excruciating pain that he was finding it extremely difficult to stop himself not so much crying out as screaming out his agony.

Meanwhile Alice continued to suck and suck at James's cock, taking its length all the way in. She moved her mouth up and down, the pace growing faster and faster still as he bucked with her movements and the rhythm of the strap with which Mistress Gale was continuing to belabour his rear so viciously.

James's breathing quickened more and more until he was panting uncontrollably and seemed to be on the verge of climaxing. Then Mistress Gale stopped beating him.

'Alice, stop blowing James,' she ordered. 'Get off your knees and stand with your legs spread.'

Alice immediately moved her lips from James's hard cock and got to her feet, parting her thighs.

'James, kneel down and crawl to the front of Alice,' Mistress Gale went on. 'I want you to eat her pussy as if your very life depended on it. And, Alice …'

'Yes, mistress,' she said in a voice that was high and unsteady

'What is it that you are not allowed to do, do you think?'

'Climax, mistress.'

'The girl's a mind reader,' Mistress Gale responded sarcastically.

James immediately got on with what he'd been told to do, subjecting Alice's pussy to a really persistent licking. His mouth licked all over Alice's hot sex, his tongue working fast and hard over her clit, licking her all wet and sticky.

While James was doing that, Mistress Gale used the same thick leather strap with which she'd just beaten him so savagely to thrash Alice's backside, doing so with equal savagery. She beat Alice until her rear cheeks were flayed a ferocious shade of red and her whole body ached with extreme pain. Then Mistress Gale stopped. But James didn't – because she hadn't told him to ...

He continued to flick-flick-flick his tongue over the lips of Alice's sex, making her ever more excited. Alice's nerves were on fire and the heat of desire swept through her body as her pussy pulsed with the tremor of the gigantic orgasm she was trying frantically to hold at bay. Faster and faster James licked her sex until she knew she was going to go over the edge. But, no, she wouldn't let herself, she *wouldn't* ...

'All right, James, stop what you're doing and stand up,' Mistress Gale commanded, much to Alice's relief. She had become slack-mouthed with lust and the pupils of her eyes were now so dilated that she seemed almost to have no iris.

'Both of you stand side by side, facing the cage,' Mistress Gale went on brusquely. 'Put your hands on its top.'

When the two sex slaves had done as they'd been told, Mistress Gale spoke again. 'Now let's see how much more damage I can do to those four inviting arse cheeks,' she said, her tone gloating.

This time using a heavy leather tawse, the dominatrix went on to beat their backsides alternately with rapid criss-cross motions of the savage implement. The thick leather snapped hard each time on their aching flesh, which smarted agonizingly from the impact.

Mistress Gale kept going mercilessly. She beat harsh strokes across their punished backsides over and over again with the tawse until Alice and James were in burning agony and both started to scream like banshees. Only then did she stop.

Chapter Twenty

Mistress Gale told Alice and James to turn around and kneel before her. 'You've endured a hell of a lot of pain, you two miscreants,' she said. 'But I think you've earned the right to some pleasure now – and so have I.'

She ordered Alice to lie flat on her back on the leather-covered bondage table with her backside as close to the edge as possible and her knees up and thighs parted.

'James, stand in front of Alice,' Mistress Gale instructed. 'Once I've straddled her face so that she can start to lick me to orgasm, I want you to fuck her hard.' Then she added, 'Let's be quite clear, though – you two *still* aren't allowed to come.'

Mistress Gale got onto the bondage table and squatted down on the heels of her thigh-high boots on either side of Alice's head. She began to sit astride her face, positioning herself over her mouth, slowly sitting lower.

Alice began to probe Mistress Gale's sex with her tongue. At the same time James started to do what he'd been instructed to do, pushing his cock hard into the hot warmth of Alice's pussy.

Straight away he began to pound his shaft in and out, his rhythm strong and quick. Each of his thrusts went deeper into Alice, penetrating her until her body was shaking to its very depths. And all the time she flicked her tongue over Mistress Gale's clit as the dominatrix rubbed her wet sex in her face, demanding constantly that she lick her even harder.

Alice was soon licking Mistress Gale's pussy voraciously, her face doused with her love juice as she took her ever closer to orgasm. And then it happened. The pleasure exploded through Gale as she shoved her sex down hard on Alice's mouth, and her climax came, making her shudder and cry out in ecstasy.

Eventually Mistress Gale came down from her orgasmic high. She lifted herself off Alice's drenched face and climbed gracefully off the bondage table. 'James, stop fucking Alice now and stand before me,' she ordered.

He immediately did as he'd been told, withdrawing his throbbing shaft from Alice's now-sodden pussy and getting into position. Mistress Gale then ordered Alice to get up from the bondage table and stand in front of her by the side of James.

'The two of you must be more than ready to climax by now,' the dominatrix suggested. 'Am I right?'

'Yes, mistress,' replied Alice, breathing very heavily.

'Yes, mistress,' echoed James, clearly in the same frantic state.

'You said earlier that I'm not as cruel as you slaves sometimes think I am,' Mistress Gale reminded Alice. 'Isn't that so?'

'Yes, mistress,' she replied, standing humbly before her. 'I'm extremely sorry for saying that.'

'Oh, I don't know,' Gale smiled. 'Maybe you were right. You see, I'm going to lock you both back in the cage again now, it's true. But once you're there, not only do I have no objection to you playing with each other, I absolutely *insist* that you do. No talking this time, though, OK?'

'Yes, mistress,' replied James in a tone of immense relief.

'Anything you say, mistress,' added Alice effusively.

'Onto your hands and knees now, both of you,' Mistress Gale ordered.

'Yes, mistress,' they replied in unison, both immediately getting onto all fours.

'Are you properly grateful to me, slaves?' Gale asked, leading them crawling to the cage and gesturing with a beckoning hand for them to enter.

'Yes, mistress,' they chorused in reply. 'Thank you, mistress.'

'There are just one or two other things I need to bring to your attention,' Mistress Gale said casually as she locked them back inside the cage. The two sex slaves turned to face her and hear what she had to say to them. 'I'm going to leave you locked in here for a long time – *hours*,' she went on. 'And you'll be doing what I wish you to do, which is precisely this: having constant sex but never allowing yourselves to climax. Now, James, if you fail you can expect to be on the receiving end of the most vicious cock and ball torture imaginable. Understood?'

'Yes, mistress,' he replied. His lips quivered and there was a break in his voice when he spoke.

'In your case, Alice,' Mistress Gale went on, her tone chilling, 'as you quite rightly said, you are really the guilty party here rather than James. Therefore your punishment will be very much more severe if you fail. I have decided that should you climax you will cease to be my slave, end of story, *finito*. If you do climax you can try lying to me about it if you want to, insist that it never happened. But you know that wouldn't work, don't you?'

She was right. Remember, Alice couldn't tell a lie to save her life. 'Yes, mistress,' she replied, hearing her voice echo hollowly against the dungeon walls.

Mistress Gale's eyes glinted malevolently. 'Who said I'm not a really cruel dominatrix!' she exclaimed with a harsh laugh.

Alice felt stunned, terrified, panic-stricken. She could feel the bottom falling out of her life. Her heart was beating wildly, crashing around inside her chest like a caged beast. Alice was caged too. But for how much longer?

She looked up at Mistress Gale beseechingly through the bars of the locked cage. But she got nothing but an icy stare in return. Then the dominatrix turned on her heels and left the dungeon, shutting the door firmly behind her.

Alice had thought that her torment this time had been nearly at an end, had thought that relief – sexual relief – was almost at hand. In fact, her torment hadn't even begun. Indeed if she failed now she would be in torment for the rest of her life because here with Mistress Gale in her dungeon domain was the only place in the world she wanted to be.

Beware of what you wish for. Those words came into Alice's head like that first time she'd spent in this dungeon, this cage. She didn't ignore the words as she had done before, though, didn't try to blank them out.

But they meant something very different this time round. Because what Alice wished for right now – what she needed, craved so desperately – was sexual release. But if she got what she wished for, *ached* for, she would be lost forever, mad with longing for her beloved Mistress Gale.

Then again, if she managed to keep herself from climaxing over the long hours ahead of her, she was sure it would be at the expense of her sanity.

Either way, madness lay ahead for Alice. But one was a madness filled with misery and loss. The other – a kind of endless erotic dementia – was her choice. Perhaps at some level it always had been.

Beware of what you wish for. Alice said those words to herself with ever-increasing urgency over the next endless hours, each of the innumerable times she felt close to climaxing as a result of James's frighteningly conscientious ministrations.

Eventually she found herself intoning the words

160

constantly inside her head – *screaming* them – like the most fanatical and frantic of prayers, in her increasingly demented efforts not to climax, in her desperate efforts to stop it all coming to an end.

BOOK THREE

DARK DELUSION

'Now you understand the suprasensual fool! Under the lash of a beautiful woman my senses first realised the meaning of woman.'
Leopold von Sacher-Masoch

Chapter One

There are some people who live to work, ambitious to succeed in the workplace at all costs and terrified of failure. There are others who work to live, many because they have no choice, but some because they choose to, essentially treating the world of work with the contempt they think it deserves. Peter Moran fell into this last category. He worked to live. And he lived to fuck.

Peter never brought any of his sexual conquests back to his apartment with him, though. I mean *never*. That was because, extremely modest though it was, he considered it to be entirely his personal space. It was sacrosanct to him. He liked to have his apartment completely to himself, spending much of his time there all on his own and in silence. Paradoxically, he'd always wanted to live alone. If he'd not been highly sexed, he'd have lived the life of a recluse, he was sure of it. But one thing he did have was a strong libido – an extremely strong libido. It ruled his life, had become the *purpose* of his life. He was a sex addict.

Peter's apartment, his solitary haven, was certainly nothing to write home about, that was for sure. It was above a scruffy parade of shops in a ragged corner of West London. The place was sparsely furnished and most of that furniture was second-hand. The apartment was small too, which at least meant it didn't need a lot of looking after. Also, partly due to the property's unprepossessing location, the rent was reasonable. That was important to Peter as he didn't earn a great deal of money; didn't deserve to, frankly.

He was a freelance journalist of no distinction to speak of. He had few journalistic talents other than a facile ability with the written word. That is, when he could even be bothered to exercise that talent – he was a dab hand at simply regurgitating press releases for the bland and mindless style magazines that were the main outlets for his work. The most you could say of his more original pieces was that he invariably got them in on time and they were clear, concise and competent. Peter wasn't at all committed to his work, though. Indeed, he actively disliked it a lot of the time. But it paid the rent, with enough left over for him to live the kind of life he chose to lead. That was the main thing, from his point of view.

That evening, the one that would change his life for ever, started out like so many others for Peter. It began with him getting ready to go out on the prowl for pussy, as he liked to think of the young women with whom he had sex. They weren't people to him but sex objects. It was unfortunate to say the least that he should have thought that way about them, but he did.

Peter would be going to one of the many dance clubs to choose from in the centre of London – he liked to ring the changes – and would be looking to hit on some foxy girl or another, with the sole intention of having sex with her. He liked best the ones who didn't hunt in pairs or packs, the ones on their own. If a sexy young woman was out looking for Mister Goodbar, Mister Goodfuck, then she need look no further: Peter was her man.

He started to get ready to go out, his preparation both relaxed and meticulous. He stripped naked and went to the bathroom, where he took a leisurely shower, standing under the hard jets of hot water. He shampooed and soaped and soaked himself thoroughly. He towelled his body and hair dry, then opened a tube of shaving cream and lathered his cheeks. He took the safety razor that sat on the edge of the porcelain sink and shaved his face.

Peter washed off the foam, doused his face in cold water and dried it. He cleaned his teeth and gargled with mouthwash. He sprayed deodorant under his arms and dabbed a little aftershave on his face and combed his thick, dark hair back from his forehead.

Then he went into his bedroom to complete the countdown to lift-off. Peter put on a white cotton shirt and a pair of tight black leather jeans, no underwear. He strapped on his watch. He put thin black socks on, shrugged on a dark blue jacket that was lightweight and nicely tailored, and slipped into a pair of comfortable black loafers.

Peter had a handsome aquiline face and vivid blue eyes with long eyelashes. He was a little over six foot in height and his body was slim and in good shape, toned. Studying himself in the full-length mirror as he dressed, he thought he looked pretty damn good, and most women would have agreed with him.

Peter was very successful with the opposite sex. Correction, he had slept with a lot of them. Despite having sex with a bewildering number of women, he resolutely avoided any personal involvement with these one-night stands of his. He didn't want to have a relationship with anyone. There was no room for it in his scheme of things.

He was well-hung and virile and was a very good lover. Correction, he was a technically expert lover. There was no emotion in it whatsoever in his case, no soul. He was addicted to cold, ephemeral sex. And that coldness was not limited to his sex life. Peter Moran was a thoroughly alienated man, couldn't engage with the world in any meaningful sense at all. Nothing, nobody, seemed entirely real to him. Everything and everyone seemed one step removed and of little significance. He was completely jaded, thoroughly cynical.

There was something missing in Peter Moran, no doubt

about it. He was so self-contained that he was sealed off. His life was so empty, hollow, that it was without meaning. He was so cold, so self-centred, as to be almost misogynistic. He was dead at heart. He didn't see it that way, of course. He thought he was the ultimate hedonist, a sex machine, a total stud.

*　　*　　*

Peter had not the slightest sense of foreboding, not even the tiniest hint of one, when he set off on his pussy hunt that mild mid-summer evening. He watched the houses and factories and shops march inexorably in the opposite direction from the window of the taxi that was taking him into London's West End. As Peter got closer to his destination he stared out of the window at the theatres and cinemas and hotels and restaurants, at the hordes of visitors and foreigners and revellers thronging the vibrant streets.

He got the taxi driver to drop him at the end of the street where the dance club he'd decided to go to that night was situated. He paid and tipped the driver and got out of the taxi. Peter walked slowly the short distance to the club, taking wide, easy strides. There was no hurry. He glanced at his watch. It was not far off ten o'clock. The sky was a darkening blue, the light dimming markedly as the sun disappeared over the horizon.

Peter paid to go into the club and made his way elegantly through its neon-lit entrance. He went to the upstairs lounge, which had dark walls and muted lighting. He could hear the thud-thud-thud of music coming from downstairs. He walked over to the bar and, taking out his wallet, rested his elbows on the bar's black lacquered surface. Peter caught the eye of the barman who had just finished serving another man. There were rows of bottles on glass shelves behind him, all illuminated from beneath. The barman took Peter's order, a rum and Coke with ice and lemon.

168

When his drink arrived he took it over to the railings that formed a gallery above the dance floor. Peter looked down at the people dancing below, mentally airbrushing out the males as he did so, focussing on the women. He sipped at his rum and Coke, ice clinking against his glass. He rolled the taste of his drink around his tongue and rolled the thought of sex around his mind.

Peter wasn't a great one for music, preferring complete silence whenever he had a choice. But he liked well enough what the DJ was playing; it was funky, sexy. He watched the pretty girls on the dance floor moving their bodies to the music, their limbs loose and limber. But nobody particularly caught his attention. Then one did. The girl had black hair cut short with a little fringe, feline cheeks, and a soft, full mouth. She seemed to float sensuously out of the darkness like some erotic ghost right into his line of vision.

He liked the look of her immediately, thought she was very attractive indeed, with bags of sex appeal. She was all in black, wearing a tight vest and short leather skirt, and strappy open-toed sandals. Her fingernails and toenails were painted dark red. She had a neat, shiny little black handbag slung over her shoulder. The girl obviously wasn't wearing a bra, couldn't have been. Her vest was very tight, causing her nipples to stick out enticingly. The leather skirt was almost obscenely short, barely skirting her thighs. Peter wondered idly if, as well as being braless, she was not wearing panties either. She had a knock-out body.

The girl looked very good to Peter. Hell, she looked better than very good. She looked great. She was irresistible. He wanted her, wanted to fuck her. He felt the beginnings of an erection at the sight of her. At that moment the girl gazed up in his direction and looked him squarely in the eyes. Peter gave her a slight smile, which she returned. He nodded, and she disappeared once more

169

into the crowd of dancers.

Peter drank the remains of his drink, put the glass on a side table, and headed down the wide staircase towards the dance floor. Again, he took his time. There was no need to hurry. He was Mr Cool. He scanned the floor for the girl until he caught sight of her. He walked over and stood before her and they started dancing, facing each other.

The girl looked even better close up. She had oval dark-brown eyes that glittered seductively and her full lips made him wonder what her pussy lips looked like. She had glossy skin too; it had a glow of sexuality to it. She was a really good dancer as well, snaked her body sinuously to the raunchy music. Peter enjoyed dancing with her. It was like foreplay, *was* foreplay.

Sometimes they were pressed together, their bodies touching. Other times they pulled apart. All the movement was in the hips. The DJ changed the pace for a while and they slow-danced, their hands on one another's waist.

'My name's Peter,' he said over the music.

'I'm Julie,' she replied.

'Fancy a drink?'

'Sure.'

'Let's go upstairs to the bar,' he said.

'OK.'

Peter's eyes lingered on the sensuous sway of Julie's leather-skirted hips as he followed her up the stairs to the lounge. 'What are you having?' he said once they'd got there.

'What are you going to have yourself?' Julie replied.

'Rum and Coke,' he said.

'Make mine a double,' she said.

'Ice and lemon?'

'Please.'

'I'll go and get the drinks,' Peter said. 'Why don't you sit down and I'll bring them over.'

Julie sat on a vacant couch, tucked against the arm with

her shapely legs together. Peter couldn't see this but as he stood at the bar, waiting for their drinks, Julie was watching him incredibly intently, her eyes burning into him. He might have been alarmed if he'd seen that intense gaze, but he didn't.

The drinks arrived and Peter took them back to Julie who was now gazing into space, toying with her hair with her darkly painted nails. As he sat down beside her, their knees touched and he felt a strong sexual frisson. Neither of them moved their legs away. Peter handed Julie's drink to her.

'Thanks,' she smiled, lifting her eyes to his. They touched glasses. The two of them sat quietly for a while and sipped their drinks, exchanging sultry glances and the smallest of small talk.

'You're very beautiful, Julie,' Peter said suddenly.

She faced him full on, her wide eyes sparkling. 'So are you,' she replied. 'We match.'

This was going to be easy, Peter thought. 'Want to do something about it?' he said.

He saw a receptive look rise in Julie's beautiful face, one that told him both of her sexual desire for him and of her availability. Then she confirmed it in words. 'Yes, I do want to do something about it, Peter,' she said, her voice husky. 'And as soon as possible.'

'I'll drink to that,' Peter said with a short laugh, raising his glass to hers once more. 'Cheers.'

'Cheers,' Julie replied, clinking her glass against his. They sipped slowly at their drinks, both of them savouring the moment.

'Is there somewhere we can go?' he asked. Because, remember, going back to his place was *never* an option.

'Oh yes,' Julie breathed. 'There's somewhere we can go all right.'

Great, Peter thought, fresh pussy and somewhere to enjoy it in the near future, somewhere they could go. And

171

he *bet* she wasn't wearing any panties. He'd soon be finding out for sure, anyway. Peter couldn't help smiling to himself. In no time at all he'd be fucking this Julie girl senseless.

Poor fool! He didn't know the half of it. He didn't know anything.

Chapter Two

Even when he was at his most animated Peter was not exactly what you might call a chatterbox. He'd always been a person of limited conversation and Julie, it seemed, had been cast from a similar mould. But that wasn't why they weren't talking, not at all. No words were necessary. There was a tense silence between them – that of sexual anticipation – as they made their way to what Julie had described as her "crash pad". Julie was anticipating something more besides straightforward sex though, something much more.

Julie's place was several roads away, walking distance from the dance club. This included a stroll past a short stretch of the Thames, the rippled surface of the river gleaming darkly in the summer night. The horny couple turned away from the river and into a street which remained busy and buzzing at that hour, people drinking outside its pubs and milling around. The city's heart still pulsed with life. The night air was warm and soft and a cool breeze was blowing. There was no moon, Peter happened to notice, but the sky was thick with stars.

After a short distance Julie steered them round a corner into a short, prosperous-looking residential street, which was a cul-de-sac. The street was empty, an oasis of quiet in the noisy city centre, and its attractively varied period buildings were doused in the amber glow of the streetlights. Julie pointed out a detached three-storey redbrick property with a garage taking up part of its ground floor frontage. She took Peter's hand and they crossed the empty street towards the property. There was a door to its side, which was the main entrance to the handful of apartments into which the building had been converted.

Julie pressed in her access code on the entrance panel and the door clicked open. 'I've got a little place on the ground floor behind the garage,' she said. 'The garage goes with the apartment, which is a godsend, of course, in central London with parking being such a nightmare. In fact it's the main reason I chose the place.'

'I see,' Peter said distractedly, the problems of parking in the nation's capital a very long way from being at the forefront of his mind.

Julie took a set of keys from her handbag and used one to unlock another door. Peter followed her along a short stretch of corridor that ran adjacent to the communal staircase on the one side and the internal wall of the garage on the other. There was a door in that wall and one at the end of the corridor, which was the entrance to Julie's apartment.

Julie selected another key, turned it in the lock and walked inside. Peter followed her in, closing the door behind him. The property was small and its curtains were drawn against the night. There were two lamps already on and they bathed the room in a soft light.

Peter liked the look of the place, could imagine living in it, not that he could ever have afforded to. It was in a considerably more salubrious part of the city than was his own apartment. They were chalk and cheese in that respect. It was much better furnished than his place too.

Julie had a stylish studio apartment, with an alcove at its left end containing a compact kitchen/dining area. There were a couple of internal doors on the wall opposite the kitchen alcove, which led respectively to the bathroom and WC, Peter assumed. In the middle of the room was a black leather couch and a thick rug, upon which stood a glass-topped coffee table, and opposite it a medium-sized television set with a flat screen.

There was a double bed at the right hand end of the room. A bedside table stood to one side of it and several feet to the other side, against the wall, there was a wardrobe and next to that a chest of drawers with a tidy, uncluttered surface.

Julie sashayed towards the bed, wiggling her backside seductively as she went. She then half-turned to Peter and raised an eyebrow. 'Time to play,' she said, turning to face him fully, and he walked towards her. The air between them was electric.

Putting her hand on his chest, Julie reached up and kissed Peter hard on the lips. Her tongue slid ardently in his mouth and his into hers. As they continued to kiss, their kisses became even hungrier and Julie started to move her head back and forth, sucking Peter's tongue. This one's really up for it, Peter thought. And she wasn't the only one. Christ, he felt horny.

Soon they were undressing together in a fever of mounting passion. Peter lifted Julie's tight black vest over her head, revealing her shapely breasts. Her nipples were dark and stone-hard. Julie took off her watch and kicked off her strappy black sandals. Peter took off his watch too, putting it into his jacket pocket. Then he shucked his jacket off his shoulders and threw it onto the couch. Julie unbuttoned Peter's shirt and pulled it off, then stroked his shoulders and kissed his chest, biting at one of his nipples excitingly. He undid the zip to her leather skirt and it slipped from her shapely hips to the floor.

Peter had been right. Julie hadn't been wearing panties. Also her pussy was entirely free of hair. He let his gaze go down her whole body, his eyes drinking her in. She looked fantastic naked, her body flawless. Peter couldn't wait to join her in nudity. He took off his loafers and his socks in double-quick time. When, lastly, he peeled off his tight leather jeans, his cock sprang out, stiff and urgent with need. '*Very* nice,' Julie breathed. 'You, Peter, are one hot stud.'

'And you, Julie,' he retorted, giving her a lascivious grin, 'are as sexy as hell.'

Julie laid herself down on the bed and Peter joined her. They lay for a moment, facing each other. Then Julie drew herself close, her body warm. She draped her leg over his, resting her face in his chest. She bit one of his nipples again. Peter really liked it when she did that, he found, rather to his surprise. She then rolled onto her back and he put his lips to her throat and licked a warm track down her collar bone to the swell of her beautiful breasts. Peter began sucking them greedily, taking Julie's erect nipples into his mouth.

At the same time he ran his hand over her stomach and down to caress her upper thighs, where his caresses rapidly became more directed. Peter let his hand slip between Julie's legs and he began to rub the opening of her pussy. She was already very wet indeed. He pressed his fingers to her stiff clitoris and she moaned with pleasure. He pushed his fingers in further, digging them in deep, plunging into all her juicy wetness over and over.

Julie jerked her hips forward again and again towards Peter's hand as it worked rhythmically between her pussy lips. His palm and wrist became soaked, she was so incredibly wet. She reached for his now achingly hard cock and started to pull at it. The feeling of sex rippled up through Peter and he groaned with her movement as she stroked and caressed at his hardness.

'Fuck me now,' Julie whispered fervently, staring into his shining blue eyes. Her breath was coming quickly, her cheeks flushed.

Peter placed himself between her legs and pushed his cock inside her, filling her with its thickness. Julie sighed with delight and turned her head to one side. He laid himself on top of her, fucking her deep and hard. She hugged him close and grasped his hair, wrapping her legs around his waist, her limbs supple and pliant, as he forged deep into her.

He pushed into her even harder. She clawed his hips, her eyes tightly shut, her breath short and shallow. Peter fucked Julie as hard as he could now, plunging his cock into her soaking wet pussy like a man possessed. He pounded away at her faster and faster, the cords standing out in his neck, his whole body shaking, his groin crashing against hers. Peter could feel himself building to the peak of excitement. Then the pulse came and he climaxed long and hard, spouting spurt after spurt of warm seed deep inside her, and grunting in satisfaction with each orgasmic spasm.

Peter's lengthy ejaculation pushed Julie ever closer to her own peak and, fighting for breath, her beautiful face screwed up, she began to rock and buck and moan. Then she shuddered to a violent orgasm, crying out deliriously as her climax exploded. She finished with a deep groan and lay there panting. 'That was fantastic,' she gasped.

Peter turned onto his back and looked at the ceiling, his face wearing a complacent smile. Another satisfied customer, he thought smugly. And a bed for the night, he sincerely hoped. Peter was done for, quite literally fucked. All passion spent, he was starting to get really sleepy. He could feel himself on the edge of dozing off, his eyes starting to close. His right arm fell loosely over the side of the bed.

Julie levered herself up on his left and, slowly swinging her legs on to the floor, sat on the edge of the bed. 'I need to use the bathroom,' she said.

Peter watched her sleepily through heavy-lidded eyes as she got to her feet and drifted over to the other side of the apartment. Jesus, she had a killer body, he thought, a

177

lovely arse. He reckoned he'd remember this one among his multitudinous conquests. Even so, by the time she'd got to the door he'd closed his eyes.

He felt utterly wiped out. His limbs were tired and heavy. It had been a long day – with a highly satisfactory conclusion, as far as he was concerned. He started to drift off. Just then his breathing, which had been slowing towards sleep, suddenly caught in his throat as he felt a flash of sharp, stinging pain in the back of his right hand.

Peter's eyes should have widened with shock but they didn't. Instead he blinked them slowly with bewilderment, then opened them to narrow slits. What the fuck was that? Peter said, or rather, thought. He didn't make a sound. The words wouldn't come out of his mouth. They froze on his tongue, which suddenly felt very heavy, too big for his mouth.

Peter could see Julie standing there beside the bed, a hypodermic needle in her hand. He understood that the sharp pain he had felt had been caused by her injecting something into his veins. He should have experienced panic but instead the only sensations he had were those of woozy surprise and a vague curiosity about why Julie should have done such a peculiar thing.

His fatigue now felt overwhelming, his head foggy and unfocused. Everything seemed to have gone into slow motion. Peter tried to lift his body up but found it had become a dead weight, that he couldn't move a muscle. He appeared to be paralysed. And that should have made him very scared indeed. Instead he felt only a kind of sleepy euphoria that flowed into every part of him, taking him over completely.

He heard a noise on the other side of the room and noticed something move at the edge of his field of vision. He saw the internal door he'd watched Julie walk toward a few moments earlier start to open and he *thought* he could make out the dim shape of another woman behind it. The trouble was that everything had gone all blurry and out of focus. His head started spinning madly, his vision rapidly darkening. Then there was blackness, blackness everywhere. Then there was nothing at all.

Chapter Three

Peter slept the profoundly deep, dreamless sleep of one who has been heavily anaesthetized. He finally started to come round, although only gradually. He dozed, he woke a little, he dozed some more, drifting in and out of consciousness in a medicated daze. Then he woke more fully but with a great sense of disorientation. At first his eyes wouldn't work properly. Things were all fogged over and unfocused.

He shook his head and blinked rapidly once, twice, three times, trying to get his vision back to normal and only partially succeeding. He looked around, still trying to adjust his eyes. At first he didn't know where he was. Oh yes, he was in his bedroom. No, that wasn't right. He was in Julie's apartment, lying on her bed. No, that wasn't right either. Where was he, then, for God's sake?

Peter lifted his head a little and looked around. He was still not even halfway alert, but at least his vision had more or less cleared now. He was in a small, dark, high-ceilinged room, that seemed from where he was lying to be all doors. A sturdy metal door stood in the wall to the right of him and there was another similar door opposite him and a third one to his left. What was behind those doors? he wondered vaguely, woozily.

The room had a stone floor and its walls were built out of brick, painted in black matt paint. There were two small low-wattage wall lights, which had been left on. There were no windows in the room but there were a couple of longish air vents that he could see.

He was in the middle of the room and was lying on his back on a single bed. No, wait, that was something else he'd got wrong. Peter was suddenly aware that it wasn't a sheet beneath his body but what felt like soft springy leather, and he tried to adjust his frame to find out what exactly he was lying on. But he found he could barely move; something was pinning him down. What on earth was it? He craned his head this way and that as best he could and found out what was hampering his movements so severely. He could barely move *because he was in chains.*

He was lying on his back, naked and spread-eagled. His wrists and ankles were being held apart by steel manacles that were shackled extremely securely by chains attached to the four corners of the black leather-covered table or whatever he was lying on.

That was when the panic should have set in, but it didn't. Given the dire circumstances – the *terrifying* circumstances – in which he'd found himself, the preternatural calmness Peter felt was totally unnatural. Just as he should have been shocked and scared when he knew he'd been injected by Julie, but hadn't reacted like that in the least, he should have been scared shitless now. But Peter wasn't afraid, not at all; it was weird. It was more than weird, it was downright nuts. He didn't feel fear or shock or panic or disbelief. He was not even surprised. It was almost as if he'd expected to find himself in this kind of situation.

But that was a crazy way of thinking, Peter berated himself. He must still be all drugged up, that was it. Certainly his mind remained incredibly slow and tangled, not unlike the way it had been immediately after Julie had injected him. Peter shuddered as he remembered the sharp pain of the hypodermic needle going into his vein. He looked up above his manacled right wrist to the back of his hand at the place where the needle had gone in. There was a slightly purple area of bruising around the vein, which ached a little.

A jumble of confused thoughts and questions cascaded through Peter's befogged brain as he started to try and take things in, tried to work them out. There was so much that puzzled and bewildered him. How long had he been unconscious and how long had he been chained up here? Fuck knows, he thought dispiritedly. It was impossible for him to know how much time had passed since he'd been put into his drugged stupor and how long he'd been here in bondage.

Where was *here* exactly anyway? Peter lay still for a moment with his head up and listened intently. There was no sound coming from outside the room, nothing to give him any kind of clue about where he might be.

And why had he been abducted? Why was he being held prisoner? Lying back and looking at the high ceiling, Peter wondered if he was being held to ransom. But that was absurd. He wasn't even remotely well-off and nor was a single one of the few relatives he had, not that he'd laid eyes on any of them for years.

So, why was he being held captive like this? And by whom? By Julie, yes, but hadn't he spotted another woman just before he'd passed out? Or had he been hallucinating by that late stage? Who could say for sure? If she did exist, was all this some kind of grudge thing? he asked himself, his mind circling lower and lower. Was the woman he thought he'd glimpsed one of his former conquests who'd taken serious umbrage at being dumped by him in his usual peremptory manner after just one night of steamy passion? Hell hath no fury, and all that.

Had she used Julie as bait to lure him into her clutches? Had one or the other or both of them been secretly stalking him before deciding to make their move? Had they followed him to the dance club? It wasn't as if it was a regular haunt of his or anything. Peter didn't *have* a regular haunt. It's a damn sight more difficult to hit a moving target, he was used to saying to himself jokingly. And what a joke that had proved to be! The point was, though, that they couldn't have waited for him to go to that particular club merely on the off chance. That wouldn't make sense. So, did that mean they *had* been stalking him? Who were the two women, for Christ's sake? Were they erotomaniacs, completely demented? Were they murderous psychotics?

Answers wouldn't come to any of Peter's questions, which were becoming increasingly frantic as the effects of the drug with which he'd been injected began rapidly wearing off. His mouth started to go dry and his heart to pound hard with anxiety. Hot fear flooded his veins. He had soon surfaced entirely from the anaesthetic and the absurdly false sense of calm it had induced in him. His heart was beating even more rapidly now, panic at last really kicking in – and with a vengeance. He had begun to sweat with fear, with terror.

Peter drew a deep, shuddering breath and let it out. What in God's name was going on and what was going to happen to him? Was he going to be left chained up here on his own to starve to death? Was he going to be killed, *murdered*? Worse, was he going to be tortured hideously before being killed? Peter became keenly aware of how completely defenceless he was, of the sheer hopelessness of his predicament. He was sure now that whoever had orchestrated his capture – that mystery woman – wanted him dead. And he didn't want to die.

Terror rapidly began to consume Peter's mind. His eyes opened wide, bulging from their sockets. He felt panic sweep over him like a storm. Blood throbbed through his temples, making the veins bulge out as he strained uselessly against the chains that held him so securely in his bondage. 'I don't want to die,' Peter whimpered. 'I don't want to die.' But he was going to die, wasn't he? He was going to die horribly, locked in this awful little room. He was going to end his days in agonizing pain in this fucking *cell*, this hideous ante-chamber to eternal damnation.

Just then Peter heard the click-click of footsteps coming down what sounded like a stone staircase outside the metal door to his right, heard the sound of a key being scraped in the door's lock, heard a squeak as its handle was turned, heard a creak as the door started to move on its hinges, heard a loud bang as the door finally swung open violently. He watched as a woman strode into the room. She wasn't Julie. He'd never seen her before in his life.

Chapter Four

Peter let out a gasp and jumped in his bonds when the door crashed open and the woman swept in. He'd been certain he would recognise her but no, he'd definitely never seen her before. He would without doubt have remembered it if he had ever set eyes on her previously because she was quite stunningly beautiful, a dark-haired Amazonian vision beyond compare.

She had exotically high cheekbones, a straight nose, a wide, sensuous mouth, and big, hypnotic eyes the colour of mahogany. Her black hair was soft and shiny and hung straight down to her shoulders. She had a lush body, with a big frame and a sumptuous well-proportioned figure. It was displayed to wondrous effect by the extremely short, almost see-through purple dress she was wearing and underneath which she was obviously naked.

The dress cupped and undulated across the defined roundness of her magnificent breasts and thighs. Her large breasts swung and swayed beneath the diaphanous material through which her stiff, thick nipples were clearly outlined. The flimsy purple dress rode up over strong thighs that quivered and rubbed together provocatively as she strode toward Peter. She was a tall woman, made even taller by the very high-heeled black shoes she was wearing.

The woman took Peter's breath away, knocked him for six, she was so incredibly beautiful. He would have been turned on as never before by this amazing Amazon, with her wonderful looks and majestic air and powerful sexual allure, if he hadn't been so terrified of the situation he was in, if he hadn't been so terrified of *her*.

Because, stunning to look at though she was, the woman gave off a decidedly sinister aura. She seemed to Peter, in the extremely panicky state he'd got himself into, to glow with malice and homicidal intent, reinforcing his conviction that he was going to be murdered. He looked at her, his eyes nearly popping out of his head with fear and his face the colour of ashes, as she stood looming over him.

'Hello Peter,' the woman said, peering down at him. Her fleshy lips drew back from her teeth into a smile that didn't travel as far as her dark eyes. Those eyes were icy cold, unnerving him even more.

'Please don't kill me,' he pleaded, blurting out the words.

'Now, why would I want to kill you?' she replied, her face expressing nothing but slight amusement, but still not in those icy dark eyes. They remained just as cold, just as hard.

'I don't know,' Peter said, flustered. 'I don't understand any of this.' Then the words tumbled out. 'Where am I and who are you and why have you brought me here? Why have you kidnapped me?'

'All will be revealed in good time,' the woman drawled, running her fingers casually through her lustrous black hair. The nails of her elegant hands were painted blood-red. 'One thing I will tell you right now is that where we are is completely secluded, miles and miles from any other properties. So, you can cry for help all you like once I've left your cell, it'll do you no good. Try, if you like, make as much noise as you wish. Be my guest. You'll soon find out I'm not bluffing and all you'll have to show for your troubles will be a sore throat.'

'I don't believe you're bluffing,' Peter said, through

trembling lips. 'But, look, there's obviously been some terrible mistake. You've kidnapped the wrong man. You couldn't get any kind of ransom for me, believe me.'

'I'm not interested in a ransom,' the woman said with an amused smile. 'It's not money I want. I have all the money I could possibly want, and then some.'

'So, if you don't want to kill me and you don't want a ransom for me, what do you want?' Peter asked, his voice still quavering.

'You, Peter,' she replied shortly, looking him straight in the eyes. 'I want you.' The full force of her personality drilled into him at that moment. It was as if she had the power with her gaze to penetrate to his innermost being.

'But it makes no sense,' Peter said frantically. 'You don't know me from Adam. So why are you doing this? *Why*, for God's sake?'

'Because I want to.' The woman's voice was coldly dispassionate. 'It's as simple as that.'

'But that doesn't tell me anything at all,' he protested.

'Well, it's as much of an explanation as you're going to get out of me.' She stared at him, her expression glacial.

'How long are you going to keep me here?' Peter asked. 'At least tell me that.'

'For as long as I like,' she said coldly, giving yet another unhelpful answer to one of his questions. It was really getting to him now, that flagrant intransigence of hers, getting right under his skin.

'What the fuck did I do to deserve this? I've never done you any harm. Christ, we're complete strangers. You've already acknowledged that much.'

'That's irrelevant,' the woman said, her face still expressing about as much emotion as a sphinx, her voice perfectly calm.

'But this is madness,' Peter said, suddenly irate but also emboldened by her assurance that she didn't want him dead. 'You can't expect me to take it lying down. I won't

187

stand for it.'

'I think you'll find you're mixing your metaphors.' The woman gave a dry laugh. 'But be that as it may, I'm now going to put the lie to what you've just said.'

With that, she reached out the long fingers of her right hand and took hold of Peter's cock. She started to slowly pull it up and down. Peter felt himself harden under her touch in spite of himself, his growing tumescence betraying him. His cock stiffened further as she squeezed it back and forth between her fingers, alternating a light pressing with a firm grip.

'Such a lovely big cock,' the woman said silkily as her hand continued moving over his ever more erect shaft. She stroked and pulled, bringing her fist up and down until erotic pleasure was coursing through Peter and his erection was pulsing and pulsing.

The throbbing in his cock began to cycle up still further and his breath deepened when the woman started to rub her fingers that much faster and harder over his erection. As she jerked ever more forcefully at his cock, Peter felt himself on the verge of climaxing. His breath was coming very quickly and his heart was beating loudly. His arousal had tightened into something painful, desperate. He was ready to burst, nearly ready to come, right on the brink. Almost there. And then she stopped.

'I'll go now,' the woman said curtly, letting go of his fiercely erect cock. She went to the metal door to the right of him through which she'd first entered, and gazed back at Peter for a long moment.

'You said you wouldn't take it lying down, but you are,' she said with a smirk, running her gaze over his prone, spread-eagled form in its chained bondage. 'You said you wouldn't stand for it,' she added, letting her gaze flit ostentatiously from his face to his angry, pulsing erection and back. 'Wrong again!'

She reached for another knob now, the doorknob. She

turned it and left without another word, giving him a backward glance and a little wave that was positively *sarcastic*. The door closed behind her with a bang. There was the scraping sound of the key turning in the lock. Then Peter heard the click-click of her footsteps going off up the stairs. He heard the more distant sound of another door opening and shutting. After that he didn't hear anything.

Peter lay still, panting, for a long time after the woman's departure, waiting for the throbbing in his shaft to slow down, waiting for his cock to go limp again. But it wouldn't do his bidding, continued to stubbornly betray him. He craved release, wanted so much to shoot his load. His cock continued to throb with blood, hard and aching. It was still hard when the woman came back much later with Julie, both of them stark naked.

Chapter Five

Peter watched the two beautiful naked women as they entered the room in silence and was struck straight away by both the similarities and the differences between them. They both had jet-black hair, dark, gleaming eyes, and completely hairless bodies, and they both positively oozed sexuality. The Amazonian one, whatever the hell her name was, had shoulder-length hair and a big, fleshy body; whereas Julie, who wasn't as tall as her, had short hair and a figure that, while being very shapely, was not as fulsome as that of her companion.

Julie, he saw, was carrying a glass of water in her left hand and a metal briefcase, rectangular in shape, in her right. *What the fuck is in that, for crying out loud?* he wondered fearfully. Julie was not looking at him nor at her companion but at the floor. The other woman was holding handcuffs and leg irons. She was gazing at Peter contemplatively, at his erection to be precise, and he watched her full lips roll into a salacious smile. He knew what was going through her mind, knew exactly what she was thinking. *Now that really is something,* she must be saying to herself. *I left the guy hours ago with a gigantic hard-on and on my return he is* still *erect.*

But Peter had news for her: all was not as it seemed. At some stage in the preceding endless hours his intense sexual arousal had transformed itself into something a lot more mundane. It had become nothing more than a desire to urinate. That desire had progressively become ever

190

more urgent, and by now had become a desperate, burning need. He was dying, *dying* for a piss.

'Very impressive,' the woman said. 'You're still turned on after all this time.'

'I hate to disillusion you,' Peter said through clenched teeth. 'It's a piss hard-on. I'm really desperate too, absolutely bursting.'

'You won't be wanting this, then.' The woman laughed, gesturing to the glass of water Julie held.

'Put it this way,' Peter replied, straining the words through his teeth again. 'It's not exactly my top priority at the moment.'

Julie all the while continued to keep her eyes downcast. She went to a corner of the room and, kneeling down briefly, placed the glass of water on the floor there and, beside it, the rectangular metal briefcase. She returned to stand beside her Amazonian companion but didn't once look Peter's way. She gave no sign that she even knew him. They might as well have not ever met, never mind fucked each other's brains out.

As much as anything in order to take his mind off his urgent need to urinate, Peter went back to thinking about the contrast between the two women. The Amazon seemed to have a personality that was as large as her frame. He could feel it radiating from her like a magnetic force field. Julie, on the other hand, displayed a much more passive nature. In fact, he'd go further. She seemed from her extremely submissive demeanour right now to actually be in the other woman's power.

'We're going to get you to the toilet, Peter,' the Amazon said. Then her voice became menacing and she looked at him sharply. 'Don't do anything stupid in the process. Don't try any funny business; don't even think about it for one tiny moment. If you try anything on I'll make you regret it like you just wouldn't believe. I'll make you wish you'd never been born.'

191

Peter said nothing in response, didn't think he had to say anything. What she'd told him couldn't have been any clearer if she'd spelled out the words.

'Well?' the woman said impatiently, her tone abrasive. 'Say you won't try any funny business.'

'I won't,' Peter assured her, swallowing hard. 'I promise on my life. But, please, I'm bursting …'

The two women removed the chained manacles from his ankles and replaced them with the leg irons. Once his legs were securely shackled, they released his wrists, sat him up and used the cuffs to fasten his hands behind his back. It looked very much to Peter like a well-practised manoeuvre.

They helped him to rise to his feet and, taking an arm each, led him across the stone floor in the direction of the door immediately opposite where he'd been lying. With his hands cuffed securely behind his back and the leg irons in place, he shuffled unsteadily across the room with the two women's assistance.

'OK, you take over now, Julie,' the Amazon said when they'd got to the door. 'Help him to take a piss then spruce him up a bit for me. Don't say a word to him, though, understood?'

Julie nodded her assent obediently and guided Peter with care through the door, flicking on the room's light as she did so. Like his cell, there were no windows in the room although there were several air vents. The room contained a WC with a low level cistern, a bidet, and a hand basin with chrome fittings. On the edge of the basin there was a fresh cake of soap, a sponge, a new toothbrush in a plastic mug and an unopened tube of toothpaste; and on a ledge above the basin there was a stick of deodorant, a can of shaving foam, a safety razor, and a black plastic comb.

The room also contained a combined bath and shower with similar chrome fittings to the hand basin. Peter could see shampoo, conditioner, soap, and shower gel on the side of the bath and, on one of the adjacent walls, a couple of towel rails on which several clean white towels hung. There was a green bath mat on the floor and a mirror-covered wall cabinet hung at face level above and slightly to one side of the hand-basin. Peter caught sight of himself in the mirror and realised he was in need of a shave.

Then Julie lifted the lid and seat of the WC, after which Peter shuffled into position and took that desperately needed piss. With Peter standing above the WC and Julie holding his penis, now thankfully only semi-tumescent, he urinated Niagara-like at great length and with a huge sense of relief. When he finally splashed and shivered to a finish Julie let go of his cock and, reaching past him, pulled the flush and lowered the seat.

She then left the room briefly and returned with the glass of water in her hand. She still wouldn't meet Peter's gaze. Julie held the glass to his lips and he gulped the water so fast that some of it spilled down his chin. He hadn't realised how thirsty he was until then, so desperate had he been to relieve himself.

Julie put the empty glass on the ledge immediately above the wash basin and then picked up and opened the can of shaving cream and lathered Peter's cheeks. She took hold of the safety razor that was also sitting on the ledge above the basin. Julie filled the basin with warm water and started shaving Peter, using careful downward strokes. She splashed warm water on his face and some cold, then let out the water.

She filled the basin with warm water again and, with Peter standing on the bath mat, went on to wash him from top to toe with the sponge and soap. Finally she towelled him dry, cleaned his teeth, applied deodorant under his arms and combed his hair. Throughout this whole process Julie continued to diligently avoid making any eye contact whatsoever with Peter. Nor, as she'd been instructed by the other woman, did she utter a single word.

Julie took Peter back to her Amazonian companion and between them they rearranged his bondage, carefully ensuring that at no point was his body completely unshackled. They removed his leg irons and handcuffs and returned him to his former spread-eagled position on top of the leather-covered table, his wrists and ankles manacled and held apart by the chains attached to its four corners.

What now, for God's sake, Peter wondered in trepidation. But when he looked up at the two women and saw the way their eyes shone, saw the hungry vulpine looks on their faces – and it was *both* of the women, Julie as much as the other one, although she *still* wouldn't meet his eye – he answered his own question immediately. Their sexual interest in him had a quality about it that was so palpable it was overwhelming.

Peter could smell sex in the air, the scent of pussy, the scent of the women's sexual excitement. It was all so obvious to him now, the reason why he'd been kidnapped, and his heart began to pound in his chest with the realisation. If he hadn't been abducted to be murdered or for a ransom the only other reason was sexual, it simply had to be. They wanted him to use for their erotic pleasure. They wanted him as their fuck-toy. Peter the sex addict felt his cock harden all over again.

Chapter Six

She stepped in really close to Peter in his chained bondage, that startling Amazonian woman, shifting her weight from one foot to the other. She stood over him, her fat, naked breasts swaying, their giant nipples as hard as rocks. Peter looked up at her and said nervously, 'May I ask you one thing?' He didn't know it but there was wonder in his eyes at the very sight of her. He couldn't help it any more than he could help his now rigidly erect cock.

'It depends what it is you want to ask,' she said warily, her full lips pursed.

'What is your name?' Peter said.

The woman smiled indulgently at the innocuous question he had asked and pushed a strand of his hair back that had fallen down onto his brow. 'My name is Serena,' she said. She let her fingers trail down Peter's cheek before drawing them away abruptly. 'But that is enough talk. Julie, you know what to do.'

Julie immediately went to the metal briefcase on the floor, knelt down and unhinged its clasps and lifted its lid. She took out a black dildo with a rubber bag of the same colour attached to the end. Hanging from the bag by a short tube was a rubber bulb. Julie closed the metal briefcase, got up from her knees and handed the item she had removed from the briefcase to Serena.

'Open your mouth wide, Peter,' Serena ordered. As he obeyed, she took the dildo and placed the rubber bag between his lips. Using the rubber bulb, she began to pump air into the bag until it filled his mouth completely, the dildo at right-angles from his face.

Peter could not disguise his growing excitement. His thick, hard cock was now throbbing constantly and jutting up from his body like a flesh-coloured version of the black dildo sticking straight up from his face.

Facing in the direction of Peter's giant, pulsing erection, Serena climbed up onto her haunches above him and straddled his face. She took the dildo in her hand and placed it at the opening of her sex. Slowly she lowered herself down on it, her pussy tight but very wet. Soon Peter's face was shiny with her juice as she ground her hips down, sinking herself onto the dildo. Serena let out a moan of pleasure as, with the fingers of her right hand, she searched out and pressed down on her clitoris. She moaned again as she jammed her fingers down once more and started to grind them hard against her clit.

Serena's body rocked with pleasure as she played with her clitoris while pushing her big, fleshy thighs into Peter's face, making the dildo sink deeper into her sex. She pressed down so hard that Peter could barely see, could hardly breathe. Then she started to move herself up and down on the dildo, the sound noisily liquid. She rode his face like this, soon drenching it with her copious pussy juice.

'Give him a blowjob,' Serena ordered Julie, while continuing to ride the dildo jutting from Peter's face. Julie immediately moved to the end of the leather-covered table and climbed lithely onto it on her knees, kneeling between Peter's shackled legs. She put her arms either side of his waist and bent further forward, fastening her lips tight to the hot flesh of his cock, which was now glittering with precome wetness. Julie began sucking Peter's shaft and he could feel it pulse and throb excitingly inside her mouth. She sucked him slow and deep at first, then picked up momentum until her lips moved faster and faster over the length of his shaft.

In this, it appeared to Peter that Julie was taking her lead from Serena who was now shoving herself up and down on the dildo jutting from his mouth with ever-increasing force, her strong thighs quivering. She began to moan and gasp and rock back and forth on his face. Her pussy contracted tightly around the large dildo and she groaned deeply as her orgasm washed through her in mighty waves.

She didn't stop shoving her sex down against Peter's gagged mouth, though, his face now awash with her juices. At the same time, Julie sucked ever more violently at his cock, sucked until he felt sharp tremors that ripped straight through him like a tsunami, bringing him to a colossal orgasm. He climaxed hard, his semen spraying warm and creamy into her mouth, filling it. Julie swallowed it all down greedily, his cock still pulsing in her throat.

Julie withdrew her mouth slowly from Peter's erection when it at last began to wilt, and she knelt up. She looked questioningly at Serena who looked back at her and smiled a lascivious smile. 'Get the handcuffs and leg irons again,' she ordered, still moving herself up and down on the dildo. 'Also, open the briefcase once more and get out the ball-gag, enema bag, lubricant, and strap-on dildo. I haven't finished with Peter today, *no way* am I done with him yet.'

Those words landed on Peter like a boulder. In their essence they were entirely unequivocal. It was obvious what was going to happen to him, couldn't be more obvious. It was perfectly clear that he would soon be losing his virginity, so to speak, that Serena would be popping his cherry. And there wasn't a thing he could do to prevent it, not a damned thing.

His reaction to this knowledge, however, took him completely by surprise. Peter didn't feel horror or disgust or dismay. Instead, he felt resignation and excitement, both at the same time. Shameful as it was, he not only accepted what was going to happen to him, he found he *welcomed* it, was excited by the prospect of it – extremely excited.

What Peter liked most about what was going to happen to him was the same as what he'd liked most about what had just happened to him: his complete powerlessness in the matter. And that was when the realisation first began to come to him, although only in the most embryonic and indistinct form. He was, he realised, but dimly as if in a dream, beginning to change in some mysterious way. He was starting to turn into another version of himself, a truer one somehow. He was still a sex addict, yes, but he was starting to become a different kind of sex addict altogether.

Peter thought excitedly about being violated by Serena, fucked in the arse by her, as he continued to feel her thighs, which remained weighed down on his face, stifling him, smothering him as she continued to push herself up and down on the dildo jutting from his mouth. He felt his cock thicken yet again; it was incredible. 'Just look at that, Julie,' he heard Serena say with a throaty laugh. 'The man's insatiable.'

Peter urgently wanted to say something too at that point. 'Use me, use me all you like,' was what he said, or tried to say. But all he was able to do with the inflated dildo-gag in his mouth was to make a sort of muffled gurgling noise from beneath Serena's mighty thighs.

Chapter Seven

Julie brought Peter back from the bathroom to his cell. The two women then removed his dildo-gag but only to gag him again, this time with the black ball-gag that Julie had removed from the briefcase along with the other items Serena had told her to take out of it.

They removed his leg irons and handcuffs and put him back into the manacles and chains attached to the leather-covered bondage table. Once again, in what appeared to him another well-rehearsed manoeuvre, the two women were careful to ensure that Peter was never at any point completely unshackled. They secured his body in a spread-eagled position as before but this time he was face down.

Peter felt even more defenceless lying on his stomach than on his back, but perhaps that was because he knew why he'd been positioned like that. Hell, there was no *perhaps* about it. It was for *exactly* that reason. Peter's outstretched palms were cold and wet, his face hot, his heart thumping and his shaft rock-hard against his stomach as he awaited the inevitable, as he awaited his deflowering.

'Continue to prepare him for me, Julie,' Serena demanded as she buckled on her strap-on dildo harness. Clearly more was being required of Julie than to give Peter the thorough enema she had already administered. And what that might be was soon made evident to him.

Julie climbed up on her knees onto the leather-covered bondage table with one fluid motion and knelt between Peter's spread legs. She leant forward and pushed her face between the cheeks of his backside, pulling them apart with her soft hands. Julie pressed her lips to Peter's smooth, clean anus and began to lick it. Her tongue was taut and wet and hot. She licked him slowly at first, flicking her tongue gently. Then she started licking faster and faster, leaving daubs of saliva. It made Peter shudder and squirm with pleasure.

Next Julie stuck one, then two fingers inside her pussy and spread her wetness over his anal hole. Peter liked that if possible even more than the anilingus and pushed his hips back, helping her slender fingers to ease in a little further. Julie pushed her fingers in deeper still. Then she extracted them and fingered her pussy again, before re-inserting the two digits into his anus. She did this several times, making him even wetter with her love juice than she'd done with her saliva. Julie lavished Peter's anus with her own lubrication, making him burn with pleasure. Then Serena told her to stop.

'That's very good, Julie, but it won't be enough for my virgin bride,' Serena announced as she doused the strap-on dildo that now protruded from her crotch with a liberal amount of lubricant. Julie climbed down from the bondage table and stood to its side.

Peter couldn't wait for what he knew was going to happen now, couldn't wait for Serena to start fucking him in the arse. He yearned for her to sodomise him, hungered for it. He pushed his splayed backside towards her, his sense of anticipation intense. Peter could feel the blood singing in his veins and his breath was coming quicker all the time. He felt Serena climb up behind him, felt her rise onto her knees and place them between his waiting thighs.

At last the moment had come. Serena pressed the tip of the dildo against Peter's anal hole, then pushed it inside, penetrating him a few inches. It hurt. She held him by the hips and pushed in a little deeper. He felt another twist of pain. Finally she entered fully, and the pain began to recede. Serena began fucking him deep and slow. She moved rhythmically, making the smooth length of the dildo enter and re-enter his anus.

Serena's body weighed Peter down as she buggered him, her breath whispering hotly in his ear, her strap-on dildo pushing in and out of his tight anus. It made his aching cock, stiffly erect between his stomach and the leather-covered bondage table, pulse with a hot insistent throb. She speeded up her thrusts, which caused his excitement to grow even more.

It was an exhilarating sensation Peter felt, a strange mixture of pain and pleasure that he had never known before. God, it felt good. Serena's glorious naked breasts bounced and bumped against his shoulders with each of her powerful thrusts as she forged deep into him with a strong, steady rhythm.

'Masturbate for me, Julie,' Serena instructed and her companion lost no time in complying. She moved near to the head of the leather-covered table in a position that ensured Serena – and Peter – would have the closest view possible of her self-pleasuring activities.

Julie began by running her hands up over her stiff nipples, squeezing them both hard. She then brought her right hand down to run across her hip and brush against the inside of her thighs before arriving at her bald, wet pussy. Julie started to circle two of her fingers over her shiny clit and then pushed them deep between the lips of her vagina. Her eyes glistened and she sighed with pleasure as she used her fingers on herself, love juice dripping down her quivering thighs. She trembled uncontrollably at the moment of orgasm, her eyes wide open, her legs shaking and buckling.

Throughout Julie's fevered masturbatory display Serena made the strap-on dildo move ever faster inside Peter. By the time Julie had finished, Serena and Peter were both in pace with each other. Groaning into his ball-gag, he pushed himself back on the dildo as Serena fucked him with it harder and harder. It felt *so* good. Peter felt mad with lust by now. He felt totally degraded too, totally *wonderfully* degraded.

Serena pounded into him hard, pounded into him so hard that all his nerves were alive. Gasping noisily, her teeth gritted, her dark hair damp against her neck, she pushed and pushed and pushed until she came, until they both came. Peter's orgasm was massive, shaking and scorching him to ecstasy, sending him off into the stratosphere.

Finally he fell back down to earth, but not for long. He suddenly felt an all-too-familiar sharp pain in the back of his right hand. He saw the hypodermic needle in Julie's hand and understood that he'd been drugged all over again. *Déjà vu.* A spasm of dizziness passed through his brain as it had done that first time, then along came that dreamy sensation of euphoria once more. He felt himself floating off, fading away.

Just before Peter blacked out Julie turned her face to him and gave him a small smile, fixing her shining oval eyes on his as she did so. It was the first time she'd made eye contact with Peter since they'd fucked like crazy in her "crash pad", the first time since this all began. Better late than never, he thought drowsily. You and I are two of a kind, that look she gave him – that half-smile - seemed to say. He would have returned her smile if he hadn't been gagged, if he hadn't been dru …

Chapter Eight

When Peter came to, for a moment he thought he was back at home, in bed in his apartment. He felt calm, warm. Then it hit him and he remembered where he was. Then another realisation hit him. His wrists and ankles were no longer manacled. But wait a minute, what was this? There was a loose but sturdy metal collar around his neck, which had an equally sturdy ring to which a long length of strong chain was attached. The chain was attached at its other end to a solid iron staple that was firmly affixed to the base of the wall several feet behind the head of the leather-covered bondage table that served as his bed and that was itself bolted to the floor.

So, the bad news was that he remained securely shackled. The good news was that he had considerably more freedom of movement now. He could stand up and also walk around – and for quite a reasonable distance too, from the look of the chain's length. Peter noticed something else. Upon the floor beside the bondage table was a metal tray. On it there was what proved, from a quick check under its wrapping, to be a cheese and tomato sandwich. Also on the tray were a bottle of water, a shiny red apple and a typewritten note. He picked up the note. *Eat the sandwich and the apple and drink the water,* it said. *Then take a bath, shave off all your body hair, and give yourself an enema. After that, come back here and wait.*

Before he did anything, Peter wanted to stretch his

limbs and check out his immediate surroundings, such as they were. His body felt stiff as he levered himself to his feet and moved towards the metal door to his right. He checked to see whether it was still locked. It was, and on closer inspection looked even heavier than he'd thought. It looked as if it weighed a ton. He tried the door to his left; just as hefty and just as locked. What the hell was behind that door? he wondered, not for the first time since he'd found himself in his cell.

Peter then went to the bathroom door, which was certainly very solid but not such a sturdy affair as the other two. It was unlocked, as he'd assumed it would be, given what the note had said. He saw that the bathroom was back in pristine order, with a new safety razor and all clean towels – Julie's work, he presumed. Peter demonstrated to himself that his chain was more than long enough to enable him to move around the bathroom with relative ease. He noticed the enema bag on the shelf above the wash basin and it brought his mind back to the note.

Peter left the bathroom and returned to the leather-covered bondage table. He sat on its edge and hungrily ate the cheese and tomato sandwich and the apple and gulped down the bottled water. It was not the most exciting meal he'd ever had in his life but it was just about the most welcome one.

He went back into the bathroom and used and then flushed the WC. He washed and dried his hands. Peter stared at himself in the mirror of the wall cabinet for a while. It didn't feel like it was his reflection looking back at him with that metal collar round the neck. It was as if somebody else occupied his skin. He felt as if he was in a sort of trance. Maybe, he pondered, the strange otherworldly sensation he felt was one of the residual effects of the powerful drug with which he'd been injected again. Yes, that must be it, he decided. He was still drugged up to some extent.

Peter shaved his face and cleaned his teeth at the wash basin while he ran himself a hot bath. Bringing with him the safety razor and the can of shaving foam, he got into the bath. First, he shampooed his hair and rinsed it using the shower attachment. Next, he shaved his entire body very thoroughly, feeling grateful for the fact that he'd never been at all hirsute. It was not difficult to achieve the completely hairless body that was now being required of him.

He soaked for a good long while in the warm water, his skin turning pink and droplets of perspiration forming on his brow. The bath was glorious. Peter let his druggy mind drift. How little he still knew about his captors. What *did* he know, exactly? He knew that Serena had been the brains behind the audacious, the *outrageous* plan to kidnap him. She was the leader, the decision maker of the two without a doubt, and Julie was her willing accomplice. He knew that Serena was incredibly – overpoweringly – dominant while Julie had a strongly submissive nature. Presumably that had been what brought them together in the first place, a case of opposites attracting. But when had that been? Months ago, years ago? Serena had indicated that she was a very rich woman. Where had all her money come from?

Where were they keeping him? And *why* him, for Christ's sake? Then a strange, illogical thought – an *insane* thought – popped unbidden into Peter's head. Would they want to keep him once they realised he was damaged goods? Because that's what he was, no question, damaged goods.

It went back to his childhood, he knew that. Peter had never known his parents, having been orphaned as a baby. He had been brought up uncaringly by a cold fish of an aunt. As a child, Peter had not been wanted, had not been loved, and had not been happy. Was that why as an adult he had always felt out of place in the world, never had any sense of belonging to anywhere or anyone? He'd always assumed so whenever he'd thought about it, which he did his best to avoid doing most of the time. He just tried to blank it all out. And what better way to blank it out than with lots of anonymous sex? That had been the theory, in any case.

Peter didn't enjoy his work. It was just an easy way of making a living, that was all. He had no friends, not a single one. He had nothing really that meant anything to him – apart from that "haven" against the outside world he'd created for himself, which was just a tatty, nondescript apartment in an equally tatty, nondescript area of London.

He'd been doing little more than passing the time, his existence meaningless, engaging in an endless and pointless succession of one-night stands. He had never connected in any meaningful way with any of the interminable number of women he'd fucked. What a pathetic excuse for a life his had been up to now, when he thought about it.

He'd been kidnapped and yet he knew nobody would be looking for him, not a soul, simply because nobody cared. Not everyone has someone who'd notice if they were gone – and actually *care*. Peter certainly didn't. Who would miss him? Nobody. There would have been no police hunt for him organised, no offered reward, nor would there be in the future. Peter knew these things for certain. And he knew them because there was nobody who loved him. There would be nobody thinking of him with affection.

No, nobody thought about him like that except, perversely, his captors of all people. Peter didn't know this logically, of course. In fact the thought itself was illogical. Even so he felt it in his bones that Serena and Julie *did* care about him. Was that why he had accepted just about everything Serena had required of him so far with such incredible docility?

Julie hadn't required anything of him in that way but she was different again. It was uncanny but there was definitely some sort of a bond between Julie and himself. Peter remembered the almost conspiratorial look she'd given him just after injecting him that last time, the look that seemed to tell him they were two of a kind. In any event, he felt close to her and that was a first in his life.

Peter had never looked for that closeness to another human being before, never felt he needed it. That had made him incomplete, it dawned on him now. He had been a man without any real character, who had been wasting his life. But why all that compulsive screwing around? What had that been all about? Had he just been blotting out his loneliness and sense of alienation? He'd always thought so on the very few occasions he'd allowed himself to question the heavily circumscribed way of life he'd devised for himself. But no, it had been more than that, Peter now realised. He had been looking for something, *obsessively* looking, without even knowing what it was he was searching for.

Then there had been this utterly bizarre turn of events. As far as Peter could work out, it appeared to be a complete chance of fate that it had happened to him. What if he hadn't gone to that particular dance club at that particular time? He could so easily have decided to go to another club that night, or not gone out at all.

It was amazing how a life could turn so dramatically on such a random decision. He *had* gone to that dance club at that time and because of that had been abducted by Serena and Julie - and because of *that* appeared to be getting closer all the time to finding whatever it was he had been searching for all his life without realising it. He might even have found it already.

Deep down, Peter realised, he'd always wanted to be cherished, and in their own perverted way Serena and Julie seemed to cherish him – Serena in particular, oddly. She was the one who had masterminded all this, after all. She'd made it all happen. She'd made a gilded cage for him, aided and abetted by the lovely Julie, and he was now her cherished pet. And he liked it, loved it.

But hold on! Hold right on, you drug-addled idiot! It was absolute madness to think that way, Peter remonstrated with himself. Madness piled on madness. He was thinking about the two women as if they'd done him a great big favour by abducting him. He was thinking about them as if they were normal, as if they weren't a couple of maniacs who'd drugged him and were keeping him prisoner in chains in a locked cell. He must be starting to go mad too. That was the effect they were already having on him. He was their madness and they were beginning to become his.

What the fuck are they doing to me? Peter asked himself, as he turned the shower onto his smoothly shaven body to remove any loose hairs. What the fuck are they doing to me? he asked himself again, as he got out of the bath and let the water start to drain away and began to vigorously towel himself dry.

And what the fuck is Serena going to do to me this time? he asked himself, as he reached for the enema bag. That last question had been rhetorical. Peter was sure he knew the answer to it. He was right but he was also wrong. This time Serena did an awful lot more than sodomise him. This time she completely blew his mind.

Chapter Nine

Peter was back in his cell. He was nude apart from his chained collar and was displaying a partial hard-on as he stood before Serena. By her side was Julie, her body completely naked and her head bowed. Serena herself was all in black leather, wearing a figure-hugging dress that was so short it barely covered her sex. She was also wearing a tight-fitting pair of tall boots with stiletto heels and pointed toes. 'Answer me this, Peter,' Serena said tantalisingly, her voice silky smooth. 'Do you like being my degraded plaything, my human sex toy?'

'I do,' Peter replied. Well, he *did*, he couldn't deny it. He could feel his cock stiffen further.

'Glad to hear it,' she said. 'By the way, from now on you must always address me as "mistress" and you may only speak to me at all if I have addressed you first. Is that absolutely clear?'

'Yes, mistress,' Peter replied, gazing back in awe at Serena. So, he thought, she was a dominatrix. Why did that not surprise him in the least? More to the point – and the real surprise here – why did it not worry him, frighten the living daylights out of him? A dominatrix specialised in hurting people, didn't she, and he didn't want to be hurt, did he? *Did he?*

'You are my slave now, Peter, just like Julie here,' Serena said. 'And slaves need to be regularly disciplined, don't they, Julie?'

'Yes, mistress,' Julie said, looking back at her

submissively, her dark eyes shining.

'Two's company,' Serena said. 'So, I'm going to discipline you two together on this occasion – on most occasions from now on, in fact. Understood, slaves?'

'Yes, mistress,' they both replied. Peter shot an anxious look in Julie's direction but the look she gave him back after a quick glance towards his crotch said she wasn't deceived for a moment. His look may have been anxious but his cock told a different story. It had now become rigidly erect. He *wanted* to be disciplined by his, by *their* mistress. Julie clearly knew that, and so did Peter's cock even if its owner didn't yet, not quite yet anyway.

'I will now take you through to your place of punishment,' Serena said. She unlocked and opened that mysterious third metal door in the cell and reached round to switch on the subdued lighting of the room beyond it. Peter followed her into the room, the lengthy chain attached to his collar clanking as he went. Then Julie followed. She left the door behind her open in order to accommodate Peter's chain, the end of which remained firmly bolted to the wall of his cell. The room they were in had walls painted matt black, like Peter's cell, but this room was a great deal bigger, and it was decked out as a dungeon.

'See how good I am to you,' Serena said. 'Your own personal dungeon, somewhere I can discipline you – with Julie usually, as I say – whenever the mood takes me. Impressive, huh, quite a turn-on?'

'Yes, mistress,' Peter replied, and it certainly was a turn-on to him, although he would have had difficulty articulating why at that point. It was a visceral thing. The sight of it made his erection begin to throb. The room was decked out beautifully with high-quality disciplinary equipment, which included a wall-mounted St Andrew's cross, a horse, a whipping bench and a horizontal torture chair.

Hanging from the high ceiling there were various sets of chains. Suspended from a couple of these were two adjacent metal spreader bars, one with a single manacle attachment at either end and the other with two. These spreader bars were near the centre of the dungeon. Not far from them there was a black rubber mat laid out on the stone floor.

The room also contained a big open cabinet up against one of its dark walls. Upon the polished wood there hung a large collection of canes, whips, paddles, chains, clamps, and other disciplinary implements.

Wasting no time, Serena ordered Peter and Julie to kneel over the whipping bench right away, side by side. 'Prepare yourselves for a thorough beating,' she said. 'I'll warm you up first, though.' She did this by using her right hand to deliver five blows to Peter's backside, each smack a sharp stab of fire – but bearable. Then she delivered five spanks to Julie's rear. She repeated the process several times and the dungeon echoed with the sound of hand on naked flesh as she followed one stinging blow with another in quick succession.

Serena gradually started to hit them harder, bringing her hand down onto their backsides with increasing energy until each blow landed like an explosion and smarted vividly – rather *less* bearable all the time, Peter found. Julie clearly felt the same way too. The pair of them tensed and squirmed and cried out with pain as the searing heat burned their flesh.

Peter felt oddly reassured to have Julie by his side sharing his punishment, as his backside received its first ever beating. From what Serena had said, they were very often to be paired together in this way for discipline. He liked that idea, a lot. It was reassuring, comforting … and exciting.

Serena next demanded that Julie lie down on her back on the black rubber mat on the floor near the middle of the dungeon. She told Peter, 'Crawl to the front of Julie and lick her pussy, slave.' Although he didn't quite know why, Peter liked that a lot too: being called Serena's *slave*. He crawled into position with all haste.

Peter pressed his mouth to the opening of Julie's sex, flicking his wet tongue gently over her clit. She evidently wanted him to lick her harder and tried to move her pussy more rapidly against his tongue. As Peter felt her do this, he felt another sensation – the sharp sting of a rattan cane as Serena brought it down hard across the middle of his rear cheeks. Fuck, it hurt! The second swipe hurt even more, a white flash of pure pain. She brought the cane down a third time and there was that white flash of sensation again, then a fourth time, sharper still. The harsh feel of the rattan cane made the spanking he'd recently received seem like very small beer indeed by comparison.

In trying desperately to withstand the searing pain Serena was now inflicting on him Peter licked Julie's pussy more voraciously. No further encouragement from her was necessary, far from it. He worked his lips and tongue over her sex with great vigour until she was panting loudly with desire. But his oral attentions got yet more frantic in response to Serena's even more remorseless caning. The smarting impact of each blow blazed through his body like an inferno as he licked and licked at Julie.

Serena stopped caning Peter eventually but told him to continue licking Julie's pussy. She unzipped and removed her short leather dress and, entirely naked now apart from her long stiletto-heeled boots, took hold of her strap-on dildo and began to buckle its harness into place. Shortly the moment Peter *had* actually anticipated would be upon him. Serena finished buckling up the harness of the strap-on and lubricated the black dildo that now extended from her pubis.

She positioned herself behind Peter and worked the

thickness of the dildo in and out of the opening of his anus. She did this a few times, pushing it in further with each thrust and stretching his tight sphincter. Peter suddenly felt the dildo spasm right into him. It caused his cock to send a throb of precome splashing onto the black rubber beneath him as he continued to frantically lick Julie's pussy.

'Don't you dare climax, Peter,' Serena warned him, a hard edge to her voice. 'You are only allowed to have an orgasm – on this or any other occasion – if and when I say so.' Now *that* was control, Peter thought; *that* was power. He was powerless. He must do Serena's bidding even when it came to having an orgasm. Why did that feel so right, so exquisite? Why did the thought of it almost make him do the very thing she'd told him not to do? Why did it nearly make him come?

Serena began to fuck Peter in the arse, slowly at first and then increasing in momentum until she was riding him hard and fast, really pounding into him. Her rhythm was strong, each thrust going deeper into his anus, filling him, penetrating him. And all the while he was licking Julie's wet pussy for all he was worth, giving her ever more pleasure until she built to an orgasm that racked her body with spasms of delight.

'Get onto your knees, Julie, and await my further instructions,' Serena ordered, still pounding the dildo into Peter. She fucked him even harder with the strap-on, making him feel indescribably excited, amazingly turned on. No direct pressure on his pulsing cock was needed. Just one touch to his shaft would have made it almost impossible for him not to ejaculate, he was sure of it.

Peter began to tremble uncontrollably, on the verge of climaxing, but he wouldn't let himself come, wouldn't disobey his mistress. His mistress, that's what Serena said she was. His *mistress*. Oh God, his *mistress*.

No, thinking like that definitely didn't help. Peter tried to close his mind to such thoughts as he strained every fibre of his being to stop himself from climaxing. He was mightily relieved when Serena at last stopped sodomising him with her strap-on dildo and removed it from his anal hole. Christ, that had been *so* close.

Serena unbuckled and removed her dildo harness next and told Peter to get to his feet. She got him to stand underneath the metal spreader bar that had one manacle attachment either end of it, which hung from the dungeon's ceiling by chains. The dominatrix told him to stretch his arms out, and manacled his wrists to the spreader bar. She removed his collar and chain now he was alternatively – and just as effectively – restrained.

Serena went on to attach very tight clover clamps to Peter's nipples, making him shudder with pain, the clamps gripping like burning pincers. His nipples throbbed painfully, sending spasms of sensation directly to his pulsing shaft. Serena began slapping the clamps with the leather tip of a riding crop, making him flinch and wince and squeal in pain.

Peter was undeniably very turned on, but even so he wondered whether he'd be able to take much more pain. He was soon to find that out - and something much more beside. He was about to discover the very essence of the masochistic experience.

'Time for you to receive a thorough whipping now, Peter,' Serena announced ominously. She selected from the cabinet full of disciplinary instruments a particularly vicious one: a whip with a tapering leather leash. When she slashed it through the air, it made a high-pitched whistle. The whip landed on Peter's backside with a resounding crack, immediately producing a thin, red weal. Two further strokes followed in quick succession, both harder than the first, both making his backside quiver, and both producing scarlet weals on his flesh. Then Serena started to lay into Peter's backside with the cruel implement with even more energy: one, two, three, four, five, six times. And it was on that sixth strike that everything changed for Peter, changed forever.

When the dominatrix brought the whip down on that sixth occasion, he felt the pain he was suffering start to dissolve into a red heat that seeped through his body, connecting with the pulsing hardness of his cock in a subtly different way, a wonderful way. Serena carried on beating Peter for some time and the resonating crack of each blow mingled with his moans and grunts of both intense pleasure and of intense pain, of intense pleasure-pain.

Serena turned to Julie, who remained on her knees. 'Crawl over and suck Peter off while bringing yourself to orgasm with your fingers,' she ordered and Julie moved immediately to obey, crawling into position. She opened her mouth and closed her lips around Peter's hard cock, circling her tongue around its wet, swollen glans before starting to blow him. At the same time she began to masturbate, her hand pressing into her pussy. Faster and faster Julie masturbated, plunging her fingers in and out of her sex, the sound moist and urgent. And all the while she sucked and sucked ...

Then Serena started beating Peter on his backside with the whip again, laying into him with such ferocity that each stroke made him cry out and shudder within his bonds. He was now in agony - and ecstasy.

'I'm going to deliver ten more lashes,' Serena said. 'On the tenth lash, you are to climax, Peter.'

And so it was. On the tenth vicious strike, Peter felt his cock swell and pulse in Julie's mouth as he reached his peak exactly on cue, tensing his body and then yielding to the ecstasy of release. He called out a wordless explosion of pain and desire as his cock erupted, flooding streams of come deep into Julie's throat, which she swallowed down thirstily.

When Peter's orgasm had subsided, Julie let his shaft

slip from her mouth. Serena instructed her to crawl to the corner of the dungeon and she duly obeyed.

The Amazonian dominatrix then came to the front of Peter. 'Good slave,' she commended him. 'I think you're a natural born masochist, I really do. In fact I *know* now that you are. You are a real pain slut and no mistake,' she added, looking into his glittering blue eyes and smiling approvingly.

Peter knew what she'd just said was true and, standing before her there in his bondage in that dark dungeon, a sensation of pure exhilaration swept through him, so powerful he felt like crying. He trembled with emotion, didn't think he had ever felt so wonderful – and so shocked. It was the wonderful shock of recognition that Peter felt, and not just that he'd discovered he was a sexual masochist like Julie.

He knew now he was deeply, profoundly submissive like Julie too. It was no wonder he'd experienced such a strong sense of fellow feeling for her. But what really caused the tremendous sense of exhilaration that now swept over Peter was the realisation at long last that what he had been searching for all his life, without even knowing it, had been a powerfully dominant woman – a dominatrix – to whom he could give himself completely, and that he had found that woman because *she* had found him.

The power of the magnificent goddess before whom he was standing in his bonds filled Peter with rapturous wonder. He knew, just knew, that Serena was the reason he had been put on earth. From now on, he vowed to himself, he would do everything he possibly could to please her and would surrender without question to her every demand, no matter how cruel and degrading those demands might be. He would give his all to her – his body, his mind, his very soul. He would forget about everything from now on except being worthy of his sadistic mistress, his goddess.

A small voice inside his head told Peter that this was all utter lunacy, told him he was starting to go stark staring mad, that he was being sent mad by this monstrous Serena woman, assisted by her partner in crime, Julie. And it *was* a crime, an extremely serious one, that they'd committed. They'd kidnapped him and made him their prisoner, in his dungeon cell. But Peter didn't care, didn't care one little bit. He felt mad – mad with happiness.

Chapter Ten

The pattern was set that day and the discipline imposed by Serena on Peter – almost invariably with Julie as co-recipient – continued to be constant, unrelenting and, to him, wonderful. Time passed: weeks, months. Not that Peter had any sense of time whatsoever. He was totally cut off from the outside world. He never saw another person apart from Serena and Julie, never saw a paper or read a book or flicked through a magazine. He never listened to a radio or heard any music or watched a television or looked at a computer. He never breathed fresh air. He never experienced fresh light. It was either artificial light or complete darkness, nothing else.

Peter drifted into a kind of lassitude. He never tried to escape, realising that he never would. And it wasn't just that he knew Serena was always careful to keep him in one restraint or another at all times. She was only human and could slip up some time, make a mistake. And that would be when he could make his move. But Peter didn't want to make any kind of "move", didn't want to escape. He liked being the cowed slave he had become, liked being one of Serena's two masochistic pets.

Anger would fuel some positive action on his part, Peter knew that. And he did sometimes try to feel the anger that, God knows, he had every right to feel – anger that he had been kidnapped by the two women, kept prisoner where he was, and forced to engage in one degraded sex act after another. But the anger wouldn't

218

come. What did come was a sense of humiliation – a *delicious* sense of humiliation that surged through his mind and found an answering throb in his cock.

Peter had a lot of time to think when he was on his own in his cell, all the time in the world. He thought about how he'd changed since his imprisonment and how remarkably quickly that change in him had occurred too, how what had been done to him early on in his incarceration had rapidly forced him to accept his own innate masochism and submissiveness.

Perhaps he was too compliant, Peter mused on occasion, reluctantly forcing himself to go into devil's advocate mode. After all, Serena had got him behaving exactly as she wanted almost from the word go. But she was his dominatrix, his mistress – and that meant something, meant an awful lot, actually. There was a relationship between them, one he deeply valued. Peter felt close to Serena, close also to Julie, who was so like himself. He'd never felt close to anyone before in his whole life, not one single person.

What would have become of him if Serena and Julie had not kidnapped him? Peter wondered. He dreaded to think. The person he was – and would have stayed – had none of this ever happened to him, was not the person he now wanted to be.

Peter realised he hadn't known himself at all before the kidnapping, not his real self. That was why he'd had such a sense of incompletion, of emptiness, why his life had felt so meaningless. And there had been all that obsessive sleeping around he'd gone in for. Peter could hardly remember any of his countless one-night stands. The women all merged in his mind: nameless, faceless, shapeless; just warm bodies he'd used to temporarily blunt his terrible sense of loneliness as he searched for - what exactly? For what it was that he had now, surely. Because Peter wasn't lonely any more, wasn't searching either. He had Serena and Julie, and they were so special it wasn't true.

Just think what most normal people would make of so-called perverts like them, like *him*, Peter said to himself. How they would sneer at them in their petty, mean, small-minded way. Well, screw normal people. And screw the real world. The real world was suffocating, stifling, miserable. His world – the one created for him by his mistress, his *goddess*, Serena – was vastly superior.

He wondered sometimes how close he was to going completely insane.

Chapter Eleven

Peter loved the idea that Serena was his mistress, that she *owned* him. The knowledge of it spoke to something deep inside him, something that felt almost primordial. He was Serena's personal property, her slave, and it felt so right. Peter was constantly in the right place to serve his mistress too, the *perfect* place to serve her – the dungeon. He was there now …

Serena had strapped Peter to the St Andrew's cross in a spread-eagled position, his back to the wall. Only once she'd done this did she remove his collar and chain. She had put a black leather hood, which had open eye holes and a mouth hole, over his head. Apart from the hood Peter was entirely naked. His cock was rock-hard, a rivulet of precome trailing from its swollen head.

Julie was kneeling submissively at Serena's feet, both women wearing nothing at all. The dominatrix told Julie to stand up and led her over to the horizontal torture chair. 'Lie on it face up with your arms and legs spread out,' she told her before binding her wrists and ankles to the chair by its strap attachments.

Serena went on to use the leather tip of a riding crop to beat Julie's clit and pussy. She did this more sensuously than sadistically, and by the time she had finished Julie was groaning with desire. Threads of love juice were dripping from her labia, making the leather surface of the torture chair beneath her wet.

Next the dominatrix freed Julie's arms and legs and released her from the horizontal torture chair. She took her over to the horse, positioning her on her front lengthwise over it and strapping her wrists and ankles to its side. She proceeded to attach metal clamps to the lips of her sex. This was clearly very painful to Julie, causing her lovely face to grimace and her pussy and anus to pulse uncontrollably.

Serena was starting to really get into her sadistic stride now. She took hold of a leather flogger and immediately set to work with it on Julie's backside. The cruel implement hissed like an angry snake when she swung it through the air before landing with a sharp crack on its fleshy target. She beat Julie with it remorselessly until her rear was covered with angry welts and she cried out in pain. 'Too much noise, slave,' Serena announced, putting a red ball-gag into Julie's mouth and buckling it firmly into place behind her head.

Julie's punishment went on relentlessly: Serena next lit several red candles and proceeded to drizzle molten wax onto her already punished backside. This caused Julie to shudder violently, her wrists and ankles straining against the leather straps that held them tightly in place. At the same time the ball-gag muffled her agonized cries of pain.

Eventually Serena detached Julie from the horse, carefully removing the metal clamps from her labia, but leaving her gagged with the red ball-gag. She also released Peter from the wall-mounted cross but only after she had locked his chained collar back into place.

Serena put the gag attachment on to Peter's black leather hood and then led him and Julie over to one of the metal spreader bars that hung by chains from the ceiling near the middle of the dungeon. The bar had two manacle attachments at each end and she stood the gagged slaves together face to face and manacled their wrists to either end. Only then did she remove Peter's collar once again.

As they stood facing one another in their bondage, Julie's eyes locked with Peter's, the only part of his face now visible beneath his leather hood. Her pupils were wide and she kept on looking straight into his shining blue eyes. We are two of a kind, you and I, her dark, gleaming eyes seemed to be saying to him once more. We are two of a kind.

Serena took hold of Peter's throbbing erection and held it at the entrance to Julie's tight wet pussy. 'Push your cock inside her, Peter,' she ordered. As he entered Julie he felt her body tremble and she groaned with desire beneath her gag, making him stiffen even further inside her.

Serena removed Julie's ball-gag and covered her eyes instead, using a blindfold of soft red leather. She also removed the gag attachment from Peter's hood and secured its blindfold attachment in place. 'When you beg for my mercy, slaves, as you most surely will,' she told them, 'you have my permission to come.'

The dominatrix picked up two canes, one in her left hand and the other in her right, and gave the thin lengths of smooth rattan a couple of experimental swishes through the air. She went on to cane Peter and Julie simultaneously with increasing ferocity, each swipe more agonizing than the last. For a long time the dungeon resounded with the double swish and crack of two canes striking two punished backsides. Serena caned their rears with ever harder strokes until they were criss-crossed with clear stripes. Throughout this ferocious beating, Julie's pussy clenched in spasms around Peter's stiffness, which was steely-hard inside her, and her body quivered against his.

At last neither of them could hold out any longer. In unison Peter and Julie cried out desperately for mercy. At the same time the extreme pleasure-pain they were experiencing tightened and then erupted through them. They came together ecstatically in orgasms that were long and savage. They came together, two of a kind.

Chapter Twelve

It took time for it to happen. How much time exactly, it is not possible to say. But it happened. At some point Peter stopped hearing that small voice inside his head, the one that told him everything that was happening to him was insane, that it was making *him* insane.

Was this because by then any last vestiges of sanity had been beaten out of him by Serena? Or was it that she had fucked with his mind so much that it finally slipped its moorings completely? Or was it the isolation of his cell that eventually did for his sanity, that made him finally lose what fragile grasp on reality he had? Being so totally cut off like that made Peter lose all his bearings, there's no doubt about that. Maybe it made him lose all his marbles too.

Disciplined with Julie constantly, *incessantly*, and locked in his cell day after day, Peter was a million miles away from everything that was normal. Serena and Julie had become the norm to him simply because he never saw anyone else. He came to almost forget what other people were like. It was as if they didn't really exist at all. To Peter, the only people in the world that mattered were Julie, who was his soul sister, and Serena, who was the goddess to them both.

He now lived in a permanently trance-like state, unaware of the slowness of real time in the dream world he inhabited. He had no desire to leave that world, none whatsoever. He felt protected there, surrounded by a strange, electric peacefulness, and didn't want to be anywhere else. He certainly didn't want to be free. It was unthinkable. The idea of it scared him, terrified him.

When he wasn't being disciplined in some way or other he was left alone, locked in his cell and in shackles. But Peter never felt lonely there. He was fed, watered, and cherished where he was. Yes, in his world – in his *mind* – he was cherished. But he knew he wasn't trusted. He was always kept in bondage, usually chained to the wall of his cell. When he was being disciplined in the dungeon adjacent to his cell, the chained collar would sometimes be removed by Serena but only because she had temporarily replaced it with some other type of restraint that was equally effective.

He didn't need to be restrained like this all the time, Peter knew. He wished Serena would realise that too. It wasn't as if he was going to make an attempt at escape or anything like that. But the dominatrix obviously wasn't prepared to give him the benefit of the doubt. From time to time, Julie would give his hair a trim, with Serena watching the whole process like a hawk. And the scissors would not even appear until his arms had been handcuffed behind him. Peter wished Serena, his adored mistress, could learn to trust him as much as he trusted her. Maybe in time she would, he could only hope against hope.

Peter worshipped Serena and loved being her slave and being abused by her. It wasn't just the pain and bondage that he loved. It was the delicious sense of humiliation too. He loved being made to crawl around on the dungeon floor and lick Serena's boots. He loved it when she fucked him in the arse, using him like a hole as she pumped her strap-on dildo in and out of him. He loved it when she tied him up to the wall-mounted cross and then beat him so harshly that he whimpered in pain and lust and mind-fuck shame …

Peter came round from his ever more lustful reverie to the sound of the key rattling in the lock and his cell door banging open. Serena and Julie stepped into the room, both of them stark naked. He could feel himself stiffen still more at the sight of them. Julie was carrying the handcuffs and leg irons, and Serena was holding a black leather blindfold. The two women glanced at each other in amusement at the sight of his erection.

'A good man is hard to find and a hard man is good to find, huh, Julie?' Serena said with a straight face.

'Yes, mistress.' Julie smiled.

'No prizes for guessing what you've been dreaming about, Peter,' Serena said, raising an ironic eyebrow in the direction of his shaft. 'Or is it another piss hard-on?'

'No, mistress, it's not.' He smiled. 'It's the real thing.' Peter got himself up to a sitting position on the bondage table and swung his legs to its side. The length of chain attached to his collar – the chain that secured him to the cell wall for most of the time, night and day – clinked and rattled.

'Sex isn't everything, slave, is it?' Serena said, fixing him with her gaze as she walked in a slow half-circle around him.

'No, mistress,' Peter agreed. 'Sex isn't everything.' *You* are everything, mistress, he wanted to add.

'Lose the erection,' Serena said sharply. And he did. Peter always did everything Serena told him to do, even that.

'I've decided that it's time you had some fresh air,' Serena said. 'I'm going to blindfold you while Julie puts you into the handcuffs and leg irons.'

She duly wrapped the black leather blindfold over Peter's eyes, making sure he could not see even a sliver of light, while Julie handcuffed his hands behind him and put him into the leg irons. Only after they'd done all that did Serena remove his chained collar.

The two women helped Peter to stand up and led him towards the metal door through which they had arrived. They passed out of his cell and started up the staircase, one either side of him, holding him by the upper arms.

The staircase was of stone, like the floor of his cell; that was evident to Peter. It was quite wide and steep, he could discern that too. But that was about all he could make out. Peter could see nothing, of course, and anything he might have heard was drowned out by the clanking sounds his leg irons made as he moved.

When they got to the head of the stairs they turned to the right, took a dozen steps and stopped. 'Unlock and open the door, Julie,' Serena said.

'Yes, mistress,' she replied, turning a key. Peter heard the door ease open with a creak.

Then they walked out and Peter felt grass beneath his bare feet. He expanded his chest and took his first breath of fresh air. It was intoxicating, that sudden influx of oxygen into his body after nothing but recycled air for God knows how long. Peter stood outside the door on the grass and breathed and breathed, taking the air deep into his lungs.

The air smelt moist. It wasn't raining, but there was rain in the air. It hadn't rained recently, Peter determined, because the grass beneath his bare feet was dry, but rain was on its way. He could imagine a sky heavy with dark-grey, scudding clouds. He took another gulp of that intoxicating fresh air, took it to the bottom of his lungs.

Peter listened for any sound that might give him a clue as to where they were. He couldn't hear any traffic, not even in the distance, but he could hear the sound of birdsong. He remembered Serena telling him they were in a very secluded location. It was right out in the middle of the countryside somewhere, he assumed. And there he was, breathing in wonderful outdoor air full of plant smells and wet smells and the smell of grass. A deep sigh came out of him. He had a feeling almost of bliss, but not quite. There would need to be an extra component for him to achieve that euphoric condition.

'You like what I've done for you, Peter?' Serena said, standing in front of his blindfolded form and touching his shoulders.

'Indeed, mistress,' he replied, his tone ingratiating. 'I'm so grateful to you.'

'Demonstrate your gratitude to me, then,' Serena snapped. 'Get onto your knees.'

'Yes, mistress,' he said humbly. He dropped to his knees before her, his hands held behind his back by the handcuffs and his ankles constrained by the leg irons. His cock began to stiffen once more.

'Worship my feet,' Serena commanded.

'Yes, mistress,' Peter said, his cock now hard against his stomach. He leant forward and pressed his lips to one of her beautiful bare feet. He kissed and licked it eagerly, tracing little circles over its toes and every inch of its outer and inner surfaces, progressing to the ankle and all the way round to the back. Then Serena raised her foot, allowing Peter to lick and kiss its sole and lap at its heel like an obedient puppy. Next she placed her other foot to his lips and he repeated the process, feeling his cock tauten even more all the while.

'That's enough,' Serena said finally. She placed her raised foot on the back of his neck, pushing down firmly until his blindfolded face was pressed into the grass, into the warm earth. To Peter that truly *was* bliss. His cock was as hard as a rock now, his arousal so sweet, so very sweet. He felt mad with lust and crazy with love for his goddess, Serena. He was at that moment as deep into his obsession with her – into his personal insanity – as he had ever been.

Chapter Thirteen

Peter felt as if being Serena's slave was what he had been born for, that before her he'd spent his whole life not being the person he really was inside his skin. He had not the slightest wish to be released by her. Released to do what, for fuck's sake? To go back to his old existence, miserable travesty of a life that it had been? Such a prospect appalled him, horrified him. No, Peter was happy – insanely happy – with his lot as Serena's slave. But there was just one thing that kept niggling away at his mind. He continued to live in the vain hope that she would some day come to trust him, just like she trusted Julie, just like he trusted both of them. Finally, surprisingly, Serena made a significant move in that direction. At least, that's what he thought …

Peter had no idea where he was other than that it was up one flight of stairs from his cell and indoors. He could feel thick carpet beneath his bare feet, not the stone floor he was used to. Where exactly was he? He was much disorientated and had been ever since Serena, on her own and resplendent in a skin-tight black leather catsuit and stiletto-heeled boots, had stood in front of him in his cell and put earplugs in his ears, and blindfolded and gagged him to ensure his almost complete sensory deprivation. She had gone on to handcuff his wrists behind his back and secure leg irons to his ankles before removing his chained collar. The dominatrix had then led him slowly out of his cell, up the stone stairs and along a similar surface for a short while before entering this carpeted space.

All of a sudden the dense silence Peter had experienced ever since his earplugs had been inserted disappeared when these were removed. 'Get onto your knees,' Serena ordered and he obeyed instantly. Peter felt a tattoo of pulses build in his chest at the touch of her fingers as she removed first his gag and then his blindfold. She did not, however, remove either the cuffs holding his wrists behind his back or his leg irons. When his blindfold was removed Peter blinked, trying to adjust his eyes, and looked around.

He saw that he was in a largish room, rectangular in shape, and that its curtains were drawn tightly and its lights illuminated. The floor was covered in a thick carpet of vaguely oriental design. At the end of the room was a fireplace, unlit, with a marble mantelpiece above it. There was an oak door to the far left of the same wall. The walls of the room were painted white, and dark beams stretched across the ceiling. The room was minimally but expensively furnished, and strangely anonymous – no pictures, no photographs, no ornaments, nothing to give it any real sense of identity.

Right in front of where Peter knelt was a black leather couch on which Serena, who had emerged from behind him, was now gracefully seating herself.

'I am very pleased with the progress you've made as a slave, Peter,' she announced once she was seated. 'In fact, I am so pleased with your progress that I would like to reward you with something you particularly want, a treat of some kind. What would you like to request? If it's reasonable I'll grant it. How about a book to read, or a drop of alcohol to drink, or a favourite meal, or maybe another trip outside into the fresh air – blindfolded and shackled again, of course; that goes without saying. But those are just a few suggestions. It's basically your call within reason, you choose.'

Peter thought for a moment and then said, 'It is information more than any specific thing that I'd like the most, mistress, if that's possible.'

'Go on,' she said guardedly.

'I'd like to know how you came to choose me as a slave, mistress.' It had always mystified Peter. Had it all been merely happenstance or had there been more to it than that?

'To explain that to you, I'd need to go back to the beginning and tell you the whole story,' Serena said. 'And then I'd have to kill you.'

Peter's eyes widened in alarm, in horror. She couldn't mean it.

She didn't. 'Only kidding.' She laughed. 'I want you to know the whole story now – or most of it anyway. Are you kneeling comfortably, slave?'

'Yes, mistress.'

'Then I'll begin. Once upon a time …'

Chapter Fourteen

Once upon a time there was a young woman we shall call
Serena, although that wasn't her real name. All the names
in this story have been changed to protect the guilty.
Serena had a serious problem. She was certain she must be
frigid because normal sex did nothing for her, left her
completely cold. Then one day one of her more sexually
adventurous boyfriends asked her if she wouldn't mind
tying him up and giving him a sound spanking. Why not?
she thought. She certainly couldn't be bothered to have
straight sex with him.

But tying up that boyfriend and beating his bare arse
until it glowed like a furnace turned out to be a revelation
to Serena. No, it was more than a revelation. It was an
epiphany. It actually made her climax – and hugely too.
And that was her "eureka" moment. She realised that she
could experience the most intense erotic pleasure as a
result of being totally in control in a sexual situation and in
inflicting pain.

Before long Serena came to realise that she didn't just
love to be sexually dominant and sadistic, she needed it as
much as a heroin addict needs the next fix. She became
hooked on the sense of total power it gave her, couldn't
get enough of it. It became a complete obsession. She
decided to turn that obsession into a career and become a
professional dominatrix.

Under the tutelage of a highly experienced pro domme,
Serena became increasingly expert in the art of erotic

domination and learned all the tricks of the trade. She ended up becoming a first rate professional dominatrix in her own right. She also became one of those few lucky people in life who can genuinely say that they love their work. Though she was very well paid for her services, it never failed to excite her to dominate and discipline a submissive man. Or a submissive woman.

A beautiful but desperately lonely young woman called Julie, a real lost soul if ever there was one, came to Serena as a client on one occasion and never left. She stayed as her devoted house slave, totally under her control from that day on. Julie developed a particular notion over time, ended up being completely convinced about it, in fact. She claimed she could always spot a fellow submissive, that it took one to know one. It was something in the eyes, she said.

Serena, with Julie by her side, became one of the best pro dommes in the business, and one of the highest paid ones too. Her rich clients paid her handsomely for the privilege of having her make them grovel at her stiletto-heeled feet; having her make them suffer so much under the cruel lash of her whip that they begged in desperation for her mercy.

There are many pro dommes who are essentially bogus, women who pretend to be dominant to earn money from their clients. Serena wasn't like that in any way. She was the genuine article. She adored disciplining the clients who came to her. And they knew that she was the real deal, returning to her time and time again to be disciplined in the wickedly imaginative ways she devised.

There was one client in particular to whom Serena seemed to be very special indeed, perhaps because he had nobody else. Robert was his name – or Roberta the sissy maid as he was always known in Serena's dungeon. When he died suddenly at work of a massive heart attack Serena was amazed to find that he had left the entirety of his substantial fortune to her in his will, including a significant property portfolio. She went from being comfortably off to filthy rich in one fell swoop.

They say that money is power. Serena was a woman seriously into exercising power and suddenly money was no object. She could have anything she wanted. And what she wanted more than anything else was a male version of Julie, but with an all-important extra ingredient this time.

Serena controlled Julie totally. She was hers to the core of her being, and they both knew it. Serena wanted something more, though, now that she could afford to indulge her most depraved fantasies.

She wanted a slave who would yield to her totally just like Julie, yes. But Julie had come to her voluntarily. Serena wanted a slave who came to her *involuntarily.* He would resist her at first, that was only to be expected. But she would then really get to work on him, making him realise in whatever time it took – and with *her* special skills she didn't think it would take long – that total submission to her was what he needed, *all* he needed.

How would she get hold of such a man? She'd kidnap someone, that's how, someone handsome and sexy – and innately very submissive. Julie could always spot them, that's what she insisted. It was in the eyes, she said.

Once Serena had conceived the idea, it really took hold with her. It all needed meticulous planning, of course, but this was much assisted by two things: the properties she'd been left in Robert's will and her own background as a professional dominatrix.

She needed a house in a very secluded situation. The house had to have a decent-sized basement that she could get converted to a cell, bathroom and dungeon. She'd inherited such a property and it was easy to get its basement converted, employing the same extremely discreet company she'd used to set up her pro domme dungeon.

She needed a property with an integral garage, in central London. She'd inherited one: the "crash pad". She needed a car with a sizeable boot and indeed had several of these in her possession from which to choose. She had plenty of money, so could get hold of the powerful drug that would be needed to anaesthetize her victim. She needed someone she could trust totally to lure a victim – the right kind of victim – into her trap. She had that someone in her devoted house slave, Julie.

She needed to cover her tracks in the event of her deciding, for whatever reason, to release the man. If she let him go he must never be able to find her again; that was crucial. The crash pad in London was transferred to a Swiss bank with a water-tight confidentiality policy, supposedly for occasional use by its employees. So the woman who would be calling herself Serena could not possibly be traced through that means.

The secluded house in the country could be any place out in the middle of nowhere to a slave locked in a cell and otherwise suitably restrained, blindfolded when necessary. If he ever came upstairs in the house he would be in shackles and it would be to an anonymous room with drawn curtains that he'd be brought. Again, it could be anywhere.

And so on. Everything was ready. The outlandish deed was done, the enslavement process was begun in earnest, and progressed systematically, and completed successfully.

'And here you are with me today,' said Serena, or whoever she was, concluding her extraordinary account.

'And here is where I want to stay, mistress,' Peter said, still kneeling before her. 'I want it with all my heart.'

The dominatrix gave him a long look. 'That is a shame,' she said finally, her face suddenly turned to stone. 'Because you will have to go very soon.'

Peter felt something hollow where his stomach used to be. 'No, mistress, please,' he cried out, panic bursting up into his mind.

'Yes Peter,' she said, her eyes cold.

Peter looked at her desperately, panic now throbbing in his chest and spinning through his brain like a cyclone. 'I'll do anything, anything,' he pleaded, hollow-eyed. 'But please, please keep me as your slave. I'm begging you.'

The dominatrix looked back at him, her face dark. She said nothing. Peter started to cry, looking up at her, tears flowing down his cheeks as he sobbed. The sobs came from deep within. He gasped between tears and his body began to shiver, making his shackles clank and clatter. 'Please, mistress,' Peter said, his voice now racked with sobs. 'I'm begging you. I'll do *anything.*'

But the face of the woman before whom he knelt grew darker still. *I'd have to kill you,* that's what she'd told him in apparent jest. She might just as well kill him, Peter thought in abject despair. What she'd just said was as good as a death sentence to him. All of a sudden he let out a terrible high-pitched keening noise that sounded as if it belonged to someone else.

Chapter Fifteen

What goes around comes around. The West End of London on that moonless, starlit night was pulsing with life just as it had been a year ago almost to the day. The weather was equally as beautiful too. It was proving to be another very mild summer. Peter Moran was out pussy hunting again. Old habits die hard, you might say.

He looked at his watch beneath the muted glow of the streetlights. It was just past 10.30. He crossed the busy street and turned into a short alley. Peter could hear the throb of the music, loud and frantic, as he approached the neon-lit entrance to the dance club. He could feel that familiar sense of predatory anticipation. It went with being a sex addict, which he still was and which he would always be.

Peter entered the crowded club. He was wearing a lightweight dark blue jacket, a crisp white shirt and form-hugging black leather jeans, no underwear. He went to the bar and ordered a rum and Coke with ice and lemon from the barman. He sipped at the tall glass, which gleamed with rivulets of condensation. His eyes gazed around the darkened room towards the dance floor. Flashing lights illuminated the dancers as they moved their bodies with abandon to the pounding music that swept in waves through the club.

He scanned the dance floor but didn't see anyone who took his fancy at first; there were so many people dancing that they seemed to blur into one big mass. Then he saw her, saw the beautiful girl with the short blonde hair and full lips, who was dancing on her own among the throng. She wore high-heeled red leather shoes and a tiny dress of the same colour that barely covered her backside and moulded itself to the contours of her seductive body. Peter could feel his groin tighten, could feel himself stiffen at the sight of her. He caught her eye and she smiled slightly in his direction before turning away into the crowd of dancers. It was uncanny. He couldn't say why but he just knew she was the one he was looking for. He felt this weird sense of predestination that she was *the one*.

Peter took a couple more pulls of his drink, the ice clinking, and put his glass down. He ambled across to the dance floor to find the girl. There was no hurry, he told himself. Yet his heart was beating fast. He found the girl in the middle of the dance floor and stood before her. Peter didn't say anything, nor did she. They just began to dance, moving their bodies sensuously to the music. Sometimes they were pressed together, their bodies merged, their arms around one another's waist. Other times they pulled apart, their arms out sideways, their hips thrusting to the rhythm of the music.

All the while they danced Peter's eyes never left the girl's face. He stared into the depths of her big grey-blue eyes, which sparkled with life and vivacity and sexuality and - something else. They also had that look of acquiescence Peter was now convinced he was able to recognise instinctively, the one that marked out the true submissive. The woman who'd called herself Julie had been right, he thought. It took one to know one. It was all in the eyes, the windows to the soul. He felt a surge of excitement, could feel an electric sensation coursing down his spine. She was definitely the one, he said to himself. There was no doubt about it.

Peter knew exactly how this was going to go now. They'd dance for a little while longer, nice and sultry.

They'd have a drink or two together, flirting all the while. She'd become slightly drunk. They'd dance some more. The dancing would get raunchier all the time and he'd get her all sexed up. Peter would invite the girl back to his place, which was a short walk away, he'd explain. It was only small, just a crash pad really, but it had its own garage, which was a godsend in central London given the difficult parking situation.

When they got to the apartment they'd strip naked and he'd fuck her as deep and as hard as he could, hammer her to the very depths of herself. He'd fuck her senseless, that's what he'd do, and then finish off the job by injecting her with a hypodermic full of anaesthetic. She would see the needle in his hand immediately after he'd injected her but she'd already be feeling very woozy, barely able to move.

Who knows, maybe just before she lost consciousness she'd hear a door open and look over and catch sight – the merest outline – of the woman who'd been hiding behind that door all the time she'd been fucking her brains out. If she did, then she'd be getting a glimpse of the woman who now wanted a female version of Peter.

She'd be glimpsing the extremely wealthy dominatrix who wanted a new female slave so she could achieve her ideal of having two female slaves and one male slave to play with to her dark heart's content. But she didn't want just any female slave.

Oh no, she wanted one who would begin her enslavement to her involuntarily and who would resist it at first as was only to be expected. But she would learn, in whatever time it took, to accept it, realising that it was what she'd wanted all along. She would end up hungering for it, living for it, just like Peter had.

He'd do anything, *anything,* if she'd only keep him as her slave. That's what a thoroughly desperate Peter had said, whimpering and blubbering as he pleaded with his mistress. And he'd meant it to the depths of his soul, poor demented creature that he'd been, that he still was. He'd have done anything if she'd only agree not to let him go. Would he even be prepared to commit a crime – a very serious one – if she'd agree to keep him as her slave? Yes, he'd do anything, he'd repeated.

She had kept him to his word. And that was more than fine by Peter, much more than fine. Once he'd done this deed – this *terrible* deed, but he didn't see it like that any more than she did – he'd have proved to his adored mistress that she could trust him completely, proved it to her once and for all.

That knowledge on her part and their shared complicity in the major felony – the kidnapping – they would have carried out would mean they'd be tied together forever. He would belong to his mistress, his *goddess*, completely then.

He would never be free of her nor would she be of him. He'd be her slave for the rest of his life until death they do part. And that was truly wonderful as far as Peter was concerned. That was his idea of a happy ending.

BOOK FOUR

ABSOLUTE SUBMISSION

'Love that is not madness is not love.'
Pedro Calderon de la Barca

Chapter One

He lay on his stomach on the four-poster bed, naked apart from his slave's collar and wrist and ankle cuffs, which were all of black leather. He was blindfolded and gagged. His arms were crossed in front of his chest, his wrist cuffs held together by a metal trigger clip; his ankle cuffs were also clipped together by the same means. Kate stood above him, wielding a leather whip. Waves of pain swept through him as she whipped his backside relentlessly.

That had been Jay's most regular fantasy for years. It helped him relax when he couldn't sleep and lay there trying not to disturb his beautiful lover, Kate, as she slumbered peacefully by his side. Ironically, the more trapped Jay felt by the circumstances of his life – specifically the daily grind and relentless pressures of his high-powered job – the more comforting he found this masochistic bondage fantasy.

The scenario had become different over time. He was still on his front, naked, blindfolded, and gagged and wearing the same slave's collar and wrist and ankle cuffs. But this time his arms were outstretched and his legs splayed apart, his wrist and ankle cuffs secured by chains to the four corners of the bed.

Kate was flogging his back and rear ferociously with a heavy leather flogger. She stopped periodically to masturbate, the sounds urgent and liquid, and each time she returned to beating him she did so with even more savagery. Agonizing pain laced through him - and he luxuriated in it. It was what he craved, what he ached for. He couldn't do without it, lived for it. It was his only reality now, complete pain slut that he was.

Suddenly Kate stopped whipping him and he heard her leave the room. Where had she gone and when would she be back? he wondered. Jay couldn't ask her because he was gagged. In any case, it wasn't his place to ask. He wasn't allowed to speak to Kate unless she spoke to him first; that was one of her rules.

You can see how Jay's original fantasy had developed very considerably. Except it wasn't a fantasy any more but reality. That was because he had become Kate's slave, to be held in bondage or disciplined or fucked or simply ignored, according to her whim. He was the chattel of this highly sadistic dominatrix to do with exactly as she saw fit.

Jay existed only for Kate's pleasure and she required complete abject obedience from him at all times. He had always to do exactly as she told him without question, no matter how humiliating that might be for him, no matter how degrading. He wasn't even allowed to masturbate or have an orgasm without her permission.

What we are talking about here is the ultimate power exchange there can possibly be between two people in the world of BDSM: a full lifestyle relationship. That's right, for 24 hours a day, 7 days a week, 365 days a year, Jay was Kate's slave. She disciplined him repeatedly and he spent his days and nights in a constant state of anticipatory arousal, trying to second guess what his next punishment would be. And when it came, he experienced the most exquisite ecstasy in the dark ritual of that punishment.

How could this be so? How could harmless fantasy have become complete, all-encompassing reality in this bizarre way? How could such a drastic change have happened in his life? How could it all have come to this?

Jay was asking himself these very questions as he lay

there in his bondage awaiting Kate's return. I guess I've just been lucky, was his answer. And he wasn't being fatuous. He put pretty much all of it down to luck. Jay knew he'd been lucky in all sorts of ways.

He'd been lucky to have come into the world hard-wired to become essentially what he was. And what he was to the depths of his being, as it had turned out, was a submissive masochist. Some submissive masochists are born, some are made, and some have submissive masochism thrust upon them. Jay felt lucky that he fell into the first category. There were no psyche-scarring incidents in his childhood or adolescence to account for it. He was just made like that, it was in his DNA.

He felt lucky to be able to live the way he wanted to live at last. And the way he wanted to live was as Kate's full-time slave. She had put no pressure on him of any kind to do that. He it was who had elected to be her slave 24/7. He'd decided to submit himself to her totally and had made that decision entirely of his own free will.

That had been a momentous decision whichever way you look at it and couldn't have happened if the couple hadn't been well advanced down that route already as a result of their commitment to BDSM. Yet when Kate and he thought back, neither of them could remember how their lovemaking had come to change quite as radically as it had. All they could say for certain was that it had happened gradually and that with every change it had become even more intense and passionate.

It all started the first time Kate suggested that she tie Jay up and blindfold him before they made love. He found the exercise in helplessness involved in this, his first experience of bondage, to be intoxicating. It caused his spirits to soar, embracing his wildest masochistic fantasies.

Kate soon started to take on those fantasies herself. 'Get over my knee,' she ordered her naked lover one day. 'I'm going to spank you hard.' The harsh sting of the spanking, combined with the delicious humiliation of this further exciting new sexual experience, ended up exceeding Jay's most feverish imaginings. In the months that followed Kate progressed to disciplining him with a paddle, cane, and flogger. Then she moved on to such things as anal play and genital whipping as the couple's BDSM games became ever more elaborate and Kate became ever more sadistic

As he lay there on his stomach, blindfolded, gagged and spread-eagled in his bondage, Jay brought vividly to mind one of those exciting games they'd played. He remembered how it had gone as if it had all happened yesterday, the images in his head remarkably vivid …

Kate and Jay were standing by their double bed, both of them stark naked. The floor beneath their bare feet was of polished, honey-coloured wood. Kate, who had a whip in her hand, looked magnificent. Her nude figure was perfection: beautifully proportioned and softly curved. Kate's dark hair was shining, her violet eyes sparkling, her sensual lips pouting.

'Let's get one thing clear before I start disciplining you, slave,' she said. Jay loved it when Kate called him that: *slave*. 'You are not to climax unless I give you my permission. Is that understood?'

'Yes, mistress,' Jay replied. He loved that too – the sound of his own voice when he called her "mistress". He said it again to himself: *mistress*.

Kate told Jay to move over to the wall opposite and stand facing it with his arms up and the palms of his hands against its surface. And he moved immediately to obey her. Jay tried to keep his breathing steady and waited for Kate to begin whipping him. He did not have long to wait.

The first crack of the whip flew through the air, shocking Jay with its ferocity. He gasped, the cheeks of his backside stinging where the whip had fallen. He gave another gasp as her next stroke landed across his rear. Kate brought the whip down again with even more ferocity with her third stroke, causing a blistering jolt of pain to rack Jay's body.

Kate carried on whipping Jay hard, each searing stroke producing a sharp, fiery sting. He moaned and gasped at the pain and his flesh quivered constantly as she increased the momentum of his beating still further. The increasing vigour, accuracy and regularity of the carefully aimed blows made him writhe and moan. His moans grew louder and in time with the swooping impact of the whip with which Kate disciplined him.

As she continued whipping Jay a red heat seemed to burn into his skin, sinking deeper and deeper. But he could also feel its heat spreading to his shaft, which had become as hard as a rock. She kept on whipping him like a demon and every strike tingled deliciously through his genitals. He was panting and shivering with both pain and pleasure.

As Kate went on beating Jay his pain started to turn to white-hot lust. His nerves were on fire, he was consumed by desire and a swelling sensation of pure carnality flowed through his body as blood flushed into his pulsing shaft. Then Kate stopped.

She told Jay to turn round to face her again, this time with his hands behind his head, and he did so straight away. Kate took hold of a small flogger and whipped his genitals with it in a dozen quick bursts, causing the veins in his testicles to fill until they appeared ready to burst. Jay's hard shaft and bulbous cockhead turned a dark purple and the pain burned hotly.

And so it continued. Kate whipped Jay's aching cock over and over again, causing his flesh to quiver and burn as sharp spasms of pain sang through him. She stopped, and the pain gradually subsided to a hard, insistent throbbing that was intense pain but intense pleasure too.

Kate put the small flogger to one side and took hold of

Jay's punished shaft at the base, her fingers wrapped around it tightly. She began to masturbate him, running her hand up and down, stroking the smooth hardness of his cock. The more Kate masturbated Jay the faster she went, her hand going up and down in the precome wetness that began to cover it, until he felt on the verge of climaxing. But he knew he must not ejaculate without having received Kate's express permission. Jay closed his eyes tight shut and willed himself desperately not to climax. She stopped.

'Get onto the bed and lie flat on your back, slave,' Kate ordered next, and he did, his erect cock rearing in the air. Gazing at Jay's erection, Kate climbed onto the bed herself and straddled his upturned face. He watched the lips of her vulva open up like two beautiful wet petals. She sat over his mouth and he found that she was completely soaking wet. He began to lick her pussy and she moaned out her pleasure. He continued as he had begun, his tongue on her clitoris insistent as she quivered with passion.

Kate then leant forward and took Jay's hot shaft into her mouth, rolling her tongue up and down its length as he flicked his over her clitoris. They carried on like this in a state of ever-mounting passion, desire coursing through them as they sucked and licked deliriously.

It was not long before Kate climaxed. Her orgasm was long and violent and she took Jay's pulsing shaft from her mouth so as to cry out her ecstasy. Jay knew he really couldn't hold out any longer this time. Every nerve in his body told him that he was going to climax. 'Permission to come, mistress,' he managed to plead indistinctly from beneath her quivering, wet thighs.

Kate sat up, pressing her pussy down harder on his face. 'Permission granted,' she gasped in reply. Jay groaned painfully into her soaking crotch and, with massive relief, spurted out thick gobs of pearly cream, which splattered back down onto his torso as his climax continued to rage …

What a delicious experience that had been, Jay remembered, blindfolded, gagged and trussed up on the bed as he was. And it was not as if it had been unique. Kate used to do things like that to him all the time once they'd got into BDSM; she still did. Jay let his thoughts wander again and the memories kept on coming. He remembered how Chloe and Simon had first come into their lives …

Chapter Two

Time flies, particularly when you are an ambitious young couple, working equally hard to be successful in your respective business careers. Eventually the inevitable happened, though, and Kate and Jay began to feel a real need to meet other people who shared similar deviant sexual tastes to their own. They started going to a local fetish club and it was at their very first visit there that they made the acquaintance of another Femdom couple, Chloe and Simon, with whom they were to strike up an extremely close and long-standing friendship.

Chloe was drop-dead gorgeous, with short blonde hair, which was tousled and curly, and piercing blue eyes. Simon was exceptionally good looking as well, with sculptured cheekbones and thick, auburn hair. He was a really nice man too, kind and thoughtful and open, with a quiet charm about him. He was someone who seemed utterly incapable of doing harm to anyone. Which was not something you would ever have said about his mistress, who was a highly experienced dominatrix – and a highly sadistic one as well.

Chloe was very inventive, with a creative imagination for all things sadistic. Beautiful, subtly elegant and commanding, she was a fount of knowledge on virtually every aspect of the arcane world of BDSM. Chloe became more than a very good friend to Kate. She became her mentor.

Up until the time Kate and Jay made their first visit to

that local fetish club and met Chloe and Simon their involvement in BDSM had been strictly private. Deciding to enter the fetish scene was not exactly going public about their particular sexual orientation. Given society's taboos, that wasn't ever going to happen as far as Kate and Jay were concerned. It was more like entering an exciting secret society. But it *was* a major turning point for the couple. It was an acknowledgement that sadomasochism had now gone beyond a mere sexual preference for them and would from that point on be an increasingly active part of the way they lived their lives.

Kate, it was clear, was acutely aware of the fact that, while she was certainly very well acquainted indeed with all the basic elements of erotic domination by that stage, she still had a lot to learn if she and Jay wanted to progress further in the BDSM lifestyle. She understood full well that she would be jeopardizing Jay's physical and psychological wellbeing should she not take the trouble to learn. And who better to show her the way than Chloe, with her great wealth of experience on the subject.

Chloe set about her task with a will, training Kate in more advanced aspects of safe domination, including the use of certain hard-to-use implements of correction like the single lash whip and the bullwhip, which, she explained, were potentially dangerous if not used properly. Her training covered different types of bondage, including Japanese rope bondage, plastic wrap, leather body bags and suspension machines, to name but a few. It was a real master class. Correction, it was a real *mistress* class, and Kate advanced to the level of well-versed player in no time.

Much of this training occurred at Chloe and Simon's house, a period property with a basement, which they'd had converted so that it could be used for their kinky play. It was decked out beautifully with all the trappings of a dungeon: a throne for the dominatrix, and for the disciplining of slaves, a whipping bench, a horse, stocks, a suspension frame, a wall-mounted cross, a horizontal torture chair, and a number of strategically placed chains hanging from the ceiling, several with spreader bars attached to them. A huge array of whips, canes, paddles, clamps, gags, and other implements of correction hung on the dark walls of the dungeon.

Obviously Chloe didn't have far to look for slaves on whom her protégée could practice the skills she was so diligently passing on to her. Jay and Simon were always willing to "volunteer".

'Let me ask you a question, Kate,' Chloe said toward the end of Kate's training. Jay and Simon, both of them naked, were kneeling submissively beneath the two women as they conversed. 'If you had to summarise the essence of BDSM in a single word, what would it be?'

Without hesitation, Kate, the star pupil, replied, 'Trust.'

'That's exactly right,' Chloe said. 'It's about trust at so many different levels. That's something people in the vanilla world seldom seem able to understand.'

Chapter Three

Jay reflected on that conversation as he lay blindfolded and gagged in his bondage, awaiting Kate's return to the bedroom. In theory she could decide not to come back, leave him there to die. In reality there wasn't the remotest chance of that happening. Jay knew that for an absolute certainty. It was all about trust, simple as that. Chloe had been so right.

He went back to his memories, bringing to mind one of the occasions Kate and he had spent in Chloe and Simon's dungeon. Jay could see it all again as clearly as a film. It was an occasion that had brought him even closer to his good friend, Simon ...

Kate and Chloe were both dressed in figure-hugging black leather catsuits and long boots with very high heels. Their shapely forms were perfectly outlined by the tight catsuits, which were like second skins.

Jay was on his feet, naked, erect, and in bondage. He was secured by the wrists to the red leather manacles at either end of one of the metal spreader bars that hung by chains from the dungeon ceiling. This particular spreader bar actually had not one but two manacle attachments at either end of it so Jay had a feeling Simon might well be joining him where he was before too long. The thought of it made his heart beat faster and his erection throb.

Simon, who was also naked and erect, was kneeling at Chloe's feet. They both watched as Kate picked out a heavy leather flogger from the rack of disciplinary implements. She swung it against Jay's backside with a couple of hefty cracks in quick succession. Jay flinched from the strength of the blows and the pain bloomed.

Kate swung the flogger across with another resounding crack, its impact so harsh this time that it made Jay sob with pain. She waited a moment and then cracked the implement harshly against his backside again. Jay trembled under the force of the blow and let out another sob.

Kate handed the flogger to Chloe, who told Simon to stand up. She led him over to the horse, positioning him on his front lengthwise over it. The blonde dominatrix immediately set to work with the flogger on Simon's backside. She cracked it against his backside, making him gasp with pain. Immediately afterwards she aimed the flogger at Simon's rear again, marking the flesh with ruthless accuracy and causing him to cough back a sob of pain.

Chloe struck him again, the thongs of the flogger landing harshly against his rear cheeks and creating another reddened pattern of pain. She followed that with another even harsher strike that caused Simon to squeal in agony in response. Chloe continued to beat Simon with the flogger remorselessly, not stopping until his backside was covered with angry welts and he was crying out constantly in pain.

Kate then came over to join Chloe and the pair of them marched Simon away from the horse and toward Jay, who remained manacled to the spreader bar that hung by chains from the dungeon ceiling. They used the other two red leather manacle attachments to cuff Simon's wrists to either end of the same spreader bar. Both slaves remained stiffly erect and their hard cocks were now rubbing together excitingly. Chloe blindfolded Simon with a soft black leather blindfold and gagged him with a red ball-gag, and Kate did exactly the same thing to Jay.

The two dominatrices pushed the naked men right against each other in their bonds, in the process pinning their erections even closer together as well. They went on to cuff the men's ankles to the end of a wooden hobble bar, which also had two red leather manacle attachments at either end of it.

Chloe then took hold of a couple of leather-covered swagger canes, handing one of them to Kate. 'Let's do what we agreed earlier and cane each other's slave in turn,' she said. 'I'll go first if that's all right with you.'

'Sure,' Kate agreed.

Chloe gave a practice swipe with her swagger cane while Jay waited, his heart pounding with excitement, his erection pulsing against Simon's throbbing shaft.

Then it began. Chloe sliced the heavy cane through the air and it cracked hard across Jay's backside. It hurt like hell, a flash of pure pain that caused him to inhale sharply.

She brought the swagger cane across a second time and there was that flash of pain again as the burning line of the implement warmed his flesh. Then across came the cane once more, slicing against the cheeks of his backside with another punishing sting that made him draw a further startled breath.

The fourth stroke swept through the air, cracking hard against Jay's rear before he'd had time to recover. Strike five came across even more swiftly, harsher and sharper still.

The sixth stroke bit hardest of all, a flash of pure agony. Chloe stopped then and the pain Jay was suffering started to dissolve, becoming a suffuse red heat that connected with the hardness of his cock as it throbbed excitingly against Simon's pulsing erection.

'You cane my slave now, Kate,' Chloe said and it was Simon's turn for a beating. Kate's swagger cane swished across and the fire followed an instant later. It happened a second time, a third, a fourth, a fifth, and a sixth.

It was Jay's turn once more then, the blows landing agonizingly across the earlier strokes. Each time Chloe caned him he bucked against Simon. Then it was Simon's turn to be caned by Kate again, then Jay's turn to be caned by Chloe once more. Finally, Kate and Chloe began to cane them both together. On and on the two women caned each other's slave, one vicious swipe of their swagger canes after another, until excruciating pain burned into their flesh like twin flames.

Then pain suddenly turned to pure lust, throbbing and hot. Jay and Simon's nerves were on fire, every cell in their bodies on red alert. The heat of desire swept through their bodies and blood pulsed in their aching erections, precipitating them both to orgasm. Their shafts pumped thick waves of come over their torsos, pressed so closely together, as they writhed and thrashed helplessly in their bondage with each new spasm.

Chapter Four

Spool forward five years from that thrilling encounter. Kate and Jay found they needed to seriously consider moving out of their apartment into something bigger. Both their careers had been progressing well and their incomes were relatively good. So, within reason, money was not a problem. Space was the problem. They either had to move or they had to carry out a ruthless cull of their, by that stage, very substantial collection of BDSM gear. No contest. Except that finding a house in which they actually wanted to live proved easier said than done. All the properties they looked at were wrong in one way or another: too small, too big, too expensive, or too threadbare. The couple were on the point of giving up the hunt when their luck suddenly turned and they came across a property that was a real find.

The house, which originally dated back to the latter part of the 19th century, stood in a tree-shaded street in one of the more cosmopolitan parts of town. The house was set back behind cast-iron railings and its solid front door was approached by wide stone steps. It was self-contained and spacious, with tall, arched windows. Inside there were high ceilings and good-sized, well-proportioned rooms. The garden at the rear wasn't large but it was a tranquil place, very secluded too.

All in all, the property was ideal for the couple and as its asking price was within their budget, they had no hesitation in snapping it up. There was so much about the house that Kate and Jay loved: the wonderfully natural flow to its layout; the graceful winding staircase; the kitchen which was so cheerful and welcoming. Oh, and the large basement. Now, what on earth could a kinky couple like them possibly do with that?

Kate and Jay had played very many times in Chloe and Simon's dungeon by then and found it wonderful to think that they would soon be able to reciprocate. But first things first. They had to create their own dungeon, which would be no mean feat if they were to make a good job of it. And Kate, for one, was determined to make an *excellent* job of it.

Jay's work had become off-the-chart demanding by that stage and he was quite stressed out, the cracks beginning to show in his workaday veneer even then if the couple had but known it. So Kate decided it would be best to leave him out of this particular equation and made the creation of a dungeon her own personal project.

She had the basement fitted out with all they would need for their BDSM games. For this she employed the same specialist firm that had helped create Chloe and Simon's dungeon. The work Kate had carried out included the installation of various pieces of dungeon equipment, much of which was made of or partially covered in soft black leather, like the horse, the horizontal torture chair, the whipping bench, the bondage table, and the St Andrew's cross. Several sets of chains hung from the ceiling. A pair of these had black leather manacles attached to them. Another pair had a metal spreader bar attached, which also had black leather manacle attachments at either end.

Kate had an open cabinet of dark wood fitted against one of the walls. Upon the polished wood she hung her large collection of disciplinary instruments. They ranged from simple straps to tawses, crops, whips, paddles, canes, gags, chains, handcuffs, and a variety of clamps.

As soon as the dungeon was ready to be put into use for the first time Kate and Jay marked the occasion by inviting Chloe and Simon to join them there ...

Jay and Simon, both entirely naked, were standing side by side in the middle of the dungeon. Their heads were bowed submissively, their cocks raised. Kate and Chloe were standing together next to them. Both women were wearing knee-length boots of shiny black leather with sharp stiletto heels but were otherwise semi-nude. Kate was naked apart from a tight black leather corset that cinched her waist and pushed her bare breasts up enticingly, and Chloe was wearing only a black leather bra that left her shapely breasts entirely exposed, merely framing them.

'Want to help me make this special occasion truly memorable?' Kate gave her friend an enquiring look.

'I'd really love to,' Chloe replied. 'What do you have in mind?'

'Think of something you've never done to my slave but would like to do.'

Chloe ran a hand through her short blonde hair as she reflected. 'Well, now you mention it, I have to admit that I'd rather like to ...'

Kate interrupted. 'No, don't tell me.'

'OK.'

'There's something I'd like to do to your slave, which I'll also keep to myself,' Kate said.

'So far so mysterious,' Chloe responded with a sardonic smile. 'Now what?'

'Now we swap slaves,' Kate said. 'We then torment, discipline and generally do whatever we like to them – culminating in something we've *never* done to them before but would like to. Are you up for this?'

'I certainly am,' Chloe replied enthusiastically. 'I'm highly intrigued to know what you've always wanted to do to Simon, by the way, so why don't you go first and I can find out.'

'How could I say no to that?' Kate laughed. She then turned to Simon and told him to come with her over to the spreader bar hanging from the ceiling chains. She got him to raise his arms and went on to attach his wrists to the black leather manacles on the ends of the spreader bar. Kate next walked round to position herself behind Simon, her breasts jiggling above her tight corset and her shapely thighs rubbing together as she moved.

'Time for a spanking,' she said gleefully before delivering a harsh spank to both cheeks of Simon's taut, curved backside with the one blow, the echo sounding from the dungeon wall. Her hand landed for a second, third, and fourth time in quick succession, each time jolting him with the force of the blow.

Kate kept on spanking Simon, doing so a dozen more times. Each of her smacks landed like an explosion and steadily accumulated, becoming an angry red heat that suffused his backside.

Next Kate switched to a leather flogger, which she used remorselessly on Simon's already punished rear. He was subjected to the harsh sting of the flogger time and time again as Kate swung it through the air faster and faster. His backside was crimson by the time Kate eventually stopped whipping him.

Kate detached Simon from the spreader bar, telling him to get onto his knees and kneel upright. His erection was pulsing as he did so. He was also breathing fast and trembling noticeably from his beating. 'Suck my nipples,' Kate said, letting Simon admire the swell of her breasts and hard nipples as she spoke.

'Yes, mistress,' Simon replied. He moved his face towards Kate's beautiful breasts, bringing his lips to one of her erect nipples. Kate sighed with arousal when his tongue touched the stiff nub. Simon teased the tip of her nipple at first with his tongue and then began to suck gently at it, making Kate moan with pleasure.

She pushed Simon's face away from her breast but only so that she could present her other one to his lips. Simon fell hungrily onto her nipple and began suckling it. Kate purred with pleasure, savouring every delicious sensation. Then she gripped Simon's hair and pulled lightly, pushing his head down and parting her quivering thighs. 'Now lick me to orgasm,' she told him.

'Yes, mistress,' Simon answered, and buried his face in Kate's sex, which was wet with passion. He snaked out his tongue and began moving it around her clitoris, licking it and licking it. Kate opened her thighs a little more to let his tongue enter her sex more fully. Simon sucked Kate's juices, plunging his sinuous tongue into her pussy. She let out a low moan of release as he brought her cresting to a climax.

Kate allowed herself a few moments to compose herself before leading Simon over to the horizontal torture chair and telling him to get onto it flat on his back. She buckled his wrists behind his head, his knees right up and his legs wide apart. Her hands began stroking Simon's muscular thighs and the mounds of his backside. She traced a finger against the rosebud opening of his anus, subjecting it to her tantalizing caress.

Then Kate removed her finger from the entrance to Simon's anal hole and put on a strap-on dildo, which she coated liberally with lubricant. She pushed it against the opening of his anus and eased it in skilfully, going deep into his rear. Simon let out a groan of anguished delight and his hard cock spurted out a throb of precome as his sphincter tightened and relaxed around the dildo. Kate began to fuck him hard, her hands gripped tight on his hips as she plunged into the depths of his anal hole. Simon moaned with pleasure at the brutal thrill of her penetration.

Kate's rhythm was fast and strong, each thrust going deeper into Simon's anus, penetrating him further. As she built up even greater momentum, really pounding into him, she also started pulling his cock hard, her fist working up and down on it fast.

Simon's body was shaking in its bondage as though electric shocks were coursing through his veins, and he was panting uncontrollably with desire. His wrists and ankles were straining against the leather straps that held them tightly in place, his body bucking as his pleasure mounted ever closer to the point of no return. Then that point arrived and he ejaculated voluminously. The come leapt out of his aching cock in spurts, spilling in pools across his stomach.

'It would appear that the thing you'd never done to Simon but wanted to do today was to fuck him in the arse,' Chloe said as she watched Kate release him from the torture chair. 'I hope you enjoyed it.'

'Oh yes,' Kate confirmed with a throaty laugh. 'Oh *very much* yes. Your turn now.'

'Don't I know it,' Chloe replied, a flash of fire in her eyes. 'I can't *wait* to get at Jay.'

'Have yourself a ball,' said Kate magnanimously as she unbuckled her strap-on.

Chloe told Jay to follow her. She then strode purposefully across the dungeon with him in tow. Chloe ordered Jay to stop when they'd arrived at the two chains that hung from the ceiling. She told him to raise his arms, and attached his wrists to the black leather manacles at either end of the two chains. Chloe next picked out a red leather paddle from the rack of disciplinary implements, positioned herself behind Jay and raised the paddle. She swung it across against Jay's backside with a heavy thud, the action forcing a winded sigh from him.

Chloe landed another blow to Jay's rear cheeks, and another and another. She struck him a dozen times in all and when she'd finished, his backside was painfully red. But its glowing heat was fuelling his sexual excitement, which was all too evident. His erection, already rock-hard, had begun to pulse.

The dominatrix put the paddle to one side and reached for Jay's backside, gently caressing its reddened curves. She then stepped away from him again, this time picking out a rattan cane from the rack of disciplinary implements.

Chloe stood behind Jay again and took aim. 'I'll give you a dozen strokes with this as well,' she said and brought the thin length of rattan sharply against his backside. Jay grunted and she brought the cane against his rear again. Chloe brought the cane against Jay's backside once more and he grunted again, his entire posture becoming rigid. And so it went on.

The dominatrix paused when she'd delivered 11 strokes and Jay tried to brace himself as he waited for the inevitable impact of her final blow. Chloe raised the rattan cane and then threw it against the striped flesh of his backside. When the blow came Jay's throbbing erection let out a squirt of precome and his backside began quivering uncontrollably as though he was on the point of ecstatic release – which he almost was.

Chloe then detached Jay from the chains and told him to kneel behind her. When he had done this she parted her thighs and pushed her backside towards Jay's face. 'I want you to lick my arsehole,' she said.

'Yes, mistress,' Jay replied. He opened his lips slightly, pressed them to Chloe's clean, pink anus and began to lick it. Then he pushed his tongue deeper inside her anal hole. He licked her slowly at first, flicking his tongue gently. Gradually he started licking her anus faster and faster, and as he did so Chloe began to masturbate.

The sound of her fingers working at herself filled Jay's ears, intensifying his arousal still further. The taste of Chloe's smooth anus and the squelching sound of her fingers working away at her sex filled Jay with desire. Chloe herself became orgasmic. She moaned and her body spasmed as a climax shuddered through her.

After allowing herself a moment or two to calm down, Chloe led Jay over to the horizontal torture chair where she told him to lie flat on his back. Her fingers working dexterously, she strapped his wrists behind his head and his legs wide apart.

She began to masturbate him, pulling on the length of his stiffness as it throbbed and flexed in her hand. She smeared her fingers with the tears that were crying from its tip as she pulled and stroked his shaft.

Next Chloe leant forward so that she could suck Jay's cock. She rounded her lips and closed them around his hardness, taking it into her mouth, pressing against its head with her tongue. She pushed herself further forward so that she could pull more of his length into her mouth. The up-and-down movement of her head went ever faster as she sucked his cock harder and harder. Finally Jay climaxed in convulsions, pumping out spurts of creamy come deep into Chloe's throat as she swallowed and swallowed.

When Jay had finished climaxing, his spent shaft still lodged in Chloe's mouth, he looked over at Kate. 'It looks like Chloe'd developed a hankering to suck you off,' she said, smiling wickedly. 'She's now got what she wanted. How do you feel about that, slave? Are you suitably honoured?'

Jay was still panting. 'Yes, mistress, I am,' he said. 'I'm extremely honoured.'

Chapter Five

Spool forward another five years. Jay arrived home one day and found to his initial bemusement that net curtains had appeared at all the windows of the house. He went into the living room to find Kate and ask her for an explanation. She was standing waiting for him – and had taken all her clothes off. 'Like the sight of me naked, slave?' she purred.

'Yes, mistress,' Jay replied, his cock beginning to swell. 'As if you need to ask.'

'Well, the feeling's mutual,' Kate said. 'Strip off too.'

'Yes, mistress,' he gasped and off came his clothes as well.

'I've always liked the look of you naked and have decided I want to see more of you that way,' Kate said, eyeing his now fully erect cock. 'That's the reason for all the net curtains,' she went on. 'From now on, when you are at home with me and I give you the word I want you to get naked and remain that way until I tell you otherwise. Understood, slave?'

'Understood, mistress,' Jay replied excitedly, his shaft beginning to throb.

'Now, do you know what I want?' Kate said, putting his slave's collar round his neck and buckling it into place.

'No, mistress.'

'I want to give you a damn good beating,' she said. 'Get on all fours.' Kate then opened a cupboard drawer and took out a leather whip. With only the most cursory of warm-ups, she went on to whip Jay harshly on the backside, one punishing sting after another. Each of Kate's vicious lashes smarted vividly, imparting a pattern of red lines on his flesh.

'Stand up, slave,' Kate ordered next.

Jay did as he'd been told. He could feel his heart pounding against the inside of his chest and his erection, more ferociously hard than ever, throbbed constantly. The hot pain he was experiencing as a result of the heavy whipping Kate had just given him had become blurred with erotic pleasure, agony and ecstasy combined.

'Go over to the dining table, slave,' Kate said. 'Put your hands on its top and push your backside out.'

Kate went on to beat Jay's rear with the whip again, even more harshly this time. Kate thrashed Jay with ever increasing savagery until his backside was completely covered in angry red lines and the pain he was enduring had become a fury burning agonizingly into his flesh.

Then she abruptly stopped whipping Jay, telling him to turn round and get back onto his knees. When he'd done this she led him crawling over to the couch. She sat down on it before him, lounged back and parted her legs. 'Now bring me off with your tongue, slave,' she ordered, looking at him greedily. And Jay moved to comply. He kissed his way up her thighs before pushing his tongue into her pussy, which was gleaming with juicy wetness.

Jay went on to lick Kate deep and hard, his mouth and tongue working vigorously on her sex, until he brought her to a trembling climax. Kate's whole body rippled with pleasure as she came and she continued to shudder for some while longer as her orgasm subsided.

She then rose gracefully to her feet. 'You've just given me the most wonderful orgasm,' she said, looking down at her kneeling slave. He was still rampantly erect, a rivulet of precome trailing from his pulsing shaft. 'I bet you'd *really* like to come too now, wouldn't you?'

Jay's breathing was laboured, halting, as if there were a valve stopping him from taking a deep breath. 'Yes, mistress,' he gasped, looking up at her with shining eyes. 'I'm desperate to come.'

There was a long silence.

'Well, you can't,' Kate finally said, her voice hard. 'Do you accept that, slave?'

'Yes, mistress,' he replied, 'if that is what you require.'

'It is,' Kate confirmed. 'Do you also accept that you must always be naked around the house when I require it of you?'

'Yes, mistress.'

And he did accept it, he honestly did, all of it. Jay had no hesitation in obeying Kate in anything she told him to do. That had always been the case and as the years had passed by, his total, unquestioning obedience to her had become ever more deeply rooted.

Being already in the nude at home, as he more often than not was from that day on, meant that when he submitted to Kate's discipline, in the living room or the dungeon or the bedroom or wherever else she chose to meet out his punishment, he became even more naked.

It was not just Jay's clothing but all his inhibitions that were stripped away, leaving him exactly where he knew Kate wanted him to be and where, to the depths of his being, he wanted to be himself – powerless and under her complete control.

Chapter Six

The thing to really understand about Jay is that when he was submitting to Kate he wasn't roleplaying in any way. It was the real him, naked and unadorned, so profound was his need to serve and surrender to her. No, his roleplaying all occurred in the vanilla world and that had been the case for almost as long as he could remember.

Jay had always been ambitious, really wanting to make a success of his life, and had realised from an early age that this would inevitably mean putting on an act to some extent. He was by nature shy, introverted, and deeply submissive, aspects of his character that he'd known would get him precisely nowhere if he wanted to get on in the world of work. So he'd hidden these traits underneath the persona of being the strong, silent type.

An act on Jay's part it may have been, but it had proved to be a very effective one. His silence had given him a quiet air of authority as he'd used other elements of his personality – a genuinely creative intelligence, a real ability to focus and not get side-tracked, resolute determination, shrewdness and empathy – to make a successful business career for himself.

The trouble was that the further up the greasy pole he climbed – the more high-powered his work became, the more he was looked upon to take the lead, the more he found himself controlling the fate of other people – the more stressful he found it and the less he liked it.

Jay could do it, sure, and do it well. It wasn't exactly

rocket science when all was said and done. But the fact was that, deep down, being in a position of authority or leadership just wasn't him. He wasn't comfortable with it at all.

The reverse was true of Kate, to whom the exercise of power had always come as second nature. Being a dominatrix outside of work made it that much easier. She dealt with colleagues in a cool, calm and collected way, employing essentially the same firm authority she used with Jay. Kate was polite at work but very much in charge.

Also, when it was appropriate to get really tough she could be as hard as nails. Kate got the reputation of being someone who was eminently reasonable but whom it was wise not to cross. Because she was a dominatrix in her private life – her *very* private life – it gave her yet more confidence, an innate self-esteem that helped her take control of even the most difficult situations at work and stay firmly in control.

In a highly competitive business environment, this gave her an extra edge, one that she was able to use to considerable effect. She achieved more and more of her career ambitions as she started to fully realise the potential of her inherent power.

BDSM served different purposes for Kate than Jay when it came to the workplace. Knowing he had that other life helped keep Jay sane as he struggled to survive in the rat-race world of commerce and hold on to the position of seniority he had achieved through his own blood, sweat, and tears.

In the case of Kate, BDSM helped her to not just survive but thrive in that same commercial world, her work persona being a natural extension of the powerful dominatrix she was in her private life. She was just as intelligent and able as Jay, more so if anything. And it was not too long before her career advancement outstretched his own – not that he minded. He couldn't have been happier for Kate or more proud of her.

Kate gave Jay what he wanted of her, that was the main thing from his perspective. And what he wanted from Kate was to be told what to do – told to walk around the house naked, told to have an orgasm or not to have an orgasm entirely as she saw fit, told to go to the dungeon to be severely disciplined, told to submit to Chloe's discipline if that was what Kate required of him, told to do whatever the hell Kate wanted him to do.

That was Jay's idea of freedom – the freedom of submission. This was because, freeing him of any feelings of guilt and shame about his deviant sexuality, it enabled him to be completely uninhibited. Because Kate didn't allow Jay to think when she was dominating him, his erotic imagination was free to go to whatever places *she* chose to take it. He had no choice but to obey her. He was not responsible for his sexuality because he had given over its control to Kate, lock, stock and barrel.

And she loved to exercise that control, revelled in it ...

Jay stood naked with his arms upraised, his wrists manacled tightly to the black leather cuffs at either end of two of the chains that hung from the dungeon ceiling. His ankles were secured in a similar manner to either end of a wooden hobble bar. He was blindfolded, gagged with a black ball-gag, and a metal cock ring encircled the base of his erection. Kate took hold of a set of clover clamps and attached these to his nipples. Jay shuddered with pain as the clamps bit into his chest.

Kate then pulled on his nipple clamps, at the same time spanking his cockhead with the leather tip of a riding crop. This twin assault caused searing pain to burn through Jay's body as he jumped and bucked within the confines of his bonds.

'Now for that cock-shaped black dildo I like to bugger you with,' Kate told her blindfolded slave. 'I'm holding it

270

in my hand and am just coating it with lubricant.' Kate then slid the dildo slowly into Jay. Its length slipped ever closer to the depths of his anus, accentuating his arousal with each further inch of its penetration. Having started slowly, Kate went on to bugger him hard with the dildo, thrusting it vigorously in and out. While continuing to do that, she went to the side of Jay and reached for his erection. 'You are not to come unless I give you my permission, slave,' she told him.

Kate began masturbating Jay hard, exciting him more and more until, with that and the vigorous buggering she was still giving him with the dildo, he just knew he was going to come. But not until he had been allowed to by Kate. Please, please, *please* let her give him permission to climax soon, he silently prayed as he got ever closer to the point of no return.

But still there was no let-up. The harder Kate played with his fiercely erect cock the more energetically she also sodomised him with the dildo. On and on she wanked and buggered Jay until ...

'Come for me now, slave,' Kate demanded and Jay, in a state by then of the most agonized ecstasy, shuddered to a cataclysmic orgasm. Convulsions shook his body and his shaft erupted, pumping out streams of creamy wetness into the air.

Chapter Seven

That was the real Jay – the complete submissive. The fake Jay, the one living a lie, was the one doing battle every working day in the cut-throat world of commerce. It seemed to him to get tougher and crazier and more wearisome all the time and increasingly all he really wanted to do was to be Kate's full-time slave. He longed to surrender his will entirely and be in a state of absolute submission to his wonderful mistress at all times. With each passing year this burning need became ever more intense and undeniable and, seemingly, unachievable.

Jay felt he had to be brutally honest with himself. It was considerably more extreme than most, but when it came down to it wasn't this need he felt little more than yet another middle-aged man's daydream? It was in essence just a fantasy, that was his sombre conclusion. But it was a powerful fantasy nonetheless, one he clung to with increasing desperation as he continued to endure the real bondage and slavery – wage slavery – that was the daily grind of his work life. At home in the dungeon at the mercy of Kate, that was where he really belonged, that was when he really came alive …

Kate and Jay were in the dungeon, he naked, she dressed in seductive fetishwear. Kate had on a leather bra that barely contained her magnificent breasts, a tiny black skirt of see-through material, which did no more than skim her shapely thighs and beneath which she was naked, and high-heeled leather boots that were polished to a fine shine. Jay was strapped face forward to the St Andrew's cross, his wrists and ankles tightly secured to its leather-covered surface.

'I'm going to beat you now, slave, and I'm going to keep on beating you until you come,' Kate announced. She then set to with a leather tawse. The quick-fire snapping sounds as its thongs connected for the first time with his backside echoed through the dungeon. She hit Jay again straight after that, bringing the sturdy leather implement down hard on his flesh and making him grimace with pain.

Kate brought the tawse down a third time onto its target. Strokes four and five landed in quick succession after that, the sharp, percussive sound of heavy leather thongs snapping against Jay's reddened backside filling the dungeon.

On and remorselessly on Kate beat Jay, his agonized face turned to the wall as he suffered each savage stroke of her punishment. He winced in anguish, his expression shielded from her view.

After numerous vicious strokes, all of them delivered with deadly precision, Kate paused to caress Jay's backside, to feel the burning heat of his flesh. He turned to her briefly at that point, a pleading look in his eyes.

But Kate knew better than to take any notice of that look. She did not stop beating him. She did not reduce the momentum of her beating either. But Jay didn't care any more because everything now was different, the livid pain he'd been experiencing having morphed into pure pleasure. He started moving with her rhythm, lifting himself in his bonds, pushing his rear back to meet each stroke. He was accepting his chastisement with delight as its ecstatic heat began to radiate through his being.

Kate paused to caress Jay's rear again and he pressed it back against her softly stroking fingers, sighing with pleasure and anticipation that his punishment would soon – what – be over? No way. He was anticipating that it would soon *recommence*. Kate did not disappoint, suddenly snapping the tawse down extra hard on his punished backside with a brisk, jagged motion. Jay found it exquisitely agonizing.

Kate upped the ante even further, her strokes growing even stronger as she made sure that every inch of Jay's backside was patterned red. Jay was ready to burst, nearly ready to come. His whole body was shaking in his bonds.

And then Jay did come – massively. A sharp tremor spasmed right through him and he reached the peak of erotic delight, come bursting out of his shaft in an abundant spray. Jay may have been in bondage, securely strapped as he was to the St Andrew's cross. But at that moment he felt so free, so joyously, wonderfully free.

Chapter Eight

They say that into every life a little rain must fall but for Kate and Jay there was a period in their lives when the downpour was nothing less than torrential. It all started when they received the devastating news that Chloe and Simon were dead. Jesus Christ, *dead*. They had been killed outright in a motorway pile-up caused by a container lorry that had jack-knifed out of control.

The passing away of their dear friends, the reality of them not being in the world any more, affected Kate and Jay deeply. They were wracked with sadness, absolutely bereft. The couple had always seemed ageless to them, as if they weren't ever going to grow old, never mind die. But die they had.

Within a few months Jay came perilously close to joining them. It was a life-threatening illness, a serious blood disease caused by a viral infection attacking an immune system weakened by years of relentless work pressure. It was dreadful for Jay. But, he realised afterwards, it had been much worse for Kate. After all, he had been blissfully unaware of his blackout, of the rush by ambulance to get him to hospital, of his time in the intensive care unit as the doctors struggled to save his life, of just how close he had come to shuffling off this mortal coil. He had no memories of the first few weeks of his illness. He was not to learn until later how far he had travelled into darkness, how nearly he had died.

He drifted out of his coma from time to time sufficient

to hear occasional sounds. He heard voices, calm and medical. He heard Kate's voice, full of compassionate concern. He thought he heard the voices of Chloe and Simon once but plainly he was hallucinating. The voices came and went. The days and nights passed by. When he finally came round the first person he saw was Kate. She smiled softly at him, her beautiful violet eyes aglow with happiness and relief, gratitude and love.

It took months for Jay to recuperate and he found the process tough and exhausting. But it did get steadily easier as time went on and he positively enjoyed the later stages. Apart from anything else, Kate and he were at long last able to resume their sex life and that represented a huge step forward …

'We'll start with a spanking,' Kate said, the words made husky by her arousal. It had been such a long time since they'd had kinky sex – since they'd had *any* kind of sex. The two of them had just taken all their clothes off and were sitting together side by side on the edge of the bed. Jay already had a powerful erection. Kate took him firmly by the hands and pulled him across her lap.

'Do you want me to start gently, slave?' she asked, erring on the side of caution under the circumstances. He felt her hand glide against his backside. 'Or do you want it hard? Just tell me what you want and I'll do it'

Jay drew a shivery breath. 'I'd like it hard, mistress,' he replied.

Kate didn't need telling twice – and hard was exactly what he got. Jay cried out when the first stinging blow came down, the flat of Kate's hand slapping firmly down on his rear cheeks. It was an explosion of pain, a raw, livid sensation that turned his skin red. Then the second stroke came down and it was as sharp as the first, the sound reverberating around the bedroom. Kate spanked Jay three more times in quick succession. The pain escalated with each blow, a fire building on his flesh.

Kate stopped briefly. She reached for Jay's backside, gently caressing its reddened curves. 'Do you want me to ease off now or to carry on spanking you hard?' she asked. 'I'll do whatever you say.'

'Hard, mistress,' Jay gasped. His reply was music to Kate's ears and, again, hard is precisely what he got. Kate cracked her hand down onto Jay's backside vigorously, following one smack after another in swift succession. The pain burned hotly on Jay's rear cheeks, sinking ever deeper. But with the pain came that old familiar pleasure and throughout the beating Jay could feel its heat build up in his shaft, which rubbed excitingly against Kate's naked thighs.

'Do you want me to stop now, slave?' Kate asked, reaching towards his reddened cheeks again and stroking the burning flesh. 'Or do you want more? Again, it's entirely up to you.'

'More, please, mistress,' Jay panted, and more was what he got.

He arched his back, lifting himself, offering the punished cheeks of his backside to Kate's fiery strokes. The pain was intense. So was the pleasure. He was rock hard, dribbles of precome leaking from his cockhead and smearing Kate's naked thighs. His erection throbbed with pleasure as he lifted himself so that Kate's slaps landed even harder on his flesh.

At last the thrashing stopped and Jay twisted round to see the curves of his cruelly spanked backside. They were dark red, the imprint of Kate's fingers on his flesh merging into a deep flush of pain. Kate ran her hand once more over the soreness of Jay's rear, feeling the burning heat that she had inflicted on his skin. 'Do you want me to leave it at that heavy spanking, slave, or do you want me to carry on chastising you, this time with a cane?' she asked. 'Again, it's entirely up to you.'

'Cane me please, mistress,' Jay gasped.

'Are you sure?' Kate asked, still stroking his punished rear. 'I warn you – it will hurt like fuck.'

'I'm sure, mistress,' he replied, breathing hard.

'One hundred per cent sure?' Kate persisted. The cheeks of Jay's backside tensed as she continued to stroke his punished globes.

'Yes, mistress,' he gasped. 'It's what I want, what I need.'

'Your decision – I did warn you,' Kate said, pushing Jay off her lap. 'Bend over the edge of the bed,' she added sharply, getting to her feet.

Jay was soon in position, breathing even more heavily. He closed his eyes and awaited the inevitable. And then it came. The smooth length of rattan whistled as it sliced through the air in a swift trajectory. Jay's eyes flew open and he cried out as the cane connected with his rear, striking a line of fire across its cheeks.

He let out another cry of pain as Kate brought the thin cutting implement down again, further inflaming his backside as it bit into his flesh. Then she sliced the cane through the air a third time and a further red-hot strike landed across Jay's rear cheeks. It was followed by another harsh stroke, and then another.

Kate began to beat Jay with even greater ferocity, slicing more and more red heat through his body. The cane struck his backside in a regular harsh rhythm, and each time it cracked against his skin it planted another line of fire on his flesh. Jay responded to each sharp strike with a cry of pain - and pleasure. A red heat seemed to be burning into his skin, sinking deeper and deeper.

Kate started to strike more quickly, inflicting even more excruciating pain on him, which brought with it even more intoxicating pleasure too, and Jay's cries came faster and faster. Shudders of pleasure-pain ran through his body and he could feel the heat blazing on the cheeks of his backside, the skin raised and imprinted with the pattern of the cane.

Jay lost count of the number of times Kate used the rattan cane on him, but when the beating was finally over and he was allowed to stand up, his flesh was quivering and burning with both great pain and great pleasure.

And that punishment had left Jay – and Kate – feeling horny beyond belief, the heat of desire sweeping through their bodies. The couple fell onto the bed and began to make love deliriously, and their lovemaking went on and on. Jay carried on thrusting in and out of Kate's sex for ages, his skin marked deeply by the heavy chastisement she had inflicted on him. His hard cock pressed into her over and over, the sensations exquisite, racking his body with spasms of erotic delight.

The pain Jay was still suffering as a result of his earlier beatings made his epic sex session with Kate infinitely more intense. He felt insatiable, wanting the waves of ecstasy to go on and on until he could do no more.

Jay, it was clear, was *definitely* on the mend from that serious illness of his. Hell, the man was as near as damn it fully recovered.

Chapter Nine

Unfortunately for Jay, being as near as damn it fully recovered – in body, if not in spirit, truth be told – meant that the so-called real world beckoned once more. He had no alternative but to bite the bullet and go back to work, back to join the senior ranks of the anonymous, soulless organisation that paid his salary. Unsurprisingly, the only contact his employers had made with him during the period of his near-fatal illness and subsequent convalescence had been cursory and formal.

It was with a heavy heart that Jay returned to the endless days on the treadmill, the interminable meetings, the never-ending influx of emails, the tedious office politics – all that jostling for position and back-biting and false bonhomie. And the pressure; that was the worst part, the constant pressure – not to stay ahead of the game like it used to be for him in the exciting early years of his career; no, nowadays it was just to keep up. That pressure was so unrelenting that in the end it became virtually all-consuming. It was true that he was well paid by his company but, my God, it certainly wanted its pound of flesh in return.

The weeks and months trudged by on leaden feet until one fine day – one very fine day – Jay got the news for which he'd silently prayed for years. He was informed by the company's stuffed shirt of an MD that his face didn't fit in the organisation any more and he would be subject to forced redundancy. With the offer of a very attractive package to go quietly - one, he realised, that would allow him financial freedom for the foreseeable future - he was asked to clear his desk and vacate the building immediately. Jay was undeniably shocked but not at all unhappy. In fact, you couldn't have seen him for dust. He'd done his time and managed to survive to tell the tale.

'So where do we go from here?' Jay asked Kate, that evening. He was elated but still demonstrably in shock.

'There's an easy answer to that question,' she replied.

'Really?'

'Yes,' Kate said. 'We go on vacation. Listen, Jay, in the recent past our two oldest and closest friends have been killed, and you've been so seriously ill that you were literally at death's door yourself. Now you've been made redundant. I think those are enough traumas to be going on with, don't you? If ever two people needed a vacation, it's you and me. Agreed?'

He agreed, but then Jay always agreed with Kate.

Chapter Ten

The remote and sparsely populated Greek island Kate and Jay chose for that desperately needed vacation was a favourite with discerning nudists during the holiday season. This was not yet the holiday season and it was almost empty, virtually deserted. Fortunately, the weather was sunny when they arrived and it stayed that way. The villa they'd rented stood right on the most westerly edge of the island. Tall and square with bright white walls, green shutters, and a red tiled roof, it sparkled magnificently on rocks strewn with wild flowers above the clear blue waters of the ocean.

The tiny island seemed to Kate and Jay to be a magical place. It had an atmosphere of tranquillity about it that subtly worked its way under the skin. Each day in its blissful, healing surroundings had a timeless quality about it that made them wish it would go on for ever. But when it did finally end and another fresh new day dawned the couple greeted it with an even more wonderful feeling of exhilaration, knowing the peaceful joys it held in store for them.

Another glorious day was drawing to a close. Kate and Jay were strolling hand in hand along the empty sugar-soft beach, the early evening sunshine washing over their naked bodies. They had their feet in the water and could hear the rhythmic sound of its gentle waves slapping the shore beside them. The sky was a deep blue without cloud and there was a slight breeze that caressed their flesh and made the expanse of ocean by their side billow like heavy silk.

Kate's judgement had been spot-on about going away on this vacation, Jay reflected. The loss of his job, while hugely welcome, had also been a traumatic experience for him. Its very suddenness had been brutal and, coming on top of all the other traumas he'd endured recently, could very easily have proved to be the last straw for him. This wonderful holiday had done the trick, though. The shock that had kept him in a punch drunk, almost trancelike state since his dismissal from his job had disappeared day by day as the island had worked its intoxicating magic on him.

It had worked its magic on Kate too. Jay didn't think he'd ever seen her look so lovely. Her body was perfectly tanned all over, her shapely breasts and thighs a honeyed brown. She looked like a goddess. She was *his* goddess.

It would be over soon, Jay reminded himself, this short time in paradise. Then what? Perhaps the island would give him a clue. It was an idyllic retreat from the outside world, a place of refuge from the rat-race existence he had grown increasingly to deplore over recent years and had only just escaped. The misery he had endured at work of late only became fully defined when he knew he wouldn't be returning; when he no longer had to condition himself to the idea that he would probably have to continue in that same stifling world until retirement. His generous redundancy package meant that he never need work again if he didn't want to. And he really didn't want to. He had grown to detest his work life even more than he had realised at the time, his hatred of it only crystallizing fully in retrospect.

This wonderful island represented the fact that there was a real alternative to such an existence, a place – not physical but spiritual – for Kate and him to start to build a different and better way of life, one where they could change and develop, where they could fully become their true selves. Life was so short. His recent brush with death had brought that message home to Jay with crystal clarity. It had made him realise just how tenuous his own existence was. He had become acutely aware of the preciousness of time and of his own mortality.

If he didn't do what he needed to do, his life would be over before he knew it. He had nearly died earlier this year. He could die tomorrow. Kate could die tomorrow, God forbid. Just think of Chloe and Simon, their lives snuffed out in such a violent way. You could not legislate for these things, it was all so random. How brittle our lives are, Jay reflected, every day of them, every moment. What was the answer? Surely it was to be bold and live one's dreams in their fullest form if one possibly could, no matter how unconventional, how extreme that form may be. Suddenly his mind became peculiarly clear.

The sun had started to go down and a soft pink glow suffused the blue of the sky. 'This wonderful vacation's nearly over,' Kate said, her own thoughts clearly not a million miles away from those of her devoted partner. 'As you asked a fortnight ago, where do we go from here?'

'I'd like to be your full-time slave,' Jay replied without hesitation, the words just tumbling out. 'It's what I've always wanted deep down and I think you have too. Why don't we go for broke with it now, what do you say?'

'What do I say?' Kate replied, her voice suddenly very commanding. 'What I say is this. Get onto your knees.' Jay instantly obeyed, kneeling down in the lapping water that edged the beach, cock beginning to stiffen. 'I want you there on your knees, slave, because as your mistress I am above you in every way and your true position is kneeling at my feet, your only function to serve, obey and please me. The number one rule, the one that you must *never* lose sight of from this moment on, is that my pleasure is everything and you are there *solely* for my pleasure. Do you understand, slave?'

'Yes, mistress.' Jay replied, his eyes shining with joy and exaltation. The power of the magnificent goddess standing above him filled him with rapturous wonder. He felt so privileged, so deeply honoured that she had agreed to his request. He was only too willing to be at her beck and call night and day, to exist only for her pleasure, his body and mind effectively her property. His place truly was on his knees before his mistress. Jay had always worshipped Kate, right from when they'd first met. He was filled with happiness at the prospect of being in total submission to her at all times from this moment on.

The sun had gone down now but it was not yet dark. The blue sky tinged with pink covered the beautiful nude dominatrix and the naked slave kneeling in the shimmering water at her feet with a tender, incandescent light.

Chapter Eleven

The night was beautifully tranquil and quiet, the noise of the waves on the shoreline languorous. Kate was on her feet and Jay was kneeling submissively beneath her as before, but this time they were in their bedroom. Both of them were naked, their tanned skin gleaming in the soft light of the bedside lamp.

'Worship my feet, slave,' Kate said.

Jay felt his heart beating faster. 'Yes, mistress,' he said before leaning forward, bringing his mouth to Kate's right foot and pressing his lips against it. He moved his lips against each one of Kate's toes, first those of her right foot, then those of her left.

'Now do it again,' Kate demanded.

'Yes, mistress,' Jay replied and got on with kissing all Kate's toes once more, raising and lowering his head each time.

When he'd pressed his lips against the tenth of Kate's toes, she told him to stand up. As he did so she picked up a black leather paddle. 'Turn towards the bed, slave,' she ordered, gesturing with the implement. 'Lean over it with your arms in front of you, hands resting on the bed.'

Jay's heart pounded even harder. 'Yes, mistress,' he said, getting into position and also spreading his thighs.

'I'm going to beat your rear two dozen times with this paddle,' Kate said. 'I want you to count off each strike. Is that clear, slave?'

'Yes, mistress,' Jay answered through quivering lips.

Kate brought her arm down vigorously. *Thwack!* The first ferocious blow brought a blast of searing pain that nearly knocked the stuffing out of Jay.

'One, mistress,' he gasped. *Thwack!* 'Two, mistress,' he panted. *Thwack!* 'Three, mistress.' *Thwack!* And on and on. Kate continued using the paddle on Jay's backside, beating him ever harder until by the 24th and final strike he felt as if his rear was ablaze.

'Now I'm going to use the kooboo cane on you, slave,' Kate announced, remaining behind him and picking up the straight armed disciplinary implement. 'I will deliver two dozen strokes as before but this time I do not want you to count them out. Instead I require *complete* silence from you until I've finished beating you. Do you understand?' Jay nodded that he did, his eyes starting to brim with tears of both pain and fear.

Kate bent the kooboo cane slightly and gave it a couple of practice strokes through the air. Then she raised it and threw a sharp blow at Jay's backside: *Swish-crack!* Jay's posture stiffened and then dissolved as he suffered the sharp sting of that first stroke of the cane. *Swish-crack!* The second stroke was even more painful and he flinched from the strength of the blow. For a long time the bedroom resonated with the swish and crack of rattan against flesh. Kate caned Jay's backside with remorselessly fierce strokes until its scorched cheeks were criss-crossed with clear stripes. But he gritted his teeth and took his punishment, uttering not a single sound throughout the duration of those two dozen agonizing strikes.

When she'd completed them Kate put the kooboo cane to one side. 'Come and join me, slave,' she demanded as she got onto the bed.

'Yes, mistress,' Jay said, and lay down beside her on his back.

'I want to fuck you,' Kate then announced, straddling his thighs and pressing the head of his shaft against her

287

slippery sex. 'Put your cock inside me.' And he did, pushing up into her dripping wet pussy. Kate took over from there, moving up and down on top of Jay with a rhythm that made them both delirious as their pleasure escalated ever higher. The couple's excitement grew and grew until they climaxed together lavishly, both of them shuddering without control as they achieved that beautiful, perfect oblivion.

After the shuddering had finally subsided they lay together in one another's arms in the afterglow. Kate pulled Jay a little closer to her and stroked his hair. 'Are you sure you want to be my full-time slave, Jay?' she asked. 'I know what I said earlier but actually it's not too late to change your mind. I wouldn't hold it against you in any way if you did.'

'I'm absolutely positive that I want to be your full-time slave, mistress,' Jay said. 'There's no doubt in my mind whatsoever.'

'So be it, slave,' Kate replied softly. 'So be it.'

Chapter Twelve

Kate and Jay were both well aware that the decision they'd made on that idyllic Greek island represented a quantum leap for them and they went into their radical new way of life with their eyes wide open. They were highly experienced BDSM players by that time, of course, and over the years had pushed the boundaries of the way they lived their lives much further than most people in the fetish world would have dared to do. But, even so, before that decision, Kate's domination of Jay had been primarily about sex. That remained at the heart of it, it's true, but it had now become something much more encompassing. It had become a full lifestyle relationship, a complete way of life.

Kate wasted no time in firmly grasping the reins. She started by taking control of all their assets and not allowing Jay any money or credit cards. He soon had very little clothing either, since she disposed of most of it, now requiring him to be naked when he was in the house, not just most of the time but as near as makes no difference *all* the time. Kate liked her collection of leather footwear to be immaculate and she imposed a strict regime of shoe and boot maintenance on Jay. In addition, he was expected to keep the dungeon scrupulously clean and tidy at all times.

But all that was just for starters. Kate went on to require Jay to do all household chores, including the cooking, washing-up, cleaning, laundry, and ironing. As well as cooking for her and doing all the domestic and other menial work around the property Jay was expected to cater to Kate's personal needs. She made him take lessons in massage, skincare, and nouvelle cuisine cooking, all to make his personal services better and more to her liking. Once Jay was up to the high standard Kate required, she arranged for him to do her nails, hair, and make-up before she went off to work each morning and serve her with cordon bleu food and fine wine when she returned in the evening.

In what seemed like no time at all Kate was barely lifting a finger around the house. Why should she? She had her very own slave to polish and buff her high-heeled leather boots and shoes, to massage her feet and neck or give her a full body massage, to feed her gourmet food, to keep her house and her dungeon looking perfect and to wait on her smallest whim. Some nights Kate didn't allow Jay to sleep with her. Instead she made him sleep on the leather-covered bondage table in the dungeon. Why did she choose to ban him from her bed from time to time like this? Sheer caprice, that's why. She just felt like it.

Jay led a life now of total submission and obedience to his mistress. This involved regular orgasm denial and a great deal of oral servitude – frequent, lengthy cunnilingus sessions – along with all the domestic and personal services he had to carry out. Kate expected excellence of Jay, having trained him accordingly. His reward was simply this: he got to worship and serve his goddess. It was more than enough. It was all he wanted.

Kate's basic ground rules for their new relationship were very strict. She instructed Jay that he should remain silent all the time in her presence unless she spoke to him and that he should always call her "mistress" when he did address her. He was expected to obey her at all times without question and carry out to the best of his abilities all the tasks she assigned to him. He was not allowed to masturbate or have an orgasm unless she said so, and it was clearly understood that she could punish him exactly as she saw fit.

There was little relaxation to speak of for Jay in his new incarnation. He no longer had to go to work to earn a living and that was a very great relief. But, ironically, his new life was not one of leisure, quite the opposite. It was all about serving his mistress constantly – doing chores for her, looking after her personal needs and her house, tending to her dungeon or spending hours chained and bound there, having to endure being whipped constantly with no sexual contact unless Kate gave her permission. Often that contact would be limited to him servicing her orally for long periods of time. On occasion, as a variation on a theme, she would make him wear a dildo chin-strap so that he could penetrate her sex and lick her anus at the same time.

Kate revelled in all the additional power she now enjoyed. It was the stuff of life to her and she found it extremely arousing to have her every command and lightest wish slavishly obeyed by Jay. Her business career continued to flourish, going from strength to strength. It was not, of course, without its travails and it felt good to her to know that when she got home she could take out all of the latent aggression built up within her by the accumulated frustrations of her day on her very own pain slut.

But how did Jay feel about the rigours of his new life? Didn't he ever want to kick against the traces? No is the honest answer. He felt as if it was what he had been born for. He wished, in fact, that it could have happened sooner. Jay couldn't go back to his old life now; nor did he want to, not one iota. Indeed, he wanted if possible to go even deeper into submission to his adored mistress.

He provided maximum backing to Kate in her alter ego of a successful businesswoman as her star continued to rise in that particular galaxy – and his own star in that same

291

galaxy disappeared for ever. And good riddance to it, as far as he was concerned.

Jay tried to be an excellent slave to Kate in every way: excellent house slave, excellent personal slave and, of course, excellent sex slave …

Kate had recently arrived home from work and had ordered Jay, who was naked as usual, to stand and wait for her in the living room while she took a shower. She had told him that when she came back to the room she intended to use and abuse him for her pleasure. By the time Kate returned to the living room, her luscious body completely nude, Jay was shivering with excitement and his cock was achingly hard. As she undulated seductively towards him he became even more aroused, his erection beginning to pulse.

Kate arrived in front of Jay and the couple stared at each other, erotic excitement sparking between them. 'You're such a good slave,' she said, beginning to caress his chest. Jay said nothing because he had not been invited to. He didn't make a move for the same reason. He simply stood and delighted in his submissiveness to his wonderful mistress as her fingers continued to travel sensuously over the musculature of his chest.

She turned away from him and walked towards the leather couch. Jay watched excitedly as Kate sat down and parted her thighs. 'Come over here and get over my lap, slave,' she demanded, and within moments he was there, his throbbing erection pressed against the warm flesh of her thigh.

Kate raised her hand and began to spank Jay's rear. He managed to muffle his cries of pain as blow after blow fell upon his backside, the sharp slapping sound filling the room with a regular rhythm. Jay took no notice of the number of smacks he received but simply luxuriated in the pleasure-pain of his lengthy spanking. Then the blows stopped as suddenly as they had begun.

'Get back on your knees before me, slave,' Kate ordered and he moved immediately to obey. Sprawling back on the leather couch and opening her thighs further, Kate brought the middle finger of her right hand to her wet pussy. As Jay looked at that finger hovering at the entrance to Kate's humid sex, he could feel his blood begin to run faster and his erect cock pulse even more.

Kate put the finger to use, teasing it against the dewy wetness of her labia and beginning to masturbate languorously. The sight of his mistress and what she was doing to herself right in front of his face, the enticingly musky scent of her sex, was making Jay ever more aroused. He began to breathe very heavily with excitement. He tried to slow down his breathing, which came in hot gasps, but found that he could not do so.

Kate next teased two fingers to either side of her pussy lips and splayed them further apart. She rested her index finger against her clitoris and began moving it in a circular motion, the hooded pearl of pleasure rotating and sliding against her slippery touch. Jay could feel his breath coming faster still. His gaze fixed on Kate's squirming index finger as it rolled against her clit before she plunged it and the middle finger next to it into her wetness.

Jay could see that Kate was dripping wet with arousal. The scent of her sex permeated his nostrils again and his erection pulsed even faster. The squelching sound of Kate's fingers thrusting away into and out of her sex rang in Jay's ears. The wet frantic sound of them and the delicious sight of them, plunging in and out vigorously, obliterated every other thought in his mind.

Kate eventually stopped masturbating, removing her fingers from her soaking vagina. 'Worship my sex with your mouth, slave,' she ordered and Jay applied his tongue to her soaking wet pussy. Kate moaned softly as her pleasure mounted, his face now buried between her thighs, his tongue within her sex.

As Jay continued to worship Kate's sex with his mouth she squirmed over his lips, pressing her quivering thighs against his cheeks. 'Push your tongue in deeper, slave,' she demanded, gripping Jay's hair and pulling him further into herself until he could hardly breathe. Kate's thighs squeezed even tighter around Jay's face and he was almost smothered by her sodden pussy.

Kate released her thighs to allow Jay to breathe. His face was now soaked with her wetness. 'Go in deeper still, slave,' Kate demanded. And Jay did as he'd been told, pushing his tongue even deeper inside her sex.

Gripping his hair tight, Kate pressed herself further on to him, the rich musk of her sex filling his mouth and fuelling his own intense arousal. Finally Jay pressed his tongue as deep into Kate's pussy as it would go. It made her cry out blissfully in orgasmic delight, erotic shivers trembling through her frame. Her climax made Jay's throbbing cock stiffen even more, until he teetered on the edge of ecstasy, his tongue continuing to pleasure her until at last she let go of his hair and told him to stop.

Kate didn't allow Jay to climax himself, though. She left him hanging instead. But that didn't matter to him – it honestly didn't – because he'd served his purpose. All that mattered to Jay was being able to please his mistress and he'd done that. It was enough for him, much more than enough. It was everything.

Chapter Thirteen

There he still lay on his stomach on the bed: blindfolded, gagged and naked apart from his slave's collar and wrist and ankle cuffs, which were secured by chains to the four corners of the bed. Jay continued to wait for Kate to return to the bedroom and was still reflecting on his life and how lucky he'd been.

He felt lucky – indescribably lucky – to have found Kate, the woman he worshipped and adored beyond all measure. She was the love of his life, his reason for being, the centre of his universe. He felt lucky that she and he had discovered the world of BDSM early on in their relationship. He felt lucky that Kate and he had made such a wonderfully close and long-standing friendship in that secret world with the late and always fondly remembered Chloe and Simon.

He felt lucky that Kate and he had found such a beautiful house all those years ago and one that was so well suited to their BDSM lifestyle. It had felt like home as soon as they'd set eyes on it. It still did, and a good thing too, since he now spent nearly all of his days naked within its walls, often within the basement dungeon that Kate had created with such typical flair shortly after they'd bought the place.

He felt incredibly lucky to have survived a life-threatening illness and to still be on the planet. It could so easily not have been the case. It was luck too, nothing to do with the indomitable persistence that was such an

295

inborn part of his character.

Not that he sold himself short, not in the slightest. He felt lucky to have been born with an innately persevering nature and sufficient intelligence and imagination to have been able to forge a successful business career for himself. He felt even luckier that he had been offered a means of escape from that career when he'd become all but burned out.

He'd been lucky to have been made redundant on terms that had given him financial independence so that he no longer had to walk within the walls of workaday conventionality and could at last live exactly the way he wanted to live. And the way he wanted to live, without the shadow of a doubt, was as Kate's full-time slave.

When Kate and he had originally fallen in love and decided to progress on life's journey together from then on, they'd had no idea that it would end up leading them into quite such dark territory. It wouldn't have felt right at that time for him to be entirely enslaved by her in the way he was these days. There were other thing he'd needed to do with his life back then and for a long time afterwards. Yet now it couldn't feel more right.

As Jay lay in his bondage, reflecting on all of this, he marvelled at how extreme his life had become as he'd adapted to an existence of complete servitude. And how it delighted him to be the slave of Kate, the one person in the world who really understood him. She could play out all his darkest fantasies for him because she could see deep into the most secret recesses of his nature, could see into the depth of his very being.

Jay worshipped his mistress and loved being dominated by such a powerful woman. He liked nothing better than to kneel at her feet and pay homage to her. And he did so with an incredible sense of pride at being owned by such a powerful dominatrix. Kate was so powerful that it radiated from her like a force field, so powerful that he had to

296

submit to all her demands without question; he had no choice.

He was there just for her pleasure to be used and punished and humiliated in whatever way she saw fit. And he loved it, loved being the slave of a woman who was a goddess. He loved bowing down before her in absolute submission, loved meeting the demands of the magnificent, cruel dominatrix who owned him body and soul.

The thought of it filled Jay with such elation that he wanted to shout for joy. But he couldn't because he was gagged. He wanted to cry with tears of happiness. But he was blindfolded. He wanted to go to his beloved mistress right there and then and prostrate himself before her to show her just how much he worshipped her. But that was not possible; he was in bonds.

Then s*he* came to him, returned to the bedroom, and Jay still couldn't do any of those things, not even when she went on to remove his blindfold and gag and release him from his bonds. That was because he was only permitted to address his mistress when she spoke to him and Kate said nothing at all on this occasion. She simply gestured to him that he should get onto his knees on the bedroom floor. She was almost as naked as her collared slave, wearing a leather choker, stiletto-heeled shoes and nothing else. She stood above Jay, looking down on him as though he lay far, far below, her expression a mixture of hauteur and desire and cruelty.

Then Kate's mood changed. She took Jay's face between both her hands, and tilted her head to one side slightly as if she was looking at him, gazing into those submissive eyes, for the very first time. She moved one hand caressingly to his hair, touching it, and then trailing over his cheeks and touching his mouth lightly.

Kate continued to stand above her kneeling slave, but looking down at him now with a much more thoughtful expression on her lovely face, compassionate even, a gentle smile on her lips. God, how she loved him, loved him more than life itself. She was his sadistic tormentor, there was no question about that, his gaoler and persecutor. But there was another side to all that, because she was also his protector, his lover, his dearest friend, his guide, his muse, his total inspiration.

Kate knew that she filled Jay with great wonder, yes, but also with a trembling fear that was just as real. She also knew this fear gave him the most tremendous erotic charge. Kate was a true sadist and loved to inflict pain on Jay, often extreme pain. But why, fundamentally, did she love to do this? Because that pain brought him the most intense pleasure. She never lost sight of that.

Nor did she ever lose sight of the fact that his submission to her was entirely voluntary. Kate knew that Jay thought she had great power. She felt differently about it. She knew she was in total control of him, but only because she had his permission, and he had only given that permission because he trusted her completely.

Power corrupts, so they say, and absolute power corrupts absolutely. Not necessarily. Kate had absolute power over Jay but there was nothing corrupt about it, nor would there ever be, she would see to that. She would continue to treat the power over him that she wielded – the power *he* had handed over to her – as the precious gift it truly was.

As if reading Kate's thoughts, Jay put his arms around her waist and drew himself gently close, cradling his head on her naked breasts and listening to the beat of her heart. He had wanted to say so much to Kate a few moments ago. He still wasn't allowed to speak. But now he thought it didn't matter at all. Words weren't necessary.

BDSM had taken over his life, of that there could be not the slightest doubt. But what was it really all about? Chloe had always insisted that BDSM was essentially about trust and she'd been right, of course. But what was the basis of that trust? It was love, pure and simple. The greater the love, the greater the trust. Jay's love for Kate was so deep, so profound that he was happy to be her slave always and for ever. He suddenly wanted to hold her even closer to him and never let go.

OTHER BOOKS BY ALEX JORDAINE

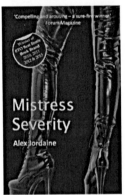

www.xcitebooks.co.uk